BAD NIGHTS

REBECCA YORK

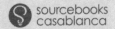
sourcebooks
casablanca

To Norman, who is always there for me.

Chapter 1

Above the muted sound of laughter coming from the television set, Morgan Rains heard a noise that made the hairs on the back of her neck prickle.

With a click of the remote, she turned off the DVD she'd been watching—of herself and Glenn in happier times—and sat very still in the darkened room, listening intently for sounds from outside.

The rustle of dry leaves came again, louder this time and closer to the little vacation retreat nestled in a hollow between two foothills of the Blue Ridge Mountains. Morgan was sure that either a person or a large animal was out there.

In the years she had been coming to this cozy cottage, there had never been any problem with intruders, but modern life might have changed that, which was one of the reasons she was here—to start getting the place in shape to sell it. She didn't need a vacation home, especially one where so many memories lurked.

Even when she'd told herself the house was perfectly safe, Morgan hadn't been foolish about staying here alone. Quietly, she walked to the desk drawer and pulled out the automatic pistol she kept with her, feeling more secure with the weight of the weapon in her hand.

Not so long ago, owning anything more deadly than a water pistol would have been as foreign to her as going back for a second PhD in quantum physics. That was before her husband had been shot and killed by a burglar, and her world had shattered.

Glenn Chandler. The love of her life.

She'd dragged herself through almost a year and a half without him, throwing herself into the psychology courses she was teaching. Although the joy had gone from the work, keeping up with research in her field, preparing lectures, giving tests, and grading term papers filled her time.

Now the semester was over, and she'd come back to the little house she'd inherited from her parents to finally pack up the clothing Glenn had left here and decide which of the furnishings should go to charity shops and which she'd move to her house in Falls Church. But when she'd come across the videos they'd made during the five years of their marriage, she'd sat down to watch. Starting with their wedding day, when they'd been smiling and happy, surrounded by family and friends.

She clicked off the gun's safety and held the weapon down by her right leg, wondering if she was going to end up like the heroine of a mystery novel who was too stupid to live.

Confronting danger was usually a bad idea, yet she didn't see any option in her present situation. This vacation retreat was in the middle of nowhere. The closest neighbor was over a mile away, even if she knew who lived in the house on the other side of the woods. And calling 911 was hardly an option, since it would take the local cops forty minutes to get here. Too late if someone outside was getting ready to break in.

She couldn't simply sit here and wait for an intruder to pounce. Of course, she reminded herself, there had been sightings of mountain lions in the area. If a big cat was prowling around out there, staying inside and opening the blinds so the cat could see her were the best alternatives. That would probably make it run away. But if it wasn't an animal, that was exactly the wrong tactic.

With her heart thumping inside her chest, she settled on a compromise. Walking to the window, she eased the curtains aside with her free hand and scanned the woods beyond the house. At first she saw nothing in the fading light. Then a flash of something that wasn't part of the natural environment made her go very still.

She was seeing flesh. Not fur. Naked flesh.

A man or a big woman. She kept her gaze trained on the figure, looking for details. It was definitely a man. He was in the woods fifty yards from the house, weaving his way through the trees on unsteady legs as though he was coming off a three-day bender.

The breath froze in her lungs. Who the hell was out there in his birthday suit? Some pervert who knew a woman was staying alone in this isolated location? A nudist who'd wandered onto the wrong property? Or an escapee from an insane asylum?

She'd seen him only briefly from the front—long enough to confirm that he was very male.

But he'd turned away from the house. Which meant that he wasn't stalking her. Unless the maneuver was designed to make her drop her guard if she was watching.

While that paranoid thought spun in her head, he wavered on his feet. His large fingers clawed at the trunk of a tree as he made a desperate attempt to stay upright.

She watched him lose his grip on the bark and slide downward to his knees.

Again he flailed out toward the tree, but his hands slipped away, and he fell onto the ground, lying on his side in a pile of dry leaves with his knees curled toward his chest. Unmoving.

She'd thought he might be stalking the house. Now it looked like he was a man in bad trouble, unless he was still pulling an elaborate scam.

But she couldn't simply leave him there. As she looked around, her gaze fell on a striped maroon and orange afghan, one of the many her mother had crocheted on long winter evenings. Snatching it off the couch, she threw it over her arm, concealing the gun as she hurried to the front door.

Outside, on the porch, she shivered in the evening chill. Not a night to be out naked, she thought as she looked around to make sure an accomplice wasn't lurking behind a tree. When she saw no one besides the guy on the ground, she crossed the patch of straggly weeds that had once been a lawn and stepped into the shade under the tulip poplars and maples. The man hadn't moved since she'd seen him claw at the tree trunk and go down.

As she approached, she took in his head full of close-cropped dark hair, broad shoulders, and narrow hips.

What in the world had happened to him? Had some disease felled him?

When she got closer, she saw well-defined muscles, and more dark hair fanned across his chest, peeking out from behind the raised knees that hid his genitals.

But that wasn't what riveted her attention. Now that she was close to him, she gasped as she realized his condition. The side of his face she could see was dark with beard stubble that didn't hide the bruises on his cheek and jaw. Or the dried blood around his nose and mouth.

There were more bruises on his back and shoulders and over his ribs. And something else made her draw in a quick breath—the small, angry red circles peppering his back, arms, and thighs.

A rash? She didn't think so.

She'd seen something similar once when she'd been a teenager. She and a bunch of kids had been out in the woods smoking. Billy Anderson had dropped a cigarette on his hand, and the mark had looked like the ones on this man, only these were deeper, angrier.

He might have gotten the bruises in an auto accident or a tumble down one of the nearby mountains, but not a dozen cigarette burns on his skin.

She shivered. Much as the idea alarmed her, the only thing she could figure was that he'd been tortured by someone.

But who would do such a thing? She couldn't ask because he was unconscious, lying out in the open with the temperature falling, his breath shallow.

Again her mind spun unwanted scenarios. There were people in these hills growing pot. Others with meth labs. Had he gotten into a dispute with one of his fellow criminals?

Her gaze landed on his hip which was covered with a particularly nasty bruise. The rational part of her mind knew that taking him into her house was dangerous. The reckless part sent a different message.

Does it matter what happens to you? You've been dead for over a year anyway. If he finished you off, it would be a kindness.

She made an angry sound, dismissing that last self-destructive thought as she turned to the injured man and murmured, "We have to get you inside."

At the sound of her voice, he stirred.

"Don't worry," she said. "Everything's going to be okay."

The words were automatic. She'd said them to Glenn when he'd lain dying on the hall floor, a pool of blood spreading around his head.

Clenching her teeth, she shoved that unwanted image out of her mind. She didn't need it now. Or any time.

"Who are you? What happened?"

He had been lying absolutely still. Now he rolled to his back. As his head moved on the bed of leaves, she saw that one of his eyes was swollen closed.

"We have to get you inside," she repeated, knowing she couldn't carry him. "Do you think you can walk?"

As she was about to come down beside him, his good eye flew open. It was dark and unfocused, until it lit on her. A kind of wily intelligence seeped into his face, and she knew he was going to attack.

"Don't," she gasped.

But it was already too late. He lunged, and she jumped back. Even in his battered condition, his reflexes were good. He closed his hand around her ankle, his grip surprisingly strong for someone who'd been unconscious a few moments ago.

She hadn't known what to expect, but it certainly wasn't this.

His voice was steely as he asked, "I don't remember you around the camp. Did they send a woman to work me over this time?"

"No," she answered automatically. "Who are they?"

He laughed. Not a pleasant sound in the gathering gloom of the forest. "What? Are you fucking Trainer? And he's having some fun letting you play with the prisoner."

"No. I'm trying to help you. Who are you? Who did this to you?"

"You know damn well." Even as he said the words, a look of confusion crossed his features.

"Please, I don't know anything about you—except that I found you in the woods outside my house. You're hurt. You need help."

The gun was still in her hand, but she didn't want to shoot him, unless there was no alternative.

"What's your name? Is there someone looking for you?"

"Looking for me? Get real."

He'd been lying unmoving on the ground, his large hand gripping her ankle. Still holding her in place, he surged up and grabbed at the afghan. As it slipped off her arm, he fell back, but the damage was already done. His gaze riveted to the gun in her hand, and she knew that a dangerous situation had just become a whole lot more deadly.

Chapter 2

"I'M TRYING TO HELP YOU," MORGAN PROTESTED, hearing her own voice go high and thin.

"Not likely." The stranger's eye stayed on the weapon, and she knew he was calculating his chances of getting it from her before she pulled the trigger.

In that moment of confrontation, she knew she couldn't shoot him point-blank.

In desperation, she tried to throw herself backward, away from him. As she fell, her finger tightened on the trigger, and the gun discharged with an ear-splitting blast. Not like on the practice range where she always wore ear protectors.

The man's grip on her ankle loosened and he flopped heavily back against the leaves, his eyes closing again and his face ashen.

"Oh God. Oh no."

Her heart was pounding wildly as she stared at him. For a long moment she was too shocked to move. Then she came down beside him on the leaves. After putting down the gun, she frantically began to check him over, looking for signs that the bullet had hit him. She ran her hands through his hair, touched his face, slid her fingers down his arms, across his chest, down his torso to his thighs, his knees, his feet, As far as she could tell, the bullet hadn't touched him. Thank the Lord.

When she'd finished her physical inspection, she took a moment to catch her breath. She hadn't hit him, but nothing had changed. He was still naked and injured, and she couldn't leave him outside on the cold ground.

Another thought skittered through her mind. What if the sound of the gun discharging brought the people who had done this to him?

Sobbing out a breath, she stared down at the stranger who had become her problem. He'd lost consciousness again, and she figured that he must have been operating on raw nerves when he'd grabbed for the weapon. He was badly beaten. She didn't even know if he had internal injuries, but she did know for sure that he needed help.

The wind was beginning to sway the branches of the trees above them. The temperature was dropping, and she knew a storm was coming.

If she'd thought it was safe to deal with him awake again, she would have tried to rouse him and help him walk to the house. Under the circumstances, that was much too risky. In fact, taking care of him was much too risky—because it was clear he thought that the men who had savaged him still had him in their custody.

Could she convince him otherwise?

Maybe after she got him inside.

That decision brought her up short. For all she knew, he could be a criminal, although she didn't think so.

She repressed a hysterical laugh. Did she think he had an honest face? Black and blue and honest all over?

While she was thinking all that, he was still lying out here, naked and cold.

After clicking the gun's safety on, she shoved the weapon into the waistband of her slacks and opened the afghan. She thought about rolling him onto it and using it to drag him to the house, but if she laid his weight on it and pulled, it would likely tear apart. Instead she spread it over him, thinking that his back was still against the cold bed of leaves.

When he moved his head and moaned, she held her breath, waiting for him to wake up and attack her again. But his eyes stayed closed.

After a silent debate, she left him where he was and ran back to the house where she found a tarp in the storage closet. Her dad had used it to cover the woodpile in winter, but she hadn't burned anything in the fireplace since forever.

Quickly she returned to the woods. When she didn't see the injured man, panic jolted through her.

Looking wildly around, she spotted him staggering a few yards farther into the trees, the afghan clutched around his shoulders. The man was obviously tough as iron—and bullheaded as a rogue elephant. As she watched, he went down again, obviously at the limit of his endurance.

She knelt beside him, murmuring soothing reassurances as she rolled him onto the tarp and breathed a sigh of relief when he didn't try to do her bodily harm. With him stretched out straight, she had a better view of his injuries. It looked like his body had taken an awful lot of punishment. Maybe some of his ribs were even broken, and she marveled that he'd gotten this far.

How far exactly?

She'd thought her nearest neighbor was a mile away. Was there someone closer? A cabin hidden in the woods, perhaps, where they'd been holding him and torturing him?

And they must know he'd escaped. Which meant they were looking for him now. That realization made her shudder.

Fat drops of rain were beginning to fall as she arranged the afghan over him again. Praying that she could get him to the house, she began to tug on the tarp, using it like a sledge, pulling his dead weight back the way she'd come, foot by slow foot.

Thoughts circled through her mind as she clenched her teeth and kept moving. Why was she doing this? She could just leave him out here and call an ambulance. Yet she couldn't shake the feeling that if she followed that route, he'd be dead.

On the other hand, he'd tried to attack her. When he woke up, would he do it again?

Even as she tugged on the tarp, then stopped to catch her breath, she questioned herself. Maybe she was trying to help him because something about him reminded her of Glenn.

Not his physical appearance. Her husband had been fair-haired with blue eyes—and a sunny disposition. This man was all dark shadows and hard angles. If she had to guess what he was, she'd call him a warrior. Whatever that meant. But there was something below the surface that she was responding to.

She made a scoffing sound. Maybe she was responding because she hadn't had a relationship with a man in more than a year.

But if she chose to have one, it wouldn't be with this guy. Would it?

The questions distracted her as she tried to hurry. The rain was only sporadic at the moment. Soon it would be coming down in buckets.

She was breathing hard by the time she reached the house. Thankful that the entrance was only one step up from the ground, she pulled him onto the porch. She'd thought about leaving him outside, but just as they reached the shelter of the porch, the storm broke in earnest, the wind blowing stinging drops of rain against her face and toward the front door.

Because she wouldn't have left a dog out in the storm, she pulled the man into the house.

Once he was inside, she wanted to slam and lock the door, but when she looked back the way they'd come, she saw a clear trail of skid marks where she'd dragged the tarp across the open ground, a dead give-away that she'd been pulling something heavy, like an unconscious man. And somehow she had the feeling that giving away his presence in her house would be a bad mistake.

Quickly she ran back, found a forked branch in the woods, and swept it over the track, the rain pelting her as she tried to hide the path she'd taken.

She was remembering the house's pre-Civil War history as she closed and locked the door. Once it had been a stop on the Underground Railroad, the chain of safe houses that had harbored escaped slaves as they made their way from servitude to the freedom of the North.

Now it was sheltering another escapee, she thought as she stood dripping by the door. Because it was the easiest thing to do, she left him where he was and ran down the hall to change her sopping clothes. Once she was dry, she brought a blanket to the living room and used it to replace the soggy afghan. Then she went to throw all the wet stuff into the dryer.

His mind flickered awake again in a swirl of confusion. Lying very still, not making a sound, he tried to separate fantasy from reality, fact from fiction.

Where was he exactly?

Still without moving, he cataloged sensations.

He'd been outside, hadn't he? Outside naked. He remembered a cold wind that had lashed his skin and seeped all the way to the marrow of his bones. Now he was warm. And lying on the hard floor with a thin sheet of something rough against his naked back and hips. But the covering on top of his body was slightly prickly. A wool blanket.

He had no idea how he had gotten from outside to this place and gotten covered with a blanket. His fingers flexed on the wool, and unconsciously he grabbed the edges and folded them closer, gripping them as he tried to grip onto reality.

Naked. Why was he naked?

He struggled to pull forth a recent memory. But now that he was awake again, his head felt like little men with pickaxes were chopping away at the inside of his skull. When he raised his hand, he felt a lump on the back of his head that was tender when he touched it.

That wasn't the only pain. Not by a long shot. One of his eyes seemed to be swollen shut, and his whole body ached, like he'd been used for a dummy lineman at a football practice. Deep muscle and bone pain. Abrasions on his skin. And something that felt like burns. Not all over. Clustered on his shoulders, chest, and thighs.

That sent an image flashing into his mind of a man with a cigarette, drawing on it to make the tip glow before pressing it into his flesh.

Maybe it was true. Maybe he was making it up to account for the raw sensations.

Screw the pain. All of it. Right now his job was to figure out where he was and why. And get away. Because he was sure that he wasn't supposed to be here.

Lying very still, he listened for clues and heard the sound of heavy rain pelting a shingled roof. And smelled the scent of soap and woman lingering in the air.

She'd been here a few minutes ago. Or was it hours? He had no way of measuring time.

He turned his head, seeing a living room with slightly shabby but comfortable-looking furniture. Sofas, chairs. A coffee table. A television set. Not one of the new flat screen ones. An old, clunky model.

It looked like he was in somebody's home, but he didn't remember coming in, and he couldn't even be sure how long he'd been here. Wait, hadn't he thought all that before?

He tried to stop the circling of his thoughts. The woman must have brought him. But how? He had an impression of a slender blonde. She certainly wouldn't have had the strength to carry him.

But she must have gotten him inside somehow and left him on the floor. Did he know her? He didn't think so, but if not, why was he here?

Not knowing who she was—or anything else— sent panic coursing through him. He tried to focus, but thoughts swam into his mind and out again too quickly for him to capture them.

For a terrible moment, he didn't even remember his own name and the fear of *not knowing* rose up like a giant wave, threatening to swallow him whole.

His name. What the hell was his damn name?

His heart pounded, and his hands clenched and unclenched as he struggled to remember his own identity.

Finally, a small part of the fog in his mind cleared away.

"Jack Brandt," he whispered aloud, feeling a wave of relief. It was followed immediately by confusion. Hadn't he been calling himself something else?

Because he'd been…

He tried to grab on to that thought and hold it, but it skittered away like a crab scrambling to escape from a seabird at the edge of the ocean.

Was the woman working for…?

Someone bad. Someone who was planning…

The name of the man and his scheme wouldn't come to him, and he gave up in frustration.

A shiver went through his body.

He wasn't in Afghanistan, was he? No. He knew that from his recent observations. He'd been in the woods. Not in the rocky terrain of that godforsaken country where you never knew if one of the friendly villagers or a provincial police officer was going to turn and put a bullet in your back. And this was the wrong kind of house. In Afghanistan, he'd be lying on a dirt floor or stone. He'd see patterned rugs, not chintz-covered furniture. And there was no way he would have seen the woman's face.

As he turned over those details, memories of his last mission jolted through him. SEAL team fifteen had been sent to take out a nest of insurgents hiding in a remote mountain village. It hadn't worked out the way anybody had expected. He remembered a woman in a burka coming toward them, her hand raised as though she wanted something from them. Then a flash, as the explosives belt she'd been wearing under the shapeless gown detonated.

Behind her, men with automatic weapons had surged forward. Insurgents who must have known the team was coming.

Recent memories eluded him. But that terrible scene ripped through his mind like an explosion in a munitions storage bunker.

He squeezed his eyes closed, trying to blot out the memory of the massacre. He'd seen the team cut down by machine-gun fire and grenades. But somehow he'd gotten out alive and staggered into the rocks. The hostiles had looked for him. But they hadn't found him because he'd covered himself with rocks and dirt. When they'd given up and moved out, he'd looked for the other members of the team. He'd only found bodies. Everyone else was dead.

A terrible feeling of loss grabbed him as he fought that memory. It was in the past. The shrinks had told him it wasn't his fault that he was alive. They'd said he could never change the past. He had to cope as best he could. But what was the present? Where was he, and why?

He strained for coherence and cursed softly when it eluded him.

As he closed his eyes and scrambled for something to ground himself, two familiar faces swam into his memory. His two best friends. Shane and Max. Guys he'd met in jail.

That stopped him again. Why had he been in jail? What jail? What city? What country?

Again, he simply couldn't remember. But he and Shane and Max had gotten each other through a long, dangerous night in a holding cell full of tough, angry men.

He recalled breaking up more than one fight between guys too drunk to think straight and stopping a couple of badasses determined to keep everyone else away from the phone. Then there had been the jerks who'd thought they could decide who could use the toilet and who couldn't.

He and Shane and Max had forced the bastards to make nice.

Yeah, he remembered that. It wasn't pleasant, but it gave him a sense of reality. It must have been in the U.S. Or perhaps Mexico because half the guys had spoken Spanish. Well, not Mexican Spanish. Cuban Spanish. Weird how he recalled that detail.

Maybe those memories brought him up to a year ago. Trying to remember more, he shifted his body, wincing as skin and bones moved against the hard floor.

How the hell had he gotten into this shape?

He must have taken a job. Something dangerous. But what was it, exactly?

He clenched his teeth, remembering pain as men punched him, burned him, beat him with a cane while a low, controlled voice spoke to him.

"You lied to me."

"No."

"No more lies. Who are you?"

"What are you doing here?"

"Who sent you?"

They were questions that he hoped he hadn't answered.

But there was something else. Something he had to remember now. Something dangerous that was going to happen. An attack? Maybe, unless he was making it up.

He scrambled to remember, but it was simply gone.

His mind snapped into the present as the woman came back into the room, and he watched her through slitted eyes. Well, through the eye that wasn't swollen shut. This time he was better able to take her measure.

She was medium height with dark blond hair worn straight and chin length. Her slender figure was covered by jeans and a long-sleeved knit shirt. Running shoes completed her fashion statement. Her breasts were medium-sized. Her hips narrow. And her blue eyes were filled with concern. Her lips parted as though she was getting ready to speak to him.

She came down beside him on the floor. "You're

awake," she said in a soft voice as she pressed her fingers to his cheek.

He liked her touch. It was the softest thing he had felt since forever.

When he didn't speak, she said, "I saw you watching me."

No use pretending he was still out cold. He made a grunting sound.

"What happened to you?"

She'd saved him. Maybe he owed her an explanation. Or was she like the Afghan villagers—pretending to be his friend? He guessed he'd find out.

His mouth was so dry he could barely speak, but he managed to say, "I don't know." It was only partly a lie. If he remembered more than the flashes that had come to him, he wasn't going to tell her. The knowledge would put her in danger. In fact, he thought with a flare of coherence that being close to him now was as risky as playing with a stick of dynamite.

Some of what he was thinking must have showed on his face.

"What?"

He tried to push himself up and fell back against the floor. "I need to get out of here."

She dragged in a breath and let it out. "You can't be serious."

"Perfectly serious."

"You were just unconscious. You're… injured. It's pouring rain. You're naked. You're not going anywhere." The last part was said with finality like a teacher informing a student of the classroom rules and giving no options.

To prove her wrong, he tried to get up again. Although he was panting from the effort, he couldn't even get to a sitting position. Unfortunately, she was correct; he wasn't going anywhere until he got a little stronger.

"I brought you some water."

Her words made him zero in on the terrible thirst he'd tried to ignore.

When she reached to ease him up, her touch was gentle. Still, he struggled not to groan as she got him to a sitting position, resting his back against her front with the blanket draped across his lap. When she lifted a cup of water to his lips, he drank eagerly before she took the cup away.

"Better take it slow."

He didn't protest. He knew that if he drank too much, he'd probably throw up.

"What's your name?" she asked.

"Jack." He didn't volunteer more, partly because he wasn't sure of his real name.

"I'm Morgan Rains."

"You came outside with a gun," he said as pictures flashed in his mind.

"I keep it for protection. Since my husband was shot by a burglar."

The clipped explanation told him she wasn't going to say any more about the weapon. Or her personal life.

"I'm going to put some salve on your burns."

He said nothing, because he was in no position to object.

Chapter 3

MORGAN STILL HELD THE MAN IN A SITTING POSITION, his back cradled against her front. Picking up the tube of burn salve, she reached around him so that she could unscrew the cap and set it on the floor.

She spread some of the salve on her fingers, then eased him forward so that she could stroke the ointment onto the angry red circles on his back, feeling his firm skin slide beneath her fingertips. Ministering to him like that was much too intimate. She should have brought a tissue to use.

But she wasn't going to get one. The best thing to do was just to finish this and let him rest because that would help him mend.

When she'd taken care of his back, she eased him down to the tarp again and adjusted the blanket.

"I should get you a sheet."

"This is fine."

His eyes were closed as though he was trying to distance himself from her as she kept working on him. And she understood why.

They were two strangers, yet she was touching him as a woman might touch a lover. And working on his broad chest with its covering of dark hair was more intimate than treating his back. Then there was the rest of him.

She stole a quick look at his face, relieved that his

eyes were still closed as she pulled the covering down, then squeezed out more salve. Some of the burns were close to his penis, and she bent her head to hide her face as she soothed on the salve. She hadn't stared at a lot of penises this close up. His was long and thick. Bigger than Glenn's.

She grimaced at that inappropriate thought. What did the size of his penis matter? She wasn't going to make love with this guy.

She pushed the sexual speculations out of her head. As quickly as she could, she finished with the salve and pulled up the blanket, covering him again. Maybe if she put some clothes on him, she wouldn't have to think about his body. She'd come up here to get Glenn's clothing out of the dresser and the closet. Although Jack No-Last-Name was taller than her husband and a bit leaner, the size wouldn't be too far off.

But she was pretty sure that the effort to dress him was more than he needed now.

"Thanks," he murmured, the weariness in his voice confirming her assessment.

"Get some rest."

"Don't have much choice," he mumbled.

She thought he was going to sleep when his good eye blinked open. "Keep the gun with you."

"Why?"

"They're looking for me."

"Who?"

"Guys you don't want to meet." He kept his gaze on her for long moments, and she saw the concern in his eyes.

"Maybe you'd better tell me about them."

"Can't," he whispered.

"Did you do something illegal?"

He hesitated for a moment, then answered, "No."

She didn't like that hesitation. What had he been doing that he thought was against the law?

"You'd better tell me."

He made a low sound. "Just push me out the door again, and you won't have to worry about it."

It was an audacious suggestion under the circumstances, but apparently the exchange had drained away his strength. She listened to the sound of his breathing change and knew he had drifted off to sleep again. Although she was relieved that he was getting the rest he needed, their conversation had unsettled her. He'd said men were looking for him. Bad men, she assumed. Did that mean she had to stand guard all night?

Or she could simply call 911 and let someone else decide what to do with him.

But before she did anything else, she'd better eat something, or she was going to fall over.

As the options for dinner ran through her mind, she made a dismissive sound. Once she had loved to cook. She'd learned the basics from her mother and continued her kitchen adventures after she'd graduated from college. She'd met Glenn in her first year of graduate school. One of the early things they'd discovered was that they both loved creating great dishes and sharing them.

They'd enjoyed paging through ethnic cookbooks for recipes to try. Then they'd shopped together and commanded the kitchen together.

Their first triumph had been a great paella, followed by beef paprikash, crème brûlée, the sugar topping caramelized with a blowtorch, chocolate lava cake, lobster bisque. She smiled as she remembered some of their kitchen adventures, then sobered. The fun had evaporated from cooking when her husband had been taken from her.

For the past year, eating had been something she did to keep up her strength because she had to go to work and make a living.

Not that she didn't like teaching, she added hastily. Too bad it wasn't the same when there was no one at home to share her victories with—or to listen to her complaints when the head of the psychology department made his power plays.

Glenn had been an engineer working for an aerospace company. Men with that background didn't necessarily want to discuss abnormal psychology. But he'd been different. He'd listened when she'd talked about the fine points of diagnosing mental illness or the pros and cons of behavior modification versus medication. He'd even given her some insights into aberrant behavior by discussing his colleagues at work.

She smiled as she recalled some of their discussions, then snapped back to the present as she opened a kitchen cabinet and began searching for something appealing.

Why was she thinking about the past now? Because a man was in her house for the first time since Glenn had died? She hadn't sought out a relationship with anyone, even the men who had made it clear that they

were interested in her. But none of them had measured up to Glenn. Not in her estimation.

Clenching her teeth to reinforce her resolve, she
reached for a can of pea soup in the cabinet next to the
sink. Just as her fingers closed around the cylinder, a
gust of wind shook the house. Setting the can on the
counter, she turned to the window and saw trees swaying wildly. A loud thud nearby told her one of them
had gone down. She was just thinking she was lucky
the house hadn't been hit when the lights went off.

Fumbling in the dark, she found a flashlight in
the utility drawer and clicked it on, grateful that the
batteries were okay. With the light in her hand, she
ran into the living room. Jack No-Last-Name was
still lying on the floor, dead to the world. The nearby
crash hadn't even made him crack an eyelid.

Her next stop was the phone, where she picked up
the receiver and found the line was dead. And she
knew her cell phone wouldn't do her any good. She'd
intended to charge it when she'd arrived here, but
she'd forgotten.

Which meant that she was stuck. Even if she'd
wanted to turn her visitor over to the cops or have him
transported to the hospital, that was impossible now.

Once again, possibilities chased themselves
through her head. He could be hiding his identity
because he was a criminal. But she suspected he was
trying to keep her from getting involved in whatever
had happened to him.

She looked down at him for long moments, then
knelt beside him and pressed her hand to his jawline.
His skin felt warm but not hot. He didn't stir when she

touched him. He'd been on alert earlier, but he was deep in sleep now. Was that dangerous? Like, what if he had a concussion? Too bad Dr. Rains didn't have a medical degree instead of a PhD.

Back in the kitchen she put the soup back into the cabinet and took out a box of crackers, then some sliced cheese from the refrigerator. After putting the simple meal on a plate, she carried it to the living room and set it on the end table beside the wingback chair where she'd been sitting before Jack had stumbled into her woods. Now the chair and everything around it felt like they'd been transported to another reality.

Munching on the cheese and crackers, she shined the beam around the room. The light fell on the simple furnishings that her mother had bought years ago, and nobody had felt the need to update. The low maple coffee table. The sofa with its faded chintz slipcover. The familiar picture was marred by the unconscious man lying near one wall, and the gun she'd set on the end table.

When she finished eating, she brought one of the coal oil lamps from the pantry and lit the wick. It seemed weird trying to go about her normal life with a guy sprawled on the floor, but what was she going to do? Sit and stare at him?

Instead, she sank back into the chair where she'd been watching the videos and picked up the book of seventeenth-century American literature that one of the women in the English department had recommended. It fell open to the poetry of Anne Bradstreet, a remarkable woman who had sailed to the Massachusetts Colony with her husband in 1629.

Married at sixteen and the mother of eight children, she'd found time to write and publish a four-hundred-page book of her verse.

Morgan had marked one of the poems: "To My Dear and Loving Husband."

> If ever two were one, then surely we.
> If ever man were lov'd by wife, then thee.
> If ever wife was happy in a man,
> Compare with me, ye women, if you can.

Maybe it wasn't as eloquently phrased as a Shakespeare sonnet, but her eyes misted as she read the lines. Once she could have boasted the same thing. Not now. Not ever again because hers had been an extraordinary partnership in an age when couples got married and divorced with alarming regularity. She'd had a match to last a lifetime. Too bad Glenn's life had been cut short at thirty-two.

With a jerky motion, she stood and walked to the window, trying to see something. It was too dark, but she could hear the wind blowing the tree branches. Too bad she hadn't already called the police and turned over her problem to them. It might be storming outside, but that wouldn't have stopped the cops from driving out here.

And why did she want to get rid of Jack? Because she was afraid of him? Or because his big cock had fascinated her?

The deliberately crude phrasing made her snort. Just because he had a big cock didn't make him a good lover. Her study of sexual functioning had taught her that some men with superior physical equipment assumed that they didn't have to do much to please a lover besides shove their dick inside her.

Shocked by the path her mind was wandering into, she returned to the chair. Tomorrow she'd find out what had actually happened to her guest. Maybe she could even drive him out of the area. Then she'd be finished with him, and she could comfort herself that she'd done the best she could under difficult circumstances.

She picked up the book of poetry again, but instead of reading she leaned back in the chair again, thinking she needed to relax. She'd just close her eyes for a moment, she thought as she let her body sink into the cushiony chair. That was a mistake. As soon as she gave into fatigue, she was lost to the world.

Chapter 4

JACK BRANDT SNAPPED AWAKE, EVERY MUSCLE tensing as he anticipated the pain of another blow or another burn at the hands of men who had been taught by an expert to inflict agony. But no fist smashed into his kidneys. No glowing cigarette pressed into his thigh.

Thank God. His mind had been fuzzy. Now it was clearer. Even if he probably had a concussion. The good news was that he wasn't dead, and when he moved his arms and legs, they seemed to be working.

The room where he lay was lit by a warm glow that he recognized as coming from an oil lamp. When he looked toward the light source, he saw the woman who'd brought him into her house. She was sitting in a wingback chair, a book in her lap, the gun on the table beside her, and her head lolling to the side. It looked like she'd tried to keep herself awake and failed.

Her name was… Morgan something. She'd told him, but he couldn't remember the rest.

Hoping not to wake her, he took an inventory of his injuries.

When he ran his tongue against his teeth, he was relieved to note they were all in place. And when he fingered his nose, he decided it wasn't actually broken—just battered.

Gingerly he touched the swollen tissue around his

eye. The massive bruise was tender, but hopefully there wasn't any permanent damage to his vision.

Still, it wasn't all good news.

When he started to sit up, he felt a sharp stab in his ribs on the right side. Moving cautiously, he pushed himself to a sitting position and fought a wave of dizziness that had him cursing silently. He was relieved when it subsided after a moment. Scooting his body to the coffee table, he got enough leverage to pull himself to his feet. He waited to be sure of his balance, then inched to the nearest window where he saw the gray light that comes before dawn. Time to get out of here, if he could manage to stay mobile.

A while ago he'd been trying to remember a name that wouldn't come to him. Now it sprang to the front of his mind like a demon leaping out of the shadows.

Wade Trainer. The self-appointed head of his own tinhorn paramilitary organization. The Real Americans Militia. RAM for short.

It was a sure bet that Trainer and his men were beating the bushes for the fugitive right now.

Jack went still. Coming up with the militia leader's name had unleashed a flood of recent memories.

Hadn't it been storming last night? Jack remembered buckets of cold rain. Maybe the downpour had slowed them down or halted their search.

He looked back toward the woman to see if his moving around had awakened her, but she was still dead to the world. Good. Maybe he could find something to wear—and find a back way out of here before she realized he was missing.

As he took a step, pain laced through him. He

gritted his teeth and drove past it. If he needed medical
attention, he'd have to get it later. When he thought
he had the pain under control, he looked toward the
yawning darkness of the hall. There must be a bathroom down there somewhere.

He found the toilet and relieved his full bladder
before peering at himself in the bathroom mirror.

The light coming through the window was low, but
the battered visage that stared back made him wince
as he saw the bruises, the crusted blood, and the eye
that wasn't yet open.

The woman had been using a kerosene lamp. Which
probably meant the electricity was out. But maybe
there was still hot water in the tank. Turning on the
tap, he let it run hot while he found a cloth and gingerly
washed the dried blood off his nose and mouth.

As he did, memories of the beating zinged back to
him. The bastards had worked him over pretty good,
but he knew they were just doing their job. Or to put
it another way, they were avoiding similar punishment, because Trainer's men ignored his orders at
their peril.

The man was a stickler for discipline. The grunt
who'd let Jack get away had made a bad mistake—
leaning over a prisoner he thought was unconscious.

Jack had surprised him with a head butt, then
slammed a fist into the guy's jaw before heaving
himself off the torture table and dashing down the
hall. Then what?

He had a vague memory of stealing an SUV and
barreling out the main gate, then ending up in a ditch.
After that he must have taken to the woods, intent on

getting the hell out of there before he ended up buried in the camp garbage dump.

Apparently he'd escaped. But how far had he gotten from the compound in his battered condition? He had no way of knowing for sure. His guess was—not far enough.

He gripped the sink, steadying himself when a wave of dizziness swept over him. It passed, and he hoped he didn't have a hematoma bleeding into his brain.

Lifting his hand, he touched the lump on the back of his head. He wasn't quite sure where he'd gotten it. Hell, he wasn't perfectly sure what he'd been doing just before the torture session. When he tried to reach for *those* memories, they simply weren't there, which was probably a consequence of the blow to the head.

He clenched his fists. He had a feeling that whatever was missing was important. But when he strained to recall the missing hours of his life, the only thing he got for his efforts was a throbbing skull.

Looking for something to relieve the pounding in his head, he opened the medicine cabinet. On the bottom shelf, he found a bottle of over-the-counter painkillers and swallowed a couple with water cupped in the palm of his hand.

The woman had put salve on his burns. He found the tube and applied more before sticking his head out of the bathroom and looking down the hall. His hostess was still sleeping in the wingback chair. Given the cold and the storm, she'd probably saved his life by bringing him inside. He'd hate to return the favor by getting her killed.

He moved quietly into one of the bedrooms farther

down the hall. The double bed was covered with a quilt. An oval rag rug lay on the pine floorboards. Across from the bed was a low dresser that held a lamp and old-fashioned washbasin and pitcher. When he tried to switch on the lamp, nothing happened, and he reminded himself about the electricity.

In the darkened room, he turned to the taller chest near the door. When he started opening drawers, he found men's folded jeans and shirts. From the husband she'd mentioned, presumably. He pulled on jeans that were a little short and a button-down cotton shirt that was an inch too short in the arms. For good measure he took an extra shirt. His luck held when he found socks and tennis shoes in the bottom of the closet. They were a size too big, but better than too tight, he thought as he kept exploring.

He'd probably have to rough it in the woods for a few days. Was there anything else he could use? He found a sleeping bag in the closet.

Again he stuck his head into the hall and saw that the woman named Morgan hadn't shifted her position in the chair. Steadier on his feet, he entered a second bedroom where he found a couple of backpacks with useful items like water bottles, ponchos, a flashlight, knife, and wooden matches.

Was there a back door? He'd take the stuff and get out of Morgan's life before she was even sure she'd really brought a naked man into the house.

Back in the bathroom, he filled two water bottles and stuffed them into the packs. Did she have any food in the kitchen that he could grab?

He shouldn't risk it, but the thought of food made his

stomach rumble. Another good sign. He wasn't too sick to eat, and apparently his stomach wasn't punctured.

He made his way quietly down the hall and slipped into the kitchen. There was a box of crackers on the counter, and he found sliced cheese in the refrigerator. Probably what she'd had for dinner. He ate some and washed the food down with water from the sink.

Feeling a twinge of guilt, he took a quick inventory of the kitchen and found granola bars and fig cookies. One of his favorites. There was also canned food, but he shouldn't spare the energy to carry it. He did, however, take a knife that looked like it would be useful, rationalizing his pilfering with the knowledge that Morgan would be well rid of him.

After wrapping the knife in a dish towel, he returned to the bedroom, where he stuffed the stolen items into his pack. He hadn't spotted a back door, but a window would do just fine, since the house was only one story.

If he'd had any money, he would have paid for the stuff he'd taken, but that wasn't an option. He'd just have to chalk it up to necessity.

As he congratulated himself on making a clean getaway, he heard a knock at the door and went stock-still.

Christ!

Morgan was in trouble. Unless that was the electric company at the door, coming to ask about her service.

Yeah, right.

He wanted to run down the hall and grab her before she could answer, but racing was still beyond him. And calling out would give him away.

As the knock came again, he moved toward the sound, judging his balance and his fighting potential.

Morgan's back was to him as she faced the door. "Who is it?" she asked, and he was glad she had the sense to keep the barrier between herself and the people outside.

"Federal Agents Richards and Becker. We need to talk to you, ma'am."

Federal agents my ass, he thought.

"What's this about?" she asked, playing dumb.

"We're looking for a fugitive reported to be in this area, and we need your cooperation."

Jack shook his head as he recognized the voice as one of Trainer's men.

"Reported by whom?"

"A local resident."

"I haven't seen anyone," she answered, her voice not quite steady.

"We need to verify that."

"You'll have to take my word for it."

"I'm afraid we can't do that."

"Hold up your identification."

Apparently the men outside had had enough of playing federal agents—and enough of Morgan's stalling tactics. Without making another plea for cooperation, they hit the door with something solid.

Chapter 5

JACK WAS IN NO SHAPE FOR A CONFRONTATION, BUT that didn't stop him. He was already halfway down the hall when the lock broke and the door burst inward. He was moving faster than he thought possible, given that he'd taken the beating of his life a few hours earlier.

But he wasn't going to let these bastards get away with whatever they had in mind for the woman who had saved his life. He kept his gaze on the two men who barreled into the room like Nazi storm troopers on a mission to round up and kill enemies of the state. Despite the false names they'd given, he knew they were Danforth and Ryder, two of Trainer's most loyal men. But not two of his smartest.

Danforth saw him coming and was dumb enough to waste his breath and precious seconds on a victory shout. "Like I thought, the lying prick's here."

Jack ignored the jibe and put on a desperate burst of speed, bashing into the militiaman with his shoulder and knocking him against the wall. It was lucky the guy stayed on his feet because Jack was so off balance himself that he would have gone down too.

Instead, he was able to follow the shoulder slam with a fist to the man's jaw.

Danforth struck back, and Jack took a blow to his already-injured cheek.

The counterattack only made him madder. He ducked low and gave Danforth a one-two punch to the gut. As the militiaman went down, Jack noted in some part of his mind how good it felt to smash the guy.

It was only a temporary victory. Danforth bent over and flailed out, grabbing Jack's foot and pulling it out from under him. He struggled to keep his balance but lost the battle and ended up sprawled on the floor, where Danforth leaped on him.

It had all happened in a few short seconds. As he grappled with Danforth, Jack saw that Ryder was still on the loose. He whipped around, his weapon pointed at Jack.

But in focusing on the escapee, the fake federal agent took his attention off Morgan. The gun was still in her hand, and Jack wondered if she could fire.

Instead, she brought the butt of her pistol down on his skull with a resounding crack, and he dropped, sprawling unmoving on the pine floorboards.

As Jack struggled with Danforth, he felt his strength failing. He was an expert at hand-to-hand combat, but he wasn't in good enough shape to finish off this bastard.

Still, he understood that failure meant Morgan's death. Calling on every ounce of reserve he possessed, he kept grappling with the attacker, each of them scrabbling to get the advantage as they rolled across the floor, punching and kicking, the fight as inelegant as it was desperate. Trainer's man was trying to get off a killing shot with the gun that was still in his hand. Jack was trying to keep himself or Morgan from getting hit.

And he was losing the fight.

In desperation, Danforth grabbed Jack's hair and tried to slam his head against the floor. Jack wrenched away, feeling hair come out by the roots. Hoping to end the struggle quickly, he raised a hand and stiffened his fingers, going for the man's eyes. Danforth screamed and jerked his head back.

Again, it was Morgan who made the difference.

"Stop or I'll shoot," she shouted.

When neither combatant paid any attention to her, she fired a round into the floor inches from Danforth's head.

The man flinched away, and Jack used the opportunity to slam an elbow into his face. To Jack's relief, the militiaman made a gurgling sound and went slack.

Jack pushed the guy to the side and sat up. His vision went murky, and he spent a few moments struggling to keep from blacking out.

"Jack!" Morgan stared at him wide-eyed.

"I'm okay. Do you have some rope?"

Morgan didn't move, obviously suffering from the shock of what had happened.

"Rope," he repeated, his voice going hard as granite. "Before these guys wake up."

She blinked. "Right."

Shaking herself into motion, she hurried to the kitchen while Jack stayed on the floor, breathing heavily and struggling to stay conscious. His plan had been to clear out of the house before Morgan woke up. That was impossible now, and he saw with new clarity that it would have been a fatally wrong move, because he could easily imagine what would have happened in his absence.

These two bozos would have broken in, seen the ground cloth and the blanket on the floor, and assumed that their quarry had been here. Then they would have dragged Morgan back to Trainer's compound, where the boss man would have started throwing questions at her. Questions Morgan couldn't answer, because she didn't know anything beyond the basics of finding a naked man stumbling around in the woods. But Colonel Trainer wouldn't have believed her story, and he would have ended up using the same methods he'd used on Jack. He shuddered, trying not to think about it. Unfortunately, vivid pictures kept flashing through his mind.

When one of the men on the floor stirred, Jack kicked him in the head, and he went still again. He would have liked to shoot these two bastards so they couldn't give Trainer any information, but he wasn't going to make Morgan accessory to what the legal system would consider murder. Never mind that the two men on the floor burst in with murderous intent.

Morgan came back with cord.

"Keep them covered."

While she held the gun on them, he worked quickly and efficiently, tying the hands and feet of both men, then testing the bonds. By the time he finished making sure they weren't going to cause any more problems, Ryder and Danforth were both stirring.

"Time to wake up." When he gave Ryder a light kick in the ribs, Morgan winced.

The man's eyes snapped open and focused on Jack, his expression turning malevolent as he realized the tables were turned. Yet his words were defiant. "You're dead meat."

"Oh yeah? You're in kind of an inconvenient position to make that statement," Jack countered.

"We're not the only guys beating the bushes for you. When we don't come back, Trainer will be all over it."

"Thanks for the heads-up." He swung toward Morgan, who was staring at him as though she couldn't quite believe what was happening.

"We'd better take his advice and get out of here," he said.

"I wouldn't count on it." Ryder gave him a satisfied smirk, and Jack felt his stomach knot. Turning to the window, he looked outside. There was only one car in sight.

"You drive a Prius?" he asked Morgan.

"Yes."

Which meant Trainer's men had come on foot, or parked their vehicle down the lane, out of sight. He searched through both men's pockets and found no keys. No cell phones. They had nothing with them except the two handguns they'd brought. And two extra clips. As per Trainer's rules, they'd carried off the operation with nothing that could identify them if they ended up dead or in police custody. Of course, if the militia leader thought they were going to keep their traps shut, he was being highly optimistic. These guys would crack like rotten eggs if they thought it would save their own miserable hides.

"You keep them covered," Jack said. "Where are your car keys?"

"In my purse. In the pantry."

He hurried to the kitchen, retrieved the purse,

and fished inside for the keys. When he returned, he took Ryder's gun. Pushing the damaged door open, he waited for signs of activity outside. When there was none, he stepped onto the porch and looked around. The ground was strewn with leaves and small branches from last night's storm. The place was a mess, but as far as he could see, there were no other men lurking in the woods. Not yet.

He crossed to the car, unlocked the door, and slid into the driver's seat, but when he tried to start the vehicle, he didn't even get a cough from the engine. Remembering Ryder's smirk, he was pretty sure the man had disabled the vehicle before ever knocking on the door.

Shit!

When he returned to the house, Morgan took in his worried expression.

"What?"

"Looks like we're not taking your car."

"Why?"

"They put it out of commission."

"What are we going to do?"

He glanced at Ryder, who was listening avidly. "Tell you later," he said as his mind worked on a plan.

They couldn't risk looking for the militiamen's car down the road. They'd have to go through the woods and take the long way around, because the road would probably be too dangerous, but he wasn't going to say that in front of the enemy.

As he sensed the problem, Ryder grinned at him.

Repressing the urge to kick the man in the face, Jack crossed to the kitchen, grabbed two dish towels, and used them as gags. Then he pulled Ryder across the living room and out the door onto the porch before doing the same with Danforth. When they were outside, he rolled them off the porch and left them lying on wet leaves in the front yard. Trying not to breathe hard, he watched them struggle for a few minutes, satisfied that they were secure before returning to the house.

Morgan was standing in the doorway, staring from him to the men he had just tossed out like sacks of garbage. "What are you doing?"

"Stowing them where there's not a chance they can hear us discussing our plans," he clipped out as he came in and closed the door. It had been kicked in, and the lock no longer worked, but he hoped nobody could tell that from the outside.

"Won't... won't someone find them if you just leave them there?"

Her shaky voice tore at him. "Like he said, when they don't come back, their buddies will be looking for them. They know their assignment, so it doesn't make any difference if they're inside or out. The main point is that we have to get out of here—fast. And we're going to have to hoof it."

She didn't move, and the doubt and confusion on her face made his chest constrict. They'd known each other for only hours, yet in some ways it felt like a lifetime. Before he could consider what he was doing, he reached for her and pulled her into his arms.

She held herself stiffly for a moment, then melted against him, her head dropping to his shoulder.

"You handled that like a pro," he murmured as he

cradled her in his arms, feeling her shaking in reaction. She might have been shocked and scared when Trainer's men had burst in, but she'd kept her head and defended herself—and him.

He stroked his hands over her back and shoulders. It felt amazingly good to hold her. Too good. He hadn't allowed a woman into his life since before Afghanistan. He hadn't been seeing anyone special, and he'd thought it wasn't fair to start something when he was leaving and might not come back.

But circumstances had thrust this woman into his path, and he was holding on to her like they meant something to each other, even when all the reasons for not getting involved with anyone still held. All those—and more. He should turn her loose immediately, but he couldn't do it. Not yet. Not when it felt like he had been out in the cold forever, and she was offering him her warmth.

Or more likely, it was the other way around. She was the one who needed him. Too bad he couldn't spare her more than a moment's comfort.

———

Morgan had been without a man since Glenn's death, and she liked it that way. Well, not liked it exactly. She knew that she was rationalizing, but she hadn't been able to imagine a relationship with anyone else besides her husband.

At this moment, she wasn't sure what she had with Jack No-Last-Name, but she allowed herself to lean on him as she tried to cope with everything that had happened in the past few minutes—or in the past eight hours, come to that. For a few moments, it was comforting to focus on the man who held her in his arms.

She was amazed by how much everything had changed since last night. When she'd found him in the woods and dragged him inside, he'd been barely functional. And when she'd examined him, she'd been appalled by his injuries. Today he seemed to be operating on what would pass for full power with most men, even when she was pretty sure he still wasn't up to par, not by his own standards.

She didn't know much about him. But she'd seen him in action a few minutes ago and knew he was capable of extraordinary bravery and of calling on hidden reserves of energy when he went into defender mode. When the knock had sounded on the door, he could have tried to get out of there before the invaders discovered him. Instead, he'd come charging down the hall to rescue her from men who had as much regard for her as they might have for a cornered mouse.

He'd knocked them out of commission, then started thinking ahead. He was a tough, decisive guy, competent and sure of his actions. Yet the way he was holding her told her that he had a tender side.

She marveled at what she was feeling now. Last night, before he'd stumbled out of the woods, she'd been dragging herself along, fighting the deadened sensations in her mind and body.

Now her heart was pounding, and all her senses were more alive than they'd been in months. She hadn't even been sure she wanted to live. Danger had convinced her otherwise. Danger and whatever she was feeling for the man who held her.

"I'm damn sorry for dragging you into this," he whispered, his lips brushing her ear and sending a shiver over her skin.

She nodded against his shoulder, then realized she couldn't simply accept the apology—or anything else—at face value.

"Those men aren't FBI agents, are they?"

"No."

"Why are they after you?"

"Long story."

Pulling herself together, she broke the contact with him, rearing back, angry with herself for giving in so easily to her needy feelings when she had to stay in control.

As much to convince herself as to convince him, she made her expression fierce. "I think you know you almost got me killed. Tell me what's going on right now—or get the hell out of here."

His features were equally vehement. "I'm not going anywhere. Not without you."

"Why not?"

"Too dangerous. Those guys came looking for me here. And before they knocked on the door, they disabled your car. That should tell you something about their intentions. When they don't come back, the big kahuna will send more of his men. And it won't be to thank you for helping me."

She made a scoffing sound. "I'm supposed to take your word for all that?"

"Yes."

"Well, they may be minions of the evil overlord, but I can't go with you unless I have more information. Who are they? What did you do to them?"

———

Jack kept his gaze on her defiant face. She wasn't bluffing. She meant what she said, and he couldn't allow her to kick him out. That was simply too dangerous for her. He dragged in a breath and exhaled to give himself another couple of seconds. He'd been in deep cover for months, and he was breaking protocol if he told her anything. But that cover was already blown, he reminded himself. That's how he'd ended up naked in her front yard.

"Okay. They belong to a homegrown militia organization that has their headquarters near here."

"I never heard of a militia around here."

"They've been in the area less than a year, and they don't advertise their presence. On the compound they wear uniforms. But if they go out in public, they change into civilian clothes."

"Why are they after you?"

The sixty-four-thousand-dollar question. He clenched and unclenched his fists.

"I was on an undercover assignment, infiltrating their group to find out what they're planning. I must have blown my cover."

"How?"

He kept his voice steady as he said the part he detested revealing. "I don't know. I mean, my memories before the interrogation are... missing." His jaw clenched. "The first thing I remember is waking up on their torture table. You saw the results."

He had the satisfaction of seeing her wince, but she was back to business immediately.

"And you're working for?"

"Rockfort Security."

"Not the government?"

He answered with a harsh laugh. "In this case, the government's using a contractor. Rockfort is doing the heavy lifting."

When she opened her mouth to ask another question, he shook his head. "Not now. We have to get out of here before the others show up. And I have to let my partners know what's going on. Do you have a working phone here?"

"The power was out last night." She raised her head and looked toward the ceiling fixture. "I had that on last night. It hasn't come back on."

He crossed to the phone and picked up the receiver, then snorted in disgust. "Dead. Where's your cell phone?"

"It was out of power, and I was going to charge it," she answered in an apologetic voice.

"Then we'd better split. And let's hope we have a little time to prepare."

"Like how?"

"I found a couple of packs in the bedroom closet. Get a change of clothes. The same for me. And some water and food that's easy to carry."

———

Morgan nodded and ran into the kitchen. As she grabbed some power bars, water, and more crackers and cheese, she could see he'd already helped himself to some food. Which made her wonder again if she could trust him and trust his story.

And trust herself. She didn't like the way she'd melted into his arms like a woman whose lover had just returned home. He wasn't her lover. He was still a stranger. And more important, still dangerous. He'd gone after those two men like a fighting machine. But he'd been defending himself, and her, she reminded herself.

And at the moment, the alternative to the man looked worse—if she believed his story. Opening one of the drawers, she took out a knife. Again she saw that he'd already raided the drawer. From the utility closet she grabbed another ground cloth.

Her mind raced as she tried to think of what they'd need. Stuff she'd taken on camping trips. But not too much. Not more than they could easily carry.

Her next stop was the bedroom, where she grabbed some clothing—for herself and for him.

She saw he'd already set out two packs and a sleeping bag, further evidence that he'd been getting ready to leave when the men had showed up at the door. Now he'd changed his mind about going solo.

She swallowed hard. His altered plans argued that he was telling the truth. It was too dangerous for her to stay here. Why else would he bring her along to slow him down?

Unless the militia were the good guys, and he didn't want her talking to them. She made a snorting sound. They hadn't acted like good guys. More like thugs.

Straining her ears, she listened for signs that men were sneaking up on the house. But it was quiet outside. Too quiet because she couldn't even hear the birds who usually sang in the morning in the trees. Quickly she stuffed socks into one of the packs.

"We should go," she called out.

From out in the living room, she heard him swear. In the next second, the rattle of gunfire made her heart stop, then start up again in double time.

Automatic weapons, it sounded like.

"Get down," Jack shouted as she heard bullets raking the wall and thudding into the door.

She dropped to the floor, flattening herself and crossing her arms over her head to ward off the noise as more bullets tore into the front wall of the cozy vacation house that had suddenly been turned into a war zone.

Oh Lord! Jack was in the living room.

Raising her head, she called his name. "Are you all right?"

When he didn't answer, her heart leaped into her throat. The barrage stopped, and she heard glass breaking, then bullets from a handgun.

He'd broken a window and returned fire. At least she knew that much, but she didn't know if he'd been hit. And if he was still all right, how long could that last? He was only one man with a pistol against guys who had brought along much more powerful weapons.

She hadn't been sure what they were up against. Now she had a much better idea.

She wormed her way to the bedroom door, trying to see down the hall. "Jack?"

Another barrage of fire came from outside the house, and she saw him hit the floor, shouting at her above the clatter of the weapons, "Stay down. Stay back. Don't come any closer."

She held her position, waiting with her heart pounding while the house seemed to shake around her like someone had thrown it into a giant cement mixer. When the noise stopped, she looked toward the living room, seeing the holes that had materialized in the wall—and Jack holding a sofa cushion in front of his body.

"Jack Barnes, come out with your hands up, and the woman won't be hurt," a voice from outside boomed.

"They're lying," he spat out as he ducked low and ran for the hallway where Morgan crouched.

"Jack Barnes? Is that your real name?"

"No. It's the name I was using with them."

"Jack Barnes, come out with your hands up," the voice boomed again.

When he ignored it, she looked toward the window. "How many are out there?"

"Three or four firing. At least around front. Is there a back door?"

"No."

"That's good. They may not have the back covered."

"What are we going to do?"

He took her shoulders and turned her toward him, his expression grim. "You're going out a back window. Do you have more bullets?"

"Yes."

"Take your gun and take more ammunition, but don't engage them unless you have to. Don't take anything with you. Run as fast as you can. Head through the woods. If you come to a road, make sure they're not patrolling it. As soon as you can get to a phone, call Rockfort Security in Rockville, Maryland.

Talk to my partners, Shane Gallagher or Max Lyon. Tell them what happened. Tell them… Jack Brandt wasn't able to discover Trainer's main mission."

Doubt and disbelief crossed his features.

"What?"

"At least I don't think I know Trainer's main mission," he clipped out.

"What does that mean?"

"Like I said, my memory's got some holes." He gave her a hard look. "You'd better get going."

"What are you going to do?"

"Draw their fire while you get away."

"No."

"It's the only way for one of us to get out of this. And one of us has to tell Rockfort what happened."

"We're both going," she said.

"I don't think so."

Chapter 6

JACK CHECKED THE CLIPS ON THE GUNS HE'D TAKEN off the two men who'd come to the house pretending to be FBI agents. He was getting low on ammunition.

When he spared Morgan a look, he saw a steely determination. "You're not going out there," she said. "I won't let you kill yourself because of me."

"Maybe I'll take them out."

She made a rough noise. "You have a couple of handguns. They've got machine guns."

He flapped an arm in frustration. "We don't have a lot of time to argue about it."

He hadn't known how right he was. The shooting was apparently over and also the offer of safe conduct for Morgan.

In the next second, a canister crashed through the living room window and landed on the sofa, spewing smoke and fire in all directions. Almost immediately, the chintz slipcover went up in flames.

Morgan gasped.

Jack grabbed her arm and herded her farther down the hall, wondering how long before the flames reached them.

Outside he could hear whoops of triumph from Trainer's men. Maybe the colonel was there himself, directing the operation.

"Come on out if you don't want to roast," someone

called. He thought it was Ryder, one of the men who had played FBI agent earlier. Cocky again now that his buddies had rescued him.

Jack didn't spare the breath to respond.

Behind him, more furnishings were catching fire, turning the living room into a suburb of hell.

The smoke was pouring into the hall and thickening around them. Jack was already coughing as he grabbed Morgan's hand. "Get down."

"This way," she said.

He hadn't expected her to take the initiative, but she seemed to know where she was going. He followed close behind as she leaned over and kept low while she sprinted down the hall, the smoke and flames at their backs.

There was still a chance they could get out a window, but now he was sure the attack was planned to herd them to the back of the house where men with machine guns would be waiting to mow them down when they tried to escape.

Morgan led him into a bedroom and slammed the door. It blocked the smoke, and he took a grateful breath of the relatively untainted air. But from the way the fire was burning, he knew the flames would reach the door soon, and then they could either burn up or take their chances at a window. He'd go first and draw their fire and hope she could get away, but he wasn't counting on it.

Morgan's voice was low and urgent as she began to speak. "This house was built in the 1830s—and it has some unusual features. It was a stop on the Underground Railroad. You know—where people helped escaped slaves travel north."

He tried to wrap his head around what she was telling him and finally thought he got the import of the history lesson.

"Are you saying there's another way out?"

She pointed to the floor. "Under there."

He watched while she pushed the rag rug aside. Under it, he could make out the outline of a rectangular shape in the wooden floor, with a small metal circle embedded in the wood at one side.

When he reached into the circle and pulled, the piece of flooring groaned with disuse.

He pulled harder, and it finally came up, almost throwing him backward. He recovered his footing and stared down into darkness from which the scent of damp earth and mold wafted upward.

"There's a ladder," Morgan said, pointing her flashlight beam at the rungs.

"Where does it come out?" he asked.

"In the woods."

"How far?"

"Maybe fifty yards."

He was making swift calculations. The house would burn for a while. Trainer might want to order his men inside, but not without special equipment. By the time they got inside, he and Morgan would be long gone, and maybe the attackers would think they had burned to crispy critters.

Morgan handed him the flashlight, and he shined it into the dark tunnel below the house, seeing a dirt floor and walls.

He knew they had to get away fast, but one more problem leaped into his mind.

"Did you leave your wallet in the living room?" he asked.

"Unfortunately, yes."

"Is there any money back here?"

"I think there's some in one of the bedroom drawers."

"Take it. We'll need it when we get out of here."

She crossed quickly to the dresser, knelt down, and opened the bottom drawer, then rummaged under some clothing. Pulling out some folded bills, she shoved them into one of the pockets of her knapsack.

"Go down," he said.

"And you'll follow?" she asked, her voice anxious.

"Yeah. After I close the trapdoor."

Outside in the woods, Wade Trainer cursed under his breath. He didn't allow his men to use foul language, and he believed in practicing what he preached, but this morning he needed an outlet for his frustration.

His hands clenched at his sides as he mentally reviewed the past eighteen hours, intent on figuring out where he'd gone wrong.

And the only thing he could fault himself on was leaving Buckman and Stanford alone with the prisoner after one of the interrogation sessions.

Wade was sure he had been close to getting Jack Barnes to talk. But he'd had to step out of the room for a few minutes when he'd gotten an urgent communication from his moneyman.

By the time he'd come back, the whole situation had gone to hell in a handbasket. Barnes was gone,

one of his men was down, and the other was working frantically to revive him.

He'd already punished the morons. At the same time, he'd ordered others to search for Barnes. The man had to be in bad shape. How far could he get?

The logical place to start was the compound. When it was clear that Barnes had somehow stolen an SUV and gotten off the property, Wade had widened the parameters. They'd found the vehicle in a ditch. At least the man had limited his escape radius.

He'd known Barnes was good. He simply hadn't realized how good—or how duplicitous the man had turned out to be.

Barnes was an ex–Navy SEAL with reasons to be disgusted with the service. Two years ago, he and eight other SEALs had been sent on what turned out to be a suicide mission in Afghanistan. Not like that operation where SEALs had killed Bin Laden. In this case, Barnes had been the only one who'd escaped alive.

Of course, Wade hadn't taken the man's word for any of that. He'd used a contact to check his military records, which had agreed with the man's story.

And the personal part had fit. Barnes had mourned the other members of his team, and as soon as he'd been able, he'd left the service, then wandered the country, like some kind of modern-day Rambo, with a chip on his shoulder and the skills to wreak havoc if he chose.

Wade had thought he'd turned the guy around.

Since joining the RAM, Barnes had accepted the militia code and followed the rules, down to the proscription against getting to be best buddies with anyone. But looking back, there were some clues that he might not be what he seemed. After their initial conversations, he'd stayed out of ideological discussions. He kept to himself more than was strictly necessary, and he had a tendency to wander off into the woods by himself when he wasn't on duty. Taken together, all those things had aroused Wade's suspicions, and he'd assigned a couple of men to keep tabs on the guy. The troops were happy to do it, because Barnes projected a grating aura of superiority.

It had taken weeks of covert surveillance. In fact, Wade had been about to give up on getting anything on the guy, until his surveillance team followed Barnes back to camp while everyone was on maneuvers. He'd ducked behind the latrine, then zeroed in on Wade's office, and he'd been sitting at the computer when Thackery had whacked him over the head with the butt of his gun.

He'd stopped breathing, and Thackery had panicked, calling out for help. Wentworth, Wade's physician's assistant, had rushed in and slapped Barnes across the face a couple of times, and that had brought him around, still groggy.

When they'd been sure Barnes wasn't going to croak, Wade had looked at his computer. The screen had been displaying the desktop, but that didn't mean Barnes hadn't somehow gotten farther in—and erased the evidence of his snooping.

Wade was sure he'd been close to finding out what Barnes knew, when the guy had escaped. He was good, but there had been no way he could get far on foot. Not naked, beaten to a pulp, and half out of his mind from torture. Once he'd abandoned the vehicle, it had been a process of elimination to track him to this house, which belonged to a widow named Morgan Rains. She must have seen the guy in the woods and taken him in, because Wade couldn't imagine Jack Barnes coming up and knocking on the door. Or maybe Jack had forced his way in and held her hostage. And there was another possibility as well. Morgan Rains could be a plant, stationed at the house and ready to rescue Jack Barnes if he got into trouble.

He took an involuntary step back as the heat from the fire he'd started threatened to set his clothing on fire.

If it was hot as hell out here, it must be unbearable inside the structure. Barnes and the woman were going to burn up in there if they didn't come out soon. Or maybe they had already passed out from smoke inhalation, and there was no way of saving them. Which was a shame, because Wade was still missing the information he needed. And his moneyman was going to want details.

He swore under his breath again. Everything had been going his way, until Barnes had come along. Wade had found a prime location for his camp in Skyline, Virginia, close enough to Washington, D.C., to easily attack the capital. He'd improved the facilities. Acquired a nice stock of weapons. Set up practice areas and trained his men to be the soldiers he needed to pull off the operation he'd planned. His troops would obey him without question, and he thought about ordering one of his men to go into the burning house and drag Barnes and the woman out.

But that option had little chance of success. And he wasn't in the business of wasting men when there was no purpose to it.

Clenching and unclenching his fists, he watched the house burn with a feeling of triumph and defeat warring inside himself. The traitor would be dead, but Wade wouldn't find out what he'd gotten out of the computer, or who had set up the spy operation. Was the government spying on the RAM? He'd have to move up his timetable.

—◆◆◆—

Jack watched Morgan climb down the ladder, testing the wooden rungs as she went. He breathed out a small sigh when they all held.

After she reached the tunnel floor, she turned and looked up anxiously.

"Come on."

"I'll be right there."

He tossed down the knapsacks and the bedroll they'd brought, then stepped onto the ladder. He was just reaching up with both hands to lower the door the rest of the way when an explosion boomed out, shaking the house to its foundations. Maybe from the propane tank or another bomb Trainer's men had lobbed inside.

Whatever the reason, the rung under Jack's feet wavered, and he scrabbled to get a grip on the side supports. When the ladder arched backward and threw him against the far wall, he lost his footing and tumbled off into space.

From below him, he heard a scream as he plummeted downward into blackness.

Chapter 7

For long moments, Jack was nowhere at all. Then, to his shock, he woke up in a place he didn't want to be. Back in Trainer's clutches, powerless to defend himself from the burns and the blows.

He was lying on a hard surface, naked and shivering from the pile of ice cubes heaped onto his chest.

"Wake up, you bastard," a harsh voice ordered. "You're not going to escape by sleeping."

He kept his eyes closed, feigning unconsciousness.

"I said wake up." The speaker was Wade Trainer himself.

Jack's brain swam with confusion. He'd thought he'd escaped from the torture room. Now he was back again.

Trainer slapped his face—hard. But it was just a bee sting compared to what had come before. To remind Jack, the man poured something hot and stinging on a couple of the cigarette burns he'd already gouged into Jack's flesh.

He couldn't hold back a groan, but he kept from screaming.

"Good. I've got your attention." The militia leader's voice turned conversational. "You find out what a man is made of by the way he responds to torture. So far, you're being stupid."

Jack clenched his teeth as he gazed up into Wade

Trainer's face. The remarkable thing was that there was nothing remarkable about Trainer's appearance. He looked ordinary, with features you might see on a guy riding the bus to work. His dark hair was straight and graying at the temples. His nose was small for a man, his lips thin, his eyes gray. They were the most notable thing about him. Not because of their color but their steely determination. When you looked into them, you knew this man had a purpose.

He made a formidable opponent. But Jack was being smart—following his SEAL training and looking for an opportunity to escape.

"You went to a lot of trouble to get into the RAM. Who are you working for?"

"Nobody."

"Don't screw with me now. That fight in the bar where I first saw you beat the crap out of a guy—that was staged, wasn't it?"

"No."

"You let me think you were a badass lone wolf, bitter about losing your buddies. You let me think you wanted to get back at the U.S. Government."

"I do."

Trainer snorted. Ignoring Jack, he went on. "You made me think you bought into the RAM ideals."

"I do."

"Bullshit. You made yourself look like the perfect recruit. You had discipline. All the skills I needed in a man. I even made you an instructor. But it was all an act."

"No."

"Cut the crap. You may think you can hold out.

But you're going to spill your guts to me like every-body does under torture. Why not make it easier on yourself and tell me now. Then I'll kill you quick."

Jack didn't waste his energy with a snappy reply. He let his mind float away—to a place where the pain was happening to someone else—only he could still feel it.

"Why were you in my office?"

He'd been in the office? Jack didn't remember that or anything else right before waking up in the torture chamber, but he filed the information away.

Trainer leaned over him, grinning as he took a drag on his cigarette and held it up, studying the glowing end. Then he pressed it against Jack's shoulder.

He called on every drop of inner strength he pos-sessed, determined to deny the militia leader the sat-isfaction of hearing him scream. But keeping silent was getting harder.

"Who are you working for?"

"Nobody."

"You're lying."

When he turned his head away, the militia leader grabbed his hair and snapped his face back, damn near breaking his neck in the process.

When he didn't respond, the man closed a hand over his shoulder, his fingers rubbing against the new burn mark as he shook him.

"Jack. Wake up. Jack. Can you hear me?" an urgent voice asked.

The voice didn't sound like Trainer, but it had to be. Or one of his men. There was nobody else in the torture room. Or was his memory wrong? He didn't recall the place smelling damp and musty.

He tensed his muscles, waiting for the right moment. "Jack?"

In the dim light, he could barely see who had spoken his name. Was that really Trainer hovering above him? His mind refused to focus, but his body reacted in the way he'd been trained. This was his chance to get away, and he took it. Springing forward, he knocked the bastard out of the way where he landed on his ass against the wall.

When he heard a grunting sound, he felt a surge of victory.

"Jack."

It didn't sound like Trainer. And as the familiar face finally came into focus, he dragged in a sharp breath.

It *wasn't* Trainer or one of his men. And he wasn't in the brightly lighted torture chamber.

He was in a dark place, illuminated only by the glow from a flashlight sitting on the floor. In the dim light, he saw Morgan picking herself up.

"Shit." He wasn't back in Trainer's clutches. His brain had made up that scenario when an explosion shook the house, and he fell down the ladder and blacked out.

"Morgan?" he asked in a strangled voice.

"Yes."

He ran a shaky hand through his hair as he thought about the short amount of time they'd spent together. "I attacked you before, didn't I? When you first found me, right?"

"You were out of it."

He snorted. "Don't make excuses for me. I'm having flashbacks to that torture session." The moment he mentioned it, he wished he hadn't reminded himself of the pain. Grimly he added, "I'm dangerous, and you need to ditch me."

Her answer was swift and decisive. "No. I won't last a couple of seconds out there without you."

Maybe it was the truth. Maybe she was saying it for effect. And maybe the idea of her ditching him made his stomach knot. He couldn't sort out facts from supposition right now. And certainly not any personal feelings.

Instead he focused on practicalities. Starting with his physical condition. He hadn't needed another injury, but his head ached again, and also his ankle. He must have twisted it in the fall. Maybe broken it. Jesus, that would be bad news.

"How long was I out?"

"Only a couple of seconds."

That was the good news, he hoped.

"You said that man's name. Trainer. The one you told me about before. He was the one torturing you?"

"His men were doing most of the work," he clipped out, hoping she'd drop the subject.

Gingerly, he moved his arms and legs. They all seemed to work, except for the pain in his ankle, but at least he didn't think it was broken. Looking up to judge how far he'd tumbled, he saw smoke seeping into the tunnel from the crack around the closed trapdoor.

When he began to cough, Morgan gripped his arm, reminding him where they were and why. Her voice was low and urgent as she said, "We have to get out of here."

"Right." No time for self-recriminations or

anything else besides the basics—survival. He'd figure out the rest of it after they got out of here. Pushing himself off the dirt floor, he winced as he felt new bruises that had joined the old ones.

She helped him climb to his feet. While she was reaching to scoop up the knapsacks, he tested his ankle.

"Careful of your head," she said.

He raised a hand above him, feeling the low earthen ceiling and stooping slightly as he steadied himself with a hand against the rough wall.

Picking up the flashlight, Morgan shined the beam down the tunnel.

It looked like no one had been here in the past century. Even with the support timbers every few feet, he didn't like the odds of the ceiling holding, especially with the fire burning above and making the house shift.

"You ever been in here?"

"I knew about the tunnel from listening to my grandma's stories about the Underground Railroad. I found it and went down a couple of times." She made a tsking sound. "Until my dad caught me and punished me for playing there."

"Why?"

"He said it was old, and it could collapse."

"Great." He looked at the equipment they'd brought. It was tempting to just leave it, but he knew that would be a mistake. If they got away from here, they'd need the survival gear.

When he scooped up a backpack and slung it over his shoulder, she did the same.

She stayed right beside him as he tried not to limp.

"You hurt your leg."

He gave her the only answer he could. "I'll manage."

He made his way awkwardly down the passage, keeping his hand on the wall and his shoulders bent so that he'd fit under the low ceiling. The position didn't help his physical condition, but after maybe two minutes, they reached another ladder. It led to another trapdoor closed by a metal bar that fit into a metal slot. When he climbed up and tried to move it to the side, the bar seemed to have rusted into place.

Behind them, the smoke was billowing more thickly, and it was worse up near the tunnel's ceiling. Then he caught the flicker of flames coming from the room where they'd first entered.

As he watched, the old timbers above the front of the tunnel began to smolder. They were damp and didn't burst into flames immediately, but soon this place would be a barbecue pit, with them as the smoked meat.

He turned back to the door, trying again to push the bar aside, but time and disuse had fixed it solidly into place.

Could they shoot their way out? Maybe. But the gunfire would alert Trainer's men that they were still alive and outside the house.

"Move over," Morgan said. As she spoke, the words triggered a coughing fit, and she stopped climbing while she recovered.

Knowing he had to focus on escape, Jack worked his way to the side of the ladder, and she stepped up beside him. He threw an arm around her shoulder, wedging her against himself.

"Sorry."

"About what?"

"Throwing you down. Just what you needed, under the circumstances."

"Don't worry about that." She was holding a T-shirt, which she wrapped around her hands before reaching for the bar, making a cushion between her palms and the rough metal.

"Now," she whispered.

He added his strength to her effort, tugging upward with everything he had. For long seconds he thought it wouldn't be enough. Then with a ripping sound, it finally came free, throwing them both off balance as it flew upward, sending leaves and other forest debris raining down on their heads, which started Morgan coughing again.

He lowered the door and rubbed her back, feeling her shoulders shake as she struggled to stop making noise.

He kept the exit closed until she had quieted.

"I'm all right," she said when she was able to speak again.

He hoped it was true. There was nobody out here who could treat either one of them for smoke inhalation.

He steadied himself and cautiously pushed the trapdoor upward again, letting in filtered light, the roar of the fire behind them, and fresh air that was tainted with smoke. They both dragged in several breaths. The oxygen helped clear his head.

"I'm going to take a look," he whispered.

Climbing up a couple more rungs, he cautiously stuck his head up just far enough to see the area around the trapdoor.

The tunnel exit was screened by brambles and small trees that must have grown up since the escape route was dug. Some of the tree roots pulled free when they wrenched the door open.

Swiveling around so that he could look in all directions, he saw that they had come up behind the rear of the burning house—about fifty yards away from the scene of the action.

Trainer's troops, dressed in combat gear with guns ready, were standing in a circle, their attention glued to the conflagration. He couldn't see all of their faces from here, but he could identify all of them by their stance and bearing. Everyone a Trainer loyalist, picked for their ideology. They weren't here to put out the blaze or save anyone's life. But what had Jack expected—that the militia leader would have called the fire department?

From Jack's position, he could see six men. Ryder, Chambers, Salter, Porter, Hamilton, and Jessup. He assumed there were more outside of his line of sight.

Ducking back inside the tunnel, he spoke to Morgan in a whisper. "I'm going out. Keep the door cracked, and keep your eyes on me. When I motion for you to follow, stay low."

She nodded, and he eased out of the tunnel, keeping almost flat to the ground as he assessed the situation. From below the trapdoor, he could hear Morgan's harsh breathing.

Satisfied that none of the militiamen was watching anything besides the blaze, he motioned to Morgan. She handed the sleeping bag up first, then flopped out onto a bed of brown leaves, imitating his low profile.

Turning, she stared back at the house that was now reduced to flames and blackened timbers.

The sad look on her face tore at him.

"Sorry," he whispered. "I guess you loved that place."

"I have mixed feelings, actually."

The way she said it made him want to know more, but there wasn't time for any personal discussion now.

They weren't out of the woods yet, so to speak.

Sweeping his arms along the ground, he gathered leaves and scattered them over the trapdoor, trying to make the spot blend back into the rest of the forest floor.

Morgan helped, gritting her teeth, probably to repress another coughing fit. He looked at her with concern, worried about her lungs and worried that she might reveal their position if she couldn't stay silent.

He pointed away from the house and started to move, easing along on hands and knees. It was an awkward way to travel, and he stopped to rest when they'd put fifty more yards between themselves and the action.

Looking around again, he spotted trouble another twenty-five yards ahead.

When he went stock-still, Morgan looked at him questioningly. He flattened himself against the ground and pointed. Ahead of them was one of Trainer's new recruits, a tall man in his thirties with sandy hair and pale skin named Gibson. Most of Trainer's troops had been in the military, but Gibson had been a truck driver who'd lost his job when his long-distance company had to lay off some men. Way behind everyone else in his level of training, he hadn't spotted them because he was facing away, taking a leak against a tree.

They stayed in position, waiting for the man to finish. He finally zipped up his pants, turned away from the tree, and fixed his gaze toward the house.

Jack looked toward Morgan and saw her face working and her jaw muscles tensing as she tried to hold back another cough. He gripped her hand, wishing there were some way to help her.

She squeezed his fingers hard, and he knew she was trying her best to stay quiet. Her body shook, and she made small choking sounds, but finally she lost the battle to stay silent.

She gave Jack a desperate look as her chest heaved, and a wracking set of coughs shook her.

Gibson went still, then turned, his gaze searching the underbrush, swinging past them as he sought the source of the noise.

It was almost comical to watch his face register surprise and then triumph as he spotted them. Raising his gun, he charged forward toward the people he'd thought were trapped in the burning house.

Shane Gallagher crumpled up a paper coffee cup and tossed it toward the trash can with a snap of his arm. It went in, and he glanced up to see Max Lyon staring at him. They were both tough-looking men in their early thirties with dark hair and dark eyes, men you wouldn't want to anger.

In fact, both were seasoned veterans of police work—Shane with the Howard County PD and Max with the Army.

They were sitting in the comfortable lounge at the

back of the Rockfort Security Agency because both of them had given up on productive work the night before.

The offices were located in an upscale industrial park that was laid out in a wooded area on the north edge of Rockville, Maryland, not far from Washington, D.C. Most of the tenants were small businesses, among them a furniture distributor, a computer repair and maintenance company, and a health food distributor; but the location suited the Rockfort men because the rent was low and there was no hassle for parking spaces.

Inside, they'd done extensive modifications. The lounge where they sat had been furnished much like a classic man cave, with tan leather couches and easy chairs, a scarred coffee table, and a neutral rug that didn't show coffee stains. There was also a small refrigerator for beer and soft drinks. They and Jack Brandt had outfitted it when they started the agency because they'd known they could be spending long hours on the job, and they wanted a place to relax. Next to the seating area was a small bedroom where they could bunk if necessary.

Shane and Max had both been in the office all night, but neither of them had tried to sleep. They were waiting for a phone call from Jack—a call that had never come. There had been no need to stay there, of course. Jack could have called either one of them on their cell phones, but when he hadn't, they'd agreed to stay together.

Max broke the silence that had stretched into the past few hours. "We're both thinking the same thing."

Shane's attention snapped to his partner. "Yeah."

They'd been expecting Jack to check in during a ten-hour window—which had come and gone eighteen hours ago.

"He's in trouble," Max said.

"Do we call Deep Throat?"

Max shook his head. "He's not going to help us."

Deep Throat was their nickname for the man who had come to Rockfort with the offer of a covert assignment.

He'd introduced himself as a government lawyer named Arthur Cunningham. Obviously not his real name. As for his real occupation, they had decided he must work for the CIA since the spy agency was supposed to focus on espionage activities in foreign countries. Because a domestic assignment was beyond their mandate, the job was being offered under the table.

Cunningham had kept his identity hidden and played his cards close to his vest, refusing to give out any details about the job until Rockfort had accepted the offer. Shane didn't like that approach. He suspected that other security agencies had turned the assignment down flat, but Jack had wanted to consider it.

After the three agents had discussed the proposal, Shane and Max had voted against taking the job. Jack had argued that the money was too good to turn down. And the others hadn't stopped him from going ahead with the risky venture, because that wasn't the way Rockfort worked.

"This whole deal was a freaking mistake," Shane muttered.

"He wanted to do it, and he said he could handle it," Max answered.

Shane made an exasperated sound. "And we should have talked him out of it."

"You know he wasn't going to let us do that."

Shane answered with a tight nod. "I'd started thinking maybe we were wrong—that it was going okay."

Max raised his hand in a gesture of frustration. "How did your mom act when you came home way late?"

Shane couldn't repress a grin. "She'd be mad as hell—and at the same time relieved. Are you saying that's the way you feel?"

"Yeah. He shouldn't have pushed it. He should have gotten the hell out of there after six weeks when he couldn't get any information on Trainer's target. He probably took some crazy chance and got himself cornered."

Max climbed out of his chair and walked to the other side of the room, where he stood leaning a shoulder against the wall.

The bond among the three men was strong. They'd gotten caught in a drug raid at a Miami nightclub. After keeping order together all night in a downtown holding cell full of druggies and petty criminals, they got out in the morning and went out for beer. They ended up forming the Rockfort Security Agency because they were all looking for a new way to apply the skills they'd learned in their former careers. When they discovered that two of them were from the Baltimore-Washington area, they picked the Rockville location because it was convenient and because they'd gotten a good deal on the rent.

They'd been together for over a year now, taking cases that had confounded other agencies, and every job had been a success.

Which might be why Jack had thought he could get away with a one-man invasion of the most dangerous militia organization in the country.

Now it looked like the assignment had blown up in his face, unless he was just in a position where he couldn't check in.

Shane had been thinking all night about how to handle the present situation. "If we try to go in there, and they're holding him, that could be the thing that gets him killed."

"And not going in could have the same effect," Max shot back.

"We have to give it a few more hours," Shane said.

"We already have."

Shane answered with a nod.

"And then what?"

They were both silent for several moments, both thinking about how long Jack could stand up under torture. This wasn't like a TV program. Eventually everyone cracked. Or died.

"I think we're on our own. Maybe our best bet is to pretend we're on a fishing trip and see how close we can get to the militia compound."

"A fishing trip. More like a fishing expedition."

Chapter 8

AT LEAST GIBSON HADN'T THOUGHT TO GIVE A shout of alarm to the other militiamen gathered around the burning house. That and his momentary hesitation gave Jack the precious seconds he needed to derail the attack. Ignoring the pain in his ankle, he sprang forward, catching the guy in the legs and bringing him down with a muffled thud in the fallen leaves. As he fell, he was already struggling like a madman to get the gun back into firing position. They rolled through a pile of leaves and sticks, Jack trying to keep the guy from firing, but the militiaman was just as desperate to hang on to the weapon and get off a shot.

Neither of them had a clear advantage. Although Jack was vastly more skilled, he was still suffering from the effects of the fall. Gibson was highly motivated, but his technique was lacking.

As Jack whacked the man's gun hand against the ground, Morgan dashed in, still coughing and holding a piece of dead wood. She circled the fighters, trying to get a crack at Gibson. Before she could, Jack pounded the man's head against a rock sticking up on the ground.

As he made a strangled sound and went still, Jack disentangled himself, looking back toward the house to see if anyone had observed the ruckus. As far as he could tell, the rest of the militiamen were still firmly focused on the burning building.

"We have to get out of here," Morgan wheezed.

Jack knew it wasn't that simple as he looked from her to the man he'd put out of commission. "Unfortunately, we can't leave him here."

"What do you mean?"

"I mean, when he comes to, he'll run back to the group and tell them he saw us. Then they'll know we got out of the house somehow. If that happens, we'll lose any advantage we had."

"What are we going to do?"

Jack was still thinking aloud. "We can't shoot him."

"Hide him?"

Jack shook his head. Earlier he'd told himself he would avoid involving Morgan in what the authorities might consider murder. Now he didn't see any choice. He was still thinking aloud when he said, "There's nowhere to hide him, and shooting him would be a dead giveaway. It's got to look like he had an accident."

He looked around and spotted a dead tree about a hundred feet farther into the woods.

"Help me carry him."

"What are you going to do?"

"Just help me carry him," he ordered, knowing she wasn't going to like his plan. But he saw no option. Not if they had a chance of making a clean getaway.

She blinked as she heard the steel in his voice. When he lifted the man by the shoulders, Morgan simply stared at him.

"You have to help me," he said, using the same tone of voice. "If I drag him, the marks will show."

She gave Jack an uncertain look, then bent and picked up the man's feet. Moving as fast as they could with Gibson's dead weight between them, they carried him farther into the forest, toward the tree Jack had spotted.

"Right here." Jack unceremoniously dropped the man's head and shoulders on the ground. Morgan lowered his feet more gently.

Jack glanced over his shoulder, making sure that the forest blocked the line of sight to the house. Then he craned his neck and looked up at the tree. The lower branches were too high for him to reach, but he could swing it if she helped him.

"Make a step with your hands and give me a boost up," he said. "And when I get up there, step way back."

This time she did as he asked without complaint, and he pulled himself up to a low branch, then higher, testing each foot- and handhold as he went, ignoring the pain in his ankle. Climbing was just what he needed at the moment.

About ten feet up, he found a rotted limb that he hoped he could bring down. Bracing himself below it, he pulled as hard as he could. At first nothing happened. After taking a moment to catch his breath and gather his strength, he pulled harder, giving it everything he had and felt it give. With one more massive yank, he brought it down. It hurtled past him and hit the ground with a muffled thump, landing on the unconscious man sprawled below.

Ignoring Morgan's gasp, he climbed back down and knelt beside the troop, feeling for a pulse in the neck. There was none.

He stepped back, examining the scene with an assessing eye. It wasn't a perfect setup, but it was the best he could do in faking an accident. Hopefully, it looked like Gibson had been standing in the wrong place at the wrong time when a branch had come down. Maybe it would work. Maybe it wouldn't, but it was their best shot.

Morgan's face was stark as she stared from him to Gibson and back again. "You killed him."

"No choice. He was going to kill us. Or turn us in to Trainer. That would be worse."

"You murdered him," she accused.

"I'm an ex–Navy SEAL. We're trained to kill if it's necessary to keep ourselves alive."

"You were a SEAL?"

"Yeah."

"You didn't kill those other two men. The ones who came to the house."

"No point in it. Trainer knew where they'd gone. He was going to come and investigate when they didn't report in."

As she continued to stare at him, he said, "We'd better get the hell out of here before somebody notices he's missing and comes looking."

When he reached for her hand, and she pulled her arm back, it felt like she'd slapped him across the face. It shouldn't matter what she thought of him, but something inside him seemed to go dead. A torrent of words clamored behind his closed lips. He longed to explain to her what it meant to be in a war and what choices you were forced to make. He suspected she probably wouldn't understand, and he didn't have the energy to spare.

Perhaps she'd come to recognize his point of view. Or perhaps she wouldn't. With a sigh he gestured toward a large oak about fifty feet farther on.

"Hide behind that tree. I'm going back for the sleeping bag—and to make sure nobody can tell there was a scuffle around here. And if they get me, run in the other direction as fast as you can."

At least she didn't give him an argument about hiding. He waited until she had taken a position behind the tree trunk, then crouched low and hurried back the way they'd come, knowing that his throbbing ankle was going to be a problem.

As he moved from tree to tree, he kept checking out the men who had come to kill him and Morgan.

They seemed totally focused on the blazing spectacle. Still, he was careful as he made sure Trainer hadn't stationed anyone else in this section of the woods.

Working as quickly as he could, he scattered dry leaves over the spot where he and Gibson had fought, then retrieved the sleeping bag and the packs before reversing his direction, finally catching up with Morgan who was peering out from behind the tree.

Her expression was still closed, but at least she hadn't taken off without him.

"We'd better split before they figure out we escaped. They may do it anyway, but at least we'll have a head start."

When she answered with a barely perceptible nod, then looked away, he felt the ache in his gut again. He wanted to reach for her and fold her close, the way he had after they'd bested the intruders. Was it possible to transmit what he was feeling from the physical contact? Perhaps if he understood his own feelings better. He'd been closed up for months, willing to take any dangerous case that Rockfort offered because he hadn't cared what happened to himself. That attitude had gotten him in big trouble.

And he understood now that his lack of success in figuring out Trainer's grand plan had made him reckless. Too bad the militia leader played his cards so close to his chest. He was pretty sure the man was planning an attack on D.C., but he had no idea of the method. Chemical weapons? Biological? Nuclear? It depended on his contacts and his funding.

Even though Wade Trainer never struck it rich in his lifetime, he'd somehow acquired enough money to fund an expensive militia operation. He'd paid cash for fifty acres in the foothills of the Blue Ridge Mountains. It was actually an old camp where wealthy parents had sent their preteen sons to toughen them up in the wild. The camp director had talked a good game, convincing moms and dads who were worried about their offspring's soft upbringing that he would turn them into men. But when a boy had finally cracked and revealed that the fifty-year-old director was taking good-looking young boys into his bed, the place had been closed down and the owner thrown into jail.

That had cut the price of the property, but it was still a lot of cash for a guy like Trainer. Ditto the money he'd spent on modifying the buildings and buying enough guns and ammo to outfit a banana republic.

His recruits were men who felt that the American system had given them the shaft. Men who were looking for a way to get even. Most had been in some branch of the armed forces, usually guys who had been less than honorably discharged.

Jack had learned all that and more before he'd put himself in a position to be noticed by Trainer by showing up at a bar the guy frequented and picking a fight with another patron. And he'd convinced himself he had enough background to fit in with the other Real Americans Militia recruits. But he understood now that he'd left out an essential ingredient—an emotional investment in the job. Or more to the point, an emotional investment in himself.

And since Morgan had rescued him, he had discovered that he cared in a way he hadn't anticipated, although now it was more about her than himself.

As those thoughts went through his head, rain began to fall again. A good thing, if you wanted to wipe out evidence. Not so good if you were roughing it in the woods on a cold night.

He struggled to repress a shudder as he considered the mess he and Morgan were in.

If he hadn't been functional when those two goons had showed up, she'd have ended up dead, and now he was obligated to get her to safety. Only it felt like more than an obligation. She wasn't just some person who'd save his life. She was Morgan Rains, a strong resourceful woman he'd very quickly come to admire.

He knew she didn't return the admiration. Not now.

Sliding her a sidewise look, he saw that her expression was still grim as she walked through the rain beside him.

Was he slowing her down now? Would she have a better chance without him? He wished he knew.

He started searching through the underbrush and cut a sapling he could use as a walking stick, a stick about four feet long. Leaning on it, he took some of the weight off the ankle.

It helped, but not enough.

As Morgan tramped along beside the man who had rescued her, she tried to evaluate his mental stability, wishing she had continued as a clinician. But she'd gone into teaching because of an incident that still made her cringe.

She'd been doing an internship at Springfield State Hospital and been working with a man named Leonard Wrigley, who was severely depressed. He'd responded favorably to her in their sessions, and she'd thought she was making progress with him—until it had all blown up in her face. One of the hospital aides had found Wrigley hanging in the shower—in time to cut him down and save his life, as it turned out.

But it had been a daunting introduction to clinical practice for Morgan, even though the hospital's chief psychiatrist assured her that the suicide attempt wasn't her fault. At the time, she knew that George Mason University was looking for an associate professor of psychology, and she'd applied for the job. With her outstanding academic record, she'd beaten out a whole slew of other candidates. She'd stayed at the school and worked her way up in the department to full professor.

Now she looked over at Jack Brandt. He'd just cold-bloodedly killed a man. Not in the heat of battle but with a cunningly conceived and executed plan. Did that mean she was in the clutches of a psychopath? Or sociopath? Or someone with an antisocial personality? Whatever you wanted to call it.

She'd taught an abnormal psychology course, and she was familiar with the type, at least in theory. Grimly she began ticking off the characteristics in her head.

Psychopaths came across as charming. They had a grandiose sense of self-worth. They were cunning and manipulative and good liars. They were emotionally shallow and lacked remorse or guilt. They failed to accept responsibility for their actions, had poor behavior control, lacked realistic long-term goals, were impulsive and irresponsible, as well as criminally versatile.

Going down the list of traits occupied her mind for a while, and when she was finished, she was feeling better about the grim-faced Navy SEAL walking beside her. Much as she hated what he'd done when he'd deliberately dropped that tree limb on the man, he wasn't following a classic psychopathic pattern.

He hadn't tried to manipulate her. He'd seemed genuinely remorseful after the episode where he'd thrown her against the wall in the tunnel. And he hadn't come across as impulsive or irresponsible.

He was trying to save his own life. And hers. And much as she hated some of his methods, she believed they might be due to his SEAL training, unless he was lying about that and everything else.

What's more, now that she had time to consider

his decision to drop the tree branch on the man, she couldn't fault his logic. If the attacker could have told Trainer that they'd escaped into the woods, then the men who'd watched the house burn would already be in hot pursuit.

Would Glenn have had the guts to do the same thing?

The question brought her up short. Why was she thinking about her deceased husband *now*? He had no place in this scenario. He never would have gotten her into this kind of trouble. He'd had a safe job. A safe life, and he'd liked it that way. They both had, until fate had stepped in and changed everything.

Too bad she hadn't played it safe yesterday. She'd gotten herself into trouble by bringing Jack inside. But she knew there was no way she would have done anything differently if she'd gotten the chance. Regardless of the consequences, she would have taken Jack Brandt in.

———

The fire had died down, and the rain helped turn the charred dwelling into a sopping mess of smoke stink and burned household items. Wade Trainer took a step closer and dragged in a breath of the tainted air, trying and failing to detect the odor of charred human flesh. But it had been pretty hot in there. Maybe Barnes and his lady friend had been reduced to ash.

On the other hand, the flames had never been as hot as a crematorium furnace. Perhaps it was possible to find some charred bones as evidence. In fact, he'd feel a lot better if he could find proof that Barnes and Morgan Rains were dead.

Wade had assumed that Barnes and the woman would try to get out, and he'd had men ready to capture or kill them the moment they emerged from the burning building. Their decision to stay inside had taken him by surprise.

"Hamilton and Chambers," he called out.

Two of his troops stepped smartly forward, ready to receive his orders.

"Take a Land Rover back to camp, and bring three shovels, three rakes, and some plastic trash bags."

"Yes, sir," they both answered.

As the two men hurried off down the road to where they'd parked the four-wheel-drive vehicles, Wade shifted his weight from foot to foot. He'd like to get confirmation of death, then go back to the compound and reassess his options.

Like for example, had Barnes gotten any messages out, and if so, what had he said? And to whom?

He thought about his own office and his quarters. A time or two, when he'd come back after being out, he'd wondered if anyone had been inside poking around. Then his man had caught Barnes in there red-handed.

But so what?

There was nothing to find, unless the man had gotten into his password-protected computer, and that was impossible.

Chapter 9

Jack's words brought Morgan out of her own thoughts.

She watched as he sat down on a log, opened the pack he'd brought from the house, and took out the T-shirt she had used to wrap her hand when she'd tugged on the door bar that was rusted shut.

Leaning down, he took off his sock and examined his right ankle. It was red and swollen, twice as big as the left.

"Too bad we don't have any ice," she murmured.

"Yeah. But I can improvise a pressure bandage."

He stopped talking again, and there was nothing to hear but the pounding of the rain. She wanted to talk to him. If they could have a normal conversation, maybe she could understand him better.

But so far nothing about her time with him had been within the realm of her everyday experience. Not since she'd first found him naked and beaten in the woods. Everything that had happened made it hard to connect with him on any kind of normal level.

On the other hand, she could evaluate what she'd seen so far—and not by checking off a list of psychopathic traits. He was a fighter. And a man who did what he had to do to get a job done. She should thank him for that, not by trying to do a psych evaluation on the fly. Probably that had been a defense mechanism on her part. Now her defenses had crumbled.

She wanted to reach out and touch his arm, but the closed expression on his face made her keep her hands to herself, because she was still trying to figure out how she felt and how she *should* feel. Or did that matter? She wasn't planning to make friends with him. Or be his lover.

She clenched her hands into fists, wondering why her mind was leaping in that direction again. Her lover?

A while ago he'd come across as a ruthless killer. Now that the shock had worn off, she understood his motivation, and she was hoping he'd come up with a plan that would save the two of them.

"Sorry," she murmured, wondering how many meanings she was giving to the apology—and how many he would take.

He gave her a small nod of acknowledgment, then pushed himself up, using the walking stick he'd found. As soon as his foot hit the ground, he clamped his teeth together. He must be in considerable pain, and if he kept walking, he might end up with a permanent injury.

"You have to get off that ankle," she said.

"We haven't put enough distance between us and the militia. We can't take a chance on sticking around here. We have to keep going."

When she clenched her fingers on his arm, his head swung toward her.

"I don't think so."

As she watched his expression change to one of resignation, she breathed out a small sigh and filled in another mental box on his psych evaluation. He was determined, but he was also practical and willing to change his plans when a more reasonable alternative presented itself.

———∿∿∿———

Jack ran a shaky hand down his wet face and into his dripping hair. Since they'd escaped from the burning house, raw nerves had kept him going as he'd tried to get as far away as possible from Trainer's men. Now he was forced to consider alternatives.

He looked toward the mountain that was ahead of them before turning to the east and west, as he called to mind the extensive research he'd done on the area. It had been part of his preparation for the assignment before he'd gone into that bar and caught Wade Trainer's attention. Probably he'd been subconsciously thinking about escape routes if he got into trouble.

"There are a lot of caves around here. Maybe we can find one," he said.

"You mean like Luray Caverns?" she asked, referring to the most famous cavern in the area. It had been lighted and outfitted with walkways for tourists, where guides told them the cutesy names given to some of the stalagmite and stalactite formations.

"Nothing quite so fancy," he answered. "Just a place where we can get dry and warm. Have you ever stumbled into one?"

"Sorry. No."

They were still in the forest, but about an eighth of a mile ahead, he could see through the trees a cliff rising in front of them.

Gesturing toward it, he said, "That's a good bet."

When she answered with a weak nod, he hoped

that he remembered his geography well enough to find the right kind of place.

As he started toward the natural wall, the impact of every step sent a painful reverberation up his leg, but he ignored the sensation. And when he saw Morgan watching him, he struggled to keep his expression neutral.

"You have to stop walking," she said.

"When we find shelter."

"What if we don't?"

"We'll make one."

"Why don't we do that now?"

"Because a cave is better, for a lot of reasons," he answered, thinking that she was speaking to him again. Had she stopped thinking of him as a cold-blooded killer, or had she simply decided that it was impractical to give her traveling companion the silent treatment?

The rain was falling harder by the time they reached an open area strewn with weeds, large boulders, and hidden rocks that made walking difficult. He picked his way carefully across, leaning on his stick and cursing when he almost went down a couple of times. Beside him, Morgan also stumbled, and he slowed his pace to accommodate both of them.

He wished he could see the surface of the wall better, but the driving rain obscured his vision as did the thick vines trailing down the rock face. Virginia creeper, wild strawberries, and honeysuckle, he thought. Along with some lichens and moss.

After stopping a few yards away from the barrier, he looked up and saw where a pile of rocks had fallen. There might be more coming down, especially in the rain, but he couldn't worry about them now.

Stepping up to the wall, he braced his knees and made sure his bad leg wasn't going to go out from under him. Then, with the walking stick, he began to pull the vines aside, looking for an opening beyond the cover of vegetation.

At first he saw nothing but stone and more stone. Choosing a direction at random, he began moving to the right, continuing to sweep the vines aside. He felt his spirits leap when the walking stick pressed through the green covering into a cavity beyond.

In the next second, he smelled something rank that made the hair on his arms prickle. A low growl of warning confirmed his fears.

"Get back," he shouted to Morgan.

Even as he called out, a large tan shape leaped from the cavern beyond the vines.

It was a two-hundred-pound mountain lion, its teeth bared and its eyes fixed on the man who had invaded its lair.

As the animal sprang, Jack acted instinctively. Raising the walking stick, he bashed at the charging animal. The blow helped deflect the attack, but he felt a ripping sensation in his shoulder as he went down under the impact of the beast's body and knew its sharp teeth had mauled him.

When he whacked at the lion again, it switched directions, heading for what looked like an easier target—Morgan.

She screamed as it sprang on her, raising her hand to protect her face.

Ignoring the pain in his shoulder, Jack swung around, pulling the gun from the waistband of his slacks. With little time to think, he fired.

Chapter 10

THE ANIMAL ROARED, THEN LEAPED AWAY. JACK saw where the bullet impacted the fur of its right shoulder, heard its scream of rage.

But before he could assess the damage, it reconsidered its options. Turning tail, it fled across the field and swiftly disappeared.

Jack felt a wave of regret. He'd taken the animal by surprise, and it had reacted by defending its den. He'd wounded it, possibly fatally. That made him feel worse than killing Gibson. What did that say about him?

No time for self-evaluation. He'd better focus on keeping himself and Morgan alive. He went absolutely still, his eyes scanning the woods behind them and the field surrounding the cliff. When none of Trainer's men emerged from behind the trees, he breathed out a small sigh. Maybe they were too far away to have heard the shot. Or if they had, maybe they'd think it was a hunter in the area.

He prayed he and Morgan were in the clear, because he suspected neither of them was going anywhere anytime soon.

Turning, he looked at Morgan who was lying on the ground, her face white as paper.

He hurried toward her, his gaze traveling swiftly over her, zeroing in on the shredded sleeve of her jacket. Blood oozed out of the fabric, mixing with the rain that was still falling steadily.

"It got you."

"Did it?" She tried to push herself up and winced, her face going even paler as she saw the blood.

When her eyes closed and she fell back against the wet ground, he feared she was going into shock.

He came down beside her, reaching to touch her shoulder. When she didn't move, he felt his chest constrict. Cautiously he pulled the torn fabric aside. The flesh beneath was mauled, but the bites didn't look deep. And the oozing blood told him that the animal hadn't chomped into an artery.

"Hang on," he murmured.

"I am," she said in the barest whisper.

He gathered her close for a moment, needing to hold her before he eased away.

"I'm going to leave you for just a minute."

She made a mumbling sound.

After taking a flashlight from his pack, he made his way cautiously toward the cave where the charging animal had emerged. With the gun in one hand and the light in the other, he shouldered the vines aside and stepped into the darkness beyond.

When he shined the light around the chamber, he saw spiderwebs in the upper reaches. On the floor were animal droppings and bones, but not what he had most feared. Thank God there were no cubs inside. The lion had not been defending her family.

Hurrying back to Morgan where she still lay in the rain, he scooped her up in his arms and carried her just inside the shelter, leaning her shoulders against the rough cave wall, before going back for the packs and the sleeping bag.

When he returned, Morgan was sitting limp and still with her eyes closed and her head canting to one side. Her hair and clothes were plastered to her from the rain. He looked down at his own clothing and saw that his condition was similar. Their light jackets were soaked through.

They'd have to do something about the wet and cold, but first things first. He took one ground cloth from a pack and spread it out. Then he unrolled the sleeping bag and laid it on top, followed by another ground cloth. When he'd finished with the bedding, he picked up Morgan and carried her over, then laid her down.

She wrinkled her nose as she took in the animal scent of the cave. "Ugh."

"Better than being cold and wet," he answered, glad that she had noticed the lion smell. It meant that she was still reacting to her surroundings.

He would have liked to clean up the cave for her, but there was no time for such niceties now. He had to make sure they were safe.

Picking up the flashlight again, he walked farther back into the cavern, noting that the ceiling sloped lower as it angled into the cliff.

He walked about sixty feet toward the back, seeing that other animals had used the shelter. Hopefully none of them were coming back anytime soon. He also saw a circle of stones and charred sticks. Other people had been in here, but not recently, he decided as he kicked at the ashes.

The idea of lighting a fire was very tempting, but he knew it wasn't a good idea. Not when the flames and smoke could lead Trainer and his men to the shelter. The cave went farther back. There might be another way out, but he wasn't going to look for it now.

When he came back to the cave entrance, Morgan's eyes fluttered open and fixed on him.

"Where were you?" she whispered.

"Making sure we didn't have any company."

Coming down beside her, he gave her a considering look. Her face was pale and wet with perspiration, and he knew she needed medical attention. Rummaging in the pack, he pulled out the first aid kit.

"I'm going to take a look at your arm."

When Morgan nodded, he tried to push back the wet sleeve of her jacket to get to her wound. But it was too waterlogged and too bulky.

"Can you take your jacket and shirt off?"

When she didn't respond, he unzipped the jacket before reaching for the buttons at the front of the shirt.

Her eyes flew open and her hand stopped him as he began to ease the top button open.

"What are you doing?"

"I've got to look at that bite. I can't do it with your shirt and jacket in the way."

She considered that. "Oh, right."

Her hand dropped back to her side.

He worked the buttons as quickly as possible, then raised her shoulders up so that he could pull her good arm out of the shirt and jacket at the same time. Then he turned to the injured side. Carefully he peeled the fabric away from the mauled flesh, trying to keep his focus on her arm. But it was impossible not to notice the front of her body.

She was wearing a light pink bra of some delicate fabric that was almost transparent from the water that had soaked through. He hadn't looked at a woman's breasts in a long time, and he didn't want to do it now, but they were on display, and there was no way to keep himself from admiring her. Her breasts were medium-sized and nicely rounded. And he could clearly see the dark circles of her nipples through the fabric. The cold had puckered them so that they stabbed against the cups, drawing a response from him that he told himself he didn't want and certainly didn't need under the present circumstances. They were still in bad trouble. The only way they were going to get out alive was if he kept his focus on the mission—not on Morgan Rains' breasts.

He didn't have a relationship with this woman. He didn't want a relationship with her. Or anybody else, he silently added. Yet circumstances had thrown them together, making it impossible for him to ignore his reactions to her.

Her shirt was stiff with blood and had stuck to her skin. He opened a water bottle and wet the fabric, peeling it away as gently as he could, but she groaned as the material came free.

"Sorry."

"Not your fault," she answered.

He spared another glance at her face. Her skin was still pale, but she seemed more alert than when he'd first started undressing her.

That was good from a medical point of view, but not so good for the awareness arcing between them.

A few moments ago, she'd been out of it. Now she was as focused on him as he was on her.

Grimly, he finished removing the shirt, then turned his attention to her injury. The animal had left teeth marks in her forearm, above her elbow.

She dragged her gaze away from him to look at her arm.

"It bled a lot."

"That's good. With bites."

"Um."

He poured on more water, then opened the first aid kit, relieved to find antiseptic, which he soaked onto a gauze pad that he used to wipe the wound.

She winced, then took her lower lip between her teeth.

"Sorry."

She gave the same answer as before. When he had finished cleaning the area, he wrapped strips of gauze around her arm and tied it off, before reaching for her pack and pulling out a dry shirt.

"Can you get into this?"

"I think so."

"An analgesic will help."

"There's some in the first aid kit, right?"

He looked in the kit again and found the tablets. He hadn't even been thinking about them, but they'd also help the sprained ankle.

They both took two, washing them down with water.

When they'd finished, she started pulling on her dry shirt, and he started unbuttoning his wet one.

Like hers, it was stiff with blood. Carefully, he wet the fabric and worked it off his shoulder so that he could look at his own injury.

More bite marks.

Morgan sat up and scooted closer, inspecting the wound. "You need antiseptic too."

He nodded.

This time she was the one who washed his wound with water and gauze, then poured pungent liquid on more gauze and stroked it onto the wounds. She also put more salve on the burn marks from the torture session.

"We should be on antibiotics," she said.

"Yeah, if we had any," he answered as he pulled on a dry flannel shirt.

Her teeth had started to chatter in reaction to the cold. So had his. "We've got to get warm."

She looked toward the cave entrance. "And we can't light a fire, right?"

"I think that might lead Trainer to us." He looked from her jeans to his and back again. "Get out of your wet pants."

"I didn't bring any more."

"Neither did I."

Standing up, he pulled off his wet jeans and laid them out on the cave floor, glad that the tails of his shirt reached to his thighs.

"You too," he said, making his voice firm as he fought to keep his teeth from clacking together.

She lay back, unbuttoning the wet pants, then working the zipper and lifting her hips so that she could wiggle out of the garment.

He took it from her and spread it on the cave floor beside his.

"We both need to get into the sleeping bag," he said.

He expected her to protest, but apparently she understood the practicalities of the situation. And perhaps she had stopped being revolted that he'd murdered a man in cold blood. He didn't discuss that with her. He simply unzipped the side of the bag so that she could slip inside.

"Move over so you've got the closed edge."

Again she did as he asked, and he slipped in after her, pulling the top ground cloth over the bag as an extra covering. He thought about turning so that his back was to her front. But that would expose his chest to the cold. Instead, he took her in his arms.

He was bone weary and in pain from everything he'd endured. Which should have made him numb, but he couldn't stop from reacting.

As he pulled her against the length of his body, he tried not to think about her tempting breasts, her narrow waist, the curve of her thigh. The position was much too intimate, with Morgan at his front and cool air at his back where the zipper of the sleeping bag was open.

She said nothing, even though she couldn't fail to be aware of his erection rising between them.

He didn't apologize.

"We've both had a rough day. We should try to get some sleep," he murmured.

She answered with an unsteady laugh. "Is that what you call it? A rough day."

"Yeah."

Without his conscious thought, his hands skimmed over her back. Maybe he was comforting her. Or comforting himself. He didn't want to examine his motives too closely. It felt good to hold on to her. Perhaps to hold on to anyone after all the months when he'd denied himself solace.

Gradually she relaxed against him, her head drifting to his shoulder.

"Get some sleep."

"I don't think I can." She dragged in a breath and let it out. "We haven't had much time to talk. Tell me something about yourself."

He didn't want to talk about himself, but maybe a conversation would help defuse the situation.

"Like what?"

"Where were you born? Where did you grow up?"

He could tell the truth or lie. Lying seemed like too much trouble at the moment, especially since he'd have to remember what he'd said. "My dad was an army sergeant. I was born at Fort Bragg. I grew up on a lot of different bases, including in Germany, but one army base is a lot like the next."

"But unsettling to a kid. When you move around all the time, you're constantly having to make new friends."

"I got used to it. And the other kids were in the same boat."

"I would have hated it. I liked staying in the same school and the same neighborhood."

Deliberately switching the focus to her, he asked, "Where did you grow up?"

"In Washington, D.C. My dad worked for the city government. We only moved once. From a little apartment on upper Connecticut Avenue to a house near Chevy Chase Circle. On Kanawha Street. Do you know D.C.?"

"A little."

"We lived in the Woodrow Wilson school district."

"That red-brick school on Nebraska Avenue?"

"Yes."

"And then you went away to college?"

"I got a scholarship from American University, so I stayed in town."

He liked listening to her talk. He wanted to ask more personal questions, like where she'd met her husband and how long they'd been married, but he kept those to himself.

Wade Trainer stood with his back straight and stiff as he watched six of his men tramp through the remains of the house, wet ashes sticking to their boots and the pant legs of their uniforms as they sifted through the charred remains. The only reason it was possible to do it was because the rain had wet down the remains of the fire.

There were still pieces of wood left. And household objects. The men would unearth a knife or a spoon from the kitchen or the frame of a lamp or a doorknob, then toss it back into the soggy black mess.

He waited for someone to call out that they'd found a bone or anything else that could be identified as human remains. Or maybe a watch Barnes or the woman had been wearing. So far, they had found no indication that the couple had been in the house.

How hot did it have to be to turn bone to ash? He pulled out his smartphone and found Google, then typed in the question. Which led him to "cremation."

In a crematorium, the temperature was between

1600 and 1800 degrees Fahrenheit. But the fire in the house couldn't possibly have been that hot. There would be something left, wouldn't there?

He was watching the men methodically working the grid he'd laid out for them, when Chambers screamed, the sound fading as he disappeared from sight.

Everyone went stock-still, looking to Trainer for guidance.

From out of sight, Chambers had started to call out frantically.

"Help me. I think my leg is broken. Help."

"Get him," Wade ordered.

The other men began converging on the spot where their comrade had disappeared.

Hamilton knelt cautiously and looked down below the level of the floor.

"Jesus Christ, you jerk; don't just stare at me," Chambers shouted.

"Where are you?" the man above asked.

"In some kind of hole."

Had the floor burned through, exposing a crawl space below? Or was there something else down there, Wade wondered.

He'd stayed outside while his men searched the house, prudently leaving the salvage work to men with fewer brains than his. And now one of them had fallen through the floor. He wouldn't make the same mistake, he thought as he stepped gingerly into the blackened structure, carefully testing each footstep before he put his weight down.

Chapter 11

WHEN JACK DIDN'T ASK ANOTHER QUESTION, Morgan shifted in the sleeping bag, conscious of his hair-roughened legs against her smooth ones. Above them were his narrow hips and his broad chest. Body heat built in the confined space. And his erection stood between them like an exclamation mark.

She told herself it was a physiological reaction to being wedged against a half-naked woman.

Physically the position was much too intimate, yet it was the only way they were going to keep warm without lighting a fire in the cave.

Closing her eyes, she let the warmth envelop her. It felt comforting. Seductive, even. But she knew there could be no real intimacy between them. They'd met by chance. Probably she'd saved his life. Then he'd saved hers. More than once, she reckoned, since those fake FBI agents had showed up at the door.

Yet she knew he was a dangerous man. Dangerous to his enemies and dangerous to her in a way she didn't want to think about in too much detail. He was the kind of man she'd never thought she'd meet, much less be lying with, half-naked in a sleeping bag.

"Did your mom have a job?" he asked, probably making another attempt to pull her attention away from the physical sensation of their bodies pressed together.

What if one of them turned around? That might be

better in the long run, but it would involve a whole lot of wiggling and rubbing against each other to get there. Cutting off the speculation, she answered the question he'd asked.

"She worked for the D.C. government too, as an administrative assistant, before I was born. But she quit to stay home with me and my brother."

"And baked cookies and led the Girl Scout troop?"

"Yes. And made our Halloween costumes and the curtains in our bedrooms. And had a wonderful flower garden. What about your mom?"

"She was less domestic," he answered, his voice sharp, and she took the hint. He didn't want to talk about his family. His tone softened when he asked, "What about your friends?"

"When I was little, we had a whole neighborhood gang. But you know how it goes when you get older. The group breaks into cliques."

"And you were in the popular group."

"No. I was one of the nerds."

"You?"

"I liked learning. That was only an acceptable occupation among a small segment of the school population."

"You sound like a teacher."

She laughed softly. "I am."

"What do you teach?"

"Psychology."

Jack barked out a laugh.

"What?"

"I'll bet you were trying to figure out what kind of psychopath I am."

She felt her face heat, since that was exactly what she had been doing.

"You're not," she murmured.

"In your professional opinion?"

"Yes."

"What am I?"

She'd been thinking he was a dangerous man, but she could say it a different way. "You're a highly trained professional who saved both our lives."

"I guess you can put it in those terms."

"How would you describe yourself?"

He sighed. "Maybe we shouldn't turn this into a therapy session."

"I'm not a shrink," she answered softly.

"Why not?"

"I'm not cut out for it."

"Okay."

They were both silent now. Maybe neither of them was sure of what to say.

She had told him she couldn't sleep, but she was dead tired and wrung out from the past few hours. Without knowing what was happening, she slipped into sleep.

Jack eased his injured ankle out of the sleeping bag, careful not to wake Morgan as he cradled her in his arms, listening to the sound of her breathing change as she drifted off.

He didn't have any ice for the sprain, but maybe the cold air would serve as a partial substitute. He'd like to ease out of the sleeping bag altogether, but the cave was no protection from the cold, and he knew he'd better stay where he was if he wanted to be in shape to travel in the morning.

The morning? Was he going to put pressure on the ankle so soon? He guessed he'd find out.

He tried to get comfortable. When his arm started to fall asleep, he moved it and found that it was curling over the rounded curve of Morgan's very appealing bottom. He couldn't stop himself from being attracted to her. And not just because he liked her figure and her face.

If asked, he would have said he didn't like shrinks. But he hadn't met her in that context, and her profession had come as a surprise to him. He'd seen her as a woman who was practical, yet at the same time so damned feminine that he couldn't help responding to her. It felt like she was everything he'd always wanted— and everything he had told himself he couldn't have, because he was the only one who had walked out of that ambush in Afghanistan. He shouldn't be alive, and when he tried to relax into the rhythm of living, he always saw the faces of his old comrades in arms staring at him. Tom Lancaster. Eduardo Blaine. Phil Armstrong. Jimmy Woo. Harrison Winters. He'd been supposed to protect them. And they'd all been wiped away before his eyes.

He'd been to the required psych sessions, which was one of the reasons he didn't like shrinks. They said what they'd been trained to say. Never mind if it was true or not. Doctor Nixon had told him the guilt would fade. He hadn't been responsible for the death of anyone on the team. He hadn't done anything wrong. He knew that on an intellectual level, but he simply didn't feel it.

He'd been drifting through his life when he'd met Shane and Max. Maybe it was divine intervention. That first night in jail, he'd felt something working among the three of them. A rhythm that they all understood without putting it into words. Maybe because they all had similar backgrounds. And all had problems they didn't want to confront. It had been easier to forge ahead with the Rockfort Security Agency, to build something that none of them could have accomplished on his own.

Shane and Max had made a difference in his life. He knew that they were replacements for the friends he'd lost. He wasn't proud of using them that way, but he suspected they understood, just the way he understood them better than perhaps they understood themselves.

They'd given him the space he needed, then tried to talk him out of taking the job of infiltrating Trainer's militia. That had only made him more determined. He'd insisted that he could handle it. Maybe he'd been secretly hoping that he'd get himself killed. But when he'd been cornered, survival instinct had taken over, and he'd fought back. He'd escaped, and now he'd dragged someone into hell with him.

Morgan Rains, a woman who'd been minding her own business when he'd stumbled into her neck of the woods.

Well, he wasn't going to let the same thing happen to her that had happened to the men of his team. He was going to get her to safety, and then he was going to walk away from her, because in the long run he was no good for her.

When his foot began to feel numb, he eased it back under the covering. He would have liked to stand on it and test the injury, but he couldn't do it without waking Morgan, and he knew the best thing for her right now was sleep.

Wade Trainer made his way toward the place where Chambers had disappeared. Looking at Rayburn, he ordered, "Get down there."

Rayburn stared back at him. "How?"

Trainer hated to reconsider an order, but in this case, he did.

"Okay. Wait for me."

Still moving cautiously, he approached the spot where Hamilton and Rayburn were waiting, looking down into a ragged hole.

Pulling a small but powerful flashlight from his belt, Wade shined the beam downward and saw Chambers lying in what could have been an earthen cellar, except that the space was too narrow, and one wall appeared to be missing.

He handed the flashlight to Rayburn. "Put this in your pocket, then grab the edge of the hole and lower yourself."

"Yes, sir." The man awkwardly swung himself over the hole and grabbed the edge of the floor. It crumbled in his fingers and he went down.

There was another scream and a string of loud curses.

"Are you all right?" Trainer called out.

"Yes, sir. But I landed on top of Chambers."

"Get off of him, and tell me what you see."

He heard scrambling noises. "There's a tunnel down here."

"The devil you say. I'm coming down."

Morgan woke after a few hours of sleep. A man was lying next to her, sleeping.

At first she thought it was Glenn. Then she realized it was Jack Brandt. A man who had no place in her life. As soon as they got back to civilization, she was getting as far away from him as she could.

He was nothing like her husband. Well, that wasn't perfectly true. They were both resourceful, capable men. And caring, she silently admitted, because she knew Jack must care about her in some way, otherwise she wouldn't still be with him.

But perhaps that was simply out of a sense of obligation. He'd gotten her into trouble, and he would do his best to get her out of it.

Maybe that was part of what must be a reckless disregard for his own safety. He'd obviously taken a job that had a good chance of getting him killed. She still didn't know much about it. And maybe she should stop jumping to conclusions about his motivation.

She closed her eyes, deliberately trying to stop thinking about the man lying next to her. The only reason they were together was because of circumstances.

Her best alternative for getting her mind off him was to pick a time when she and Glenn had been happy and focus on those memories. That wasn't difficult. They'd been happy through most of their marriage. But one of the best times was when they'd gone to the Eastern Shore of Maryland to poke around the quaint little towns that hadn't changed much since the nineteenth century—except for the influx of tourists.

She slipped from thinking about that trip to being back in that moment. Once again she saw herself and Glenn buying a picnic lunch, then wandering over to the little harbor of St. Michaels where they rented a motorboat to explore the creeks off the Miles River.

They motored out of town, along the river where big estates dominated the scenery, looking at the boat docks where large cabin cruisers were tied up and speculating about the lifestyle of the people who owned them.

They turned in at a wide creek, throttling down the motor, moving slowly through the green water until they found a secluded cove.

"This looks like a good place for lunch," Glenn had said.

"And a swim."

They grinned at each other, because they were both thinking about more than lunch and a swim.

Both of them had been wearing bathing suits under their clothing. Careful not to tip the boat, they discarded their sandals, shorts, and T-shirts and slipped over the side into the water.

"It's cold," she sputtered.

"You'll get used to it."

They both warmed up quickly, playing in their own private Eden. Finally they climbed back onto the deck and flopped down on a beach towel, both of them cold and wet. But she knew they wouldn't be cold for long.

Glenn reached for her, and she came into his arms, kissing him, stroking her hands over his broad shoulders. It was so good to be with him. It had been so long since she'd held him, touched him.

She stopped to question that last thought. So long? No, they'd been together every moment on this trip.

She pushed any doubts out of her mind. A smile curved her lips as she felt him harden against her. She didn't have to tell him what she liked. He knew. When she pressed her center against his erection, he slid his hands to her bottom, anchoring her more tightly against himself as his other hand cupped her breast, stroking across her nipple.

She moved closer, moaning as the blood raced hotly through her veins. Why had she thought she'd lost Glenn? He was here with her, wasn't he?

Yet something didn't seem right.

She'd been dreaming, and she didn't want to wake up. But she forced herself to raise her lids—and she found herself staring into a man's smoldering eyes. But not Glenn's blue eyes. The dark eyes belonged to Jack Brandt.

She had her arms around him. She was moving her body against him, and he was lying absolutely still, his erection rock hard against her middle and an expression on his face that told her he was fighting the physical sensations she was generating.

She pushed at his chest, and he rolled away from her, flopping to his back on the cold stone floor of the cave.

"Oh, Lord. I'm so sorry," she mumbled as she stared at him, trying to explain to herself and to him what had happened. "I… I was… I was dreaming about my husband."

Jack answered with a tight nod. Pushing himself up, he turned away and stood up, breathing deeply, his shoulders rigid and his back straight. She watched him walk to the front of the cave and push the vines aside so that he could look out.

In the dimming light, she saw that the rain had stopped.

He stayed there for long moments before returning to the cave and picking up the pants he'd discarded.

"Still wet," he said. He put them back down and riffled through one of the packs they'd brought. Pulling out a granola bar, he handed it to her. "Eat something."

With shaky hands she unwrapped the bar, glad to have something to do. Jack pulled another bar out of the pack and moved so that his back was propped against the cave wall before unwrapping it and starting to eat.

Neither one of them spoke, and she wished they'd had the option of two sleeping bags.

But like everything else that had happened in the past day and a half, there were no choices.

Chapter 12

"MOVE OUT OF THE WAY," WADE TRAINER ORDERED.

"Yes, sir."

He waited while Rayburn pulled Chambers away from the opening above them, the injured man cursing as his buddy jostled his injured leg.

Trainer turned his head and looked at Hamilton. "Get a first aid team on Chambers as soon as I've cleared the area, and get him back to camp."

"Yes, sir."

He looked around at the remaining men. "Jessup and Porter, you're with me. Bring flashlights."

"Yes, sir," they both answered.

When the path was clear, Wade watched the two men lower themselves into the dark, dank space below the house. As Chambers had said, it wasn't a basement but a tunnel, dug into the earth, with post and crossbeam reinforcements. Not the safest place, Wade thought. But he stayed with the men, and they regrouped a few yards down the tunnel. The house had had a hidden asset. Was it an escape hatch to the outside or a hiding place where Barnes and the woman were still holed up?

"Draw your sidearms," he ordered. "They could still be down here. Check the wall for hidden doors. Stay on alert for an ambush or a booby trap."

"Yes, sir."

Tension crackled in the group as they made their

slow way forward, running their hands along the wall and shining their lights ahead of them. They found no hiding places along the walls, but after about fifty yards, they came to a ladder that led to a trapdoor. To the surface or to a hiding place where Barnes and the woman were holed up.

Once again, Wade hung back, not because he was afraid, he told himself, but because the leader didn't have to take the risks. That's why he commanded troops. "Open it," he ordered Porter.

The troop climbed the ladder and moved a metal bar aside. As Porter pushed at the door, Wade braced himself for an attack from the other side of the barrier.

But there was only silence as the man's head and shoulders disappeared from view.

"Where are you? What do you see?" Trainer called out.

"I'm looking outside. About fifty yards from the house."

"Climb out. We'll follow."

Wade was the last to reach the surface, where he took a breath of the fresh air while he looked back at the blackened remains of the structure.

The exit from the tunnel wasn't all that far away from the house. If anyone had come out this way, he and his men should have seen them. Except that everyone had been focused on the blaze, which meant that Barnes and the woman could have slipped out while nobody was looking in this direction.

He wanted to let loose a string of curses. All this time he'd been searching for proof that Barnes and Rains were dead. Now he was pretty sure why he hadn't found anything. But he knew Barnes and the woman had been damned unlucky. If it hadn't been raining, Wade and his men wouldn't have been able to go into the house so soon, and the couple would have had hours to get away. That wasn't true now.

He addressed the men waiting for more orders. "Spread out. See if you can find which way they went."

His thoughts were interrupted by a sound that set the hair bristling on the back of Trainer's neck. In the distance he heard a siren. Someone must have finally reported the fire.

He tightened his grip on his comms unit. "Is Chambers out of there?"

"Yes, sir."

"Okay. Rayburn, pick up what's left of the firebomb canister, and take it with you. Everybody out of the area. Now. I don't want any evidence that we were here."

It might not be good enough. The authorities could probably figure out that arson had been involved. But hopefully there would be no evidence linking the incident to the Real Americans Militia.

Wade looked at the men who were gathered around him.

"We'll circle around and get back to our vehicles. And keep watch. When they're gone, we'll come back and search the area."

Porter cleared his throat. "Permission to speak, sir."

"Yes?"

"Didn't you send Gibson over this way?"

Trainer gave him a sharp look. In all the uproar, he'd forgotten one of his men wasn't accounted for.

"Where is he?"

"No idea, sir."

"Well, he'd better not get caught by the firefighters, and he'd better have a damn good reason for not showing up."

"Maybe something happened to him," Porter said.

"Like what?"

"An accident. Or maybe he met up with Barnes."

Trainer answered with a curt nod. He was considering the same possibilities.

—∿∿—

Nothing much had changed since Shane Gallagher had tossed the coffee cup into the trash. He and his partner, Max Lyon, had put their other business on hold, and neither one of them had left the office, even to get something to eat. Neither one of them was hungry, but they'd both eaten some power bars because they might have to split at a moment's notice if Jack called.

That possibility was seeming more and more remote.

When the phone rang, both men leaped toward the instrument, hoping against hope that it was Jack.

But the familiar number made them both go still. It was Deep Throat, aka Arthur Cunningham, the government operative who had hired them to infiltrate the Real Americans Militia.

"Can we let it ring?" Max asked.

"Bad idea. We're working for him."

Max nodded. "Maybe we'll pick up some information."

Shane pressed the speaker button so they could both hear.

"Gallagher. I have Max Lyon on the phone with me," he added.

"What's going on with Jack Brandt?" Cunningham asked immediately.

Shane hesitated.

"According to my project notes, you were expecting him to report in, right? And I was expecting to hear from you."

"We were waiting for his call. But he can't always get back to us on schedule."

"Have you heard from him?"

"No."

"Do you have any idea what's going on at the militia camp?"

"No."

"There was a fire reported in the area."

Max and Shane exchanged glances.

"What's your source of information?" Shane asked.

"I'm keeping tabs on the local situation."

"A fire—where?"

"At the vacation home of a woman named Morgan Rains."

"Who is she?"

"A college professor. I don't know much else yet. Except that her house was about a mile and a half from the militia compound, which means that she could have run into Brandt."

"What else can you tell us?"

"The local fire department is on the way."

"We're going down there," Shane said.

The voice on the other end of the line turned steely. "Stay away from the area," Cunningham ordered. "I don't want Trainer to know he's being observed."

"He already knows, if he's figured out that Jack was a plant," Shane shot back.

"Jack may have gotten away. I mean, why burn the house down?" Cunningham answered.

"You think Trainer did it?"

"You think it's a coincidence?"

"It could be," Shane said, but he heard the doubt in his own voice.

Cunningham was speaking again. "Even if he caught Jack poking his nose in where it didn't belong, that may be the sum total of his information. I don't want Jack traced back to Rockfort—or to me."

"You just want us to abandon him?"

"If he screwed up and got caught."

"He didn't screw up."

"We're just speculating. Nobody knows what happened. Stay out of the area. That's a direct order."

"And if we don't agree with you?"

"There will be consequences."

When the line went dead, the two Rockfort agents looked at each other.

"We're just supposed to leave Jack twisting in the wind?" Max asked.

"Maybe that's what he thinks is going to happen, but he's dead wrong," Shane responded. "On the other hand, he's right about secrecy. We can't just go charging in there. We need a cover story."

"Campers? Hunters?" Max asked.

"It's not hunting season," Shane responded. "But like you said before, fishing makes sense. We can get organized and drive down there tonight. Then be ready to go to the burned house in the morning."

"Where's our starting place?" Max asked.

"Skyline, Virginia. Unless you have a better suggestion."

His partner shook his head.

————∿————

Jack stood with his back to Morgan, dragging in air and letting it out. He'd dozed off, then awakened with Morgan touching him, sliding her lips against his face and neck.

He'd known she was sleeping, and probably dreaming of her dead husband. He'd known he should wake her immediately, but he simply hadn't been able to do it. Not right away.

He'd lain still, enjoying the hot sensations coursing through him as she'd made love to him. He'd been caught between wanting it to go on to its logical conclusion and knowing that he would have to stop her before she did something that both of them would regret.

Then her eyes had blinked open. He'd seen her confusion. Her disappointment. Her embarrassment and regret.

He was the wrong man at the wrong time in the wrong place, and he'd better remember that.

He tested his ankle. He'd given it a few hours' rest and gotten some cold air on it. It seemed better, but he wouldn't want to press it to the limit at the moment.

Anyway, it was getting dark. Not a good time to travel through the woods, particularly when you couldn't risk using a flashlight. They'd get out of here in the morning, but tonight he wanted to make sure their hideout was a bit more secure. He stepped outside, glancing up at the thick vines that partially screened the cave mouth.

He went back inside and got one of the knives they'd brought.

"What are you doing?"

"Making sure anyone who tries to come in here gets a surprise." He looked back at her. "But first you might want to go out and find a nearby place where you can pee."

She flushed, and he was sorry he was embarrassing her again, but they had to take care of practicalities.

"Better than in here," he added.

"Yes."

"Don't go too far. Take a gun, and don't stay any longer than you have to."

"You think those men are looking for us?"

"If not now, we have to assume they will be," he answered.

"They won't think we burned up?"

"Not if they find the trapdoor to the tunnel. And they have a better chance of doing that if the rain put out the fire."

She got up and went to her knapsack, rummaging inside and pulling out a small pack of tissues.

"Make sure you bury the used ones under some leaves," he said.

She nodded tightly, and he watched her disappear around a boulder. She was back in a few minutes.

He followed her example, finding a spot that would give him some privacy while he relieved himself.

When he came back, he got to work on improvising an early warning system.

She watched as he cut some of the vines. Next he found a thin branch and broke off two nine-inch lengths, which he hammered into the ground across the cave entrance, using one of the many rocks strewn around the area. He stretched a length of vine between the sticks, then ran another piece up into the tangle at the top of the cave mouth. After securing it, he searched for rocks about the size of goose eggs, which he salted into the mass of vines.

When he was finished, he ducked back into the cave, being careful not to catch his foot on the vine he'd stretched between the sticks.

"A booby trap?" Morgan asked.

"Yeah. If anyone hits that vine on the ground, he's going to pull on the vertical one and bring the rocks down. That should send an animal running in the other direction. And warn us that a man's found our hiding place."

"Good idea."

"Best I can do without equipment." He looked toward the cave mouth. "I suggest we move farther from the entrance so that booby trap will give us time to react."

They picked up the sleeping bag, the packs, and the wet clothing and moved them farther from the cave entrance. Jack shined the flashlight along their path as they went.

When they came to the old campfire, Morgan stared at the charred wood.

"Someone else has been here."

"Not recently."

He kept going until he found a spot that was around a bend from the entrance. The wall of rock would block any wind coming from the cave mouth.

After spreading out the sleeping bag again, he glanced at Morgan. Neither one of them had put on their wet jeans. "Get inside to keep warm."

She slipped inside and picked up the flashlight again.

"Is it all right to have some water?" she asked.

"Yeah. It's a good idea, actually, unless we're digging in for a siege."

"Are we?"

"I don't think so, but keep the light off most of the time to save the batteries, after we check our bite wounds."

"Right." He watched her work in a businesslike fashion as she unbuttoned her shirt and slipped her arm out of the sleeve, obviously trying to expose as little of her front as possible. And he tried to minimize his contact with her skin as he took off the dressing and looked at the bite.

"I think it's healing okay. Probably we can leave the bandage off."

"Good." She sat very still, staring into space as he applied more antiseptic. When she'd put the shirt back on, she said, "Now you."

He would have liked to avoid having her touch him, but it would be dumb to refuse. Instead of protesting, he took off his shirt, turned, and focused on the wall as she unwrapped his dressing. "I think you're okay too," she said with a little catch in her voice.

When she got out the tube of burn salve, he said, "I think we can skip that part."

"Okay."

He stood, rolling up the bandages.

"I'm going to see if I can find another way out," he said. It was a logical next step, but it also gave him a good reason to get away from Morgan, because everything they did now felt much too intimate.

He watched her pull her knees up to her chin and wrap her arms around her legs as he walked away.

Chapter 13

WADE TRAINER LEFT A SPOTTER IN THE WOODS TO keep tabs on the firemen. Then he took the rest of the team back to the RAM compound. He figured that since there wasn't much for the firemen to do besides making sure the embers were cold, they'd clear out relatively quickly.

Sure enough, his man called an hour later to report that the coast was clear.

"Did the fire marshal show up?"

"I don't know."

"Okay. Sit tight. We'll be back in fifteen."

It was just before sunset when they returned. They parked in the woods and walked to the house. Instead of going back through the tunnel, Wade led his men directly to where they'd found the exit that came out in the woods. He examined the trapdoor and the area around it but couldn't determine if it had been opened recently.

"We'll fan out," he said, "and look for evidence that Barnes and the woman escaped. And look for Gibson."

The men obeyed orders, moving through the woods, looking for clues.

Five minutes later, Jessup called out, "Over here, sir."

Trainer clenched his teeth. The man was supposed to use the comms unit, but apparently that had slipped his mind.

Trainer hurried toward the sound of Jessup's voice and felt his chest compress again when he saw what had elicited the shout.

Gibson was lying face down, unmoving on the ground, his body pinned under a dead tree limb.

The militia leader went to him and knelt. When he felt for a pulse at the man's neck, he encountered only cold skin. And when he lifted one of the man's arms, he found that rigor mortis had set in. Which probably meant that Gibson had bought the farm not long after they'd started the fire.

"He's dead," he informed the men. But the question was, what had happened here?

Trainer looked up, determining where the tree limb had fallen from.

"Get up there and see if it's been cut or if it's broken off," he ordered Jessup.

The man inspected the lower branches which were several feet above his head.

"I need a boost up."

"Help him," he ordered Porter.

The other man made a stirrup with his hands, and Jessup stepped in, straining to reach a branch. When he got his hands around it, he pulled himself up, then began to climb.

Halfway up the tree, the trooper stopped.

"You reached the place where the limb fell?" Wade called out.

"Yes."

"What do you see?"

Jessup inspected the area. "No cuts," he reported. "I mean, the edge is jagged like it broke off."

Or was it pulled down, Wade wondered. He wished he could get up there himself, but he had never liked heights. "What about the color of the wood?" he asked.

"What do you mean?" Jessup asked.

"The tree looks like it was dead for a while, and it's bleached from the elements. What about the place where it broke? Is it the same color?"

"That's darker," Jessup reported. "But it's hard to tell in this light."

Which didn't prove anything one way or the other, Wade decided. Obviously the limb had fallen recently—and come down on Gibson. Whatever the reason. Maybe the storm last night had weakened it.

Trainer went back to the body and looked for evidence that the man hadn't simply been caught in an unfortunate accident. Gibson's clothing was scuffed up, but that could have happened when the limb fell.

Had the blow from the branch been enough to kill him? Again Wade had no way of really knowing. He could have been hit, then died of internal injuries or something. They could find out if someone did an autopsy, but that wasn't going to happen, because nobody was going to report the death.

Still, it was interesting that Gibson had been in the vicinity of the man and woman, at least if they had emerged from the tunnel and come this way.

Trainer examined the ground, walking back toward the tunnel exit. About thirty-five feet from the fallen log, he thought he saw where something might have been dragged across the ground, but he couldn't be sure. And now that the light was fading, he wasn't sure what else they were going to see. But he had the gut feeling that Barnes and his girlfriend had gotten out through the tunnel, killed Gibson, and kept going.

If Barnes had staged this accident, it would be to keep Gibson from talking. A pretty cold-blooded decision, but he'd always known Barnes was a warrior.

And determined. As evidenced by his escape. How far could he and the woman have made it on foot in the rain, with Barnes still in bad shape from the torture session? Their quickest route out of the area would be the road, where they could hitch a ride. But that would be taking a chance that the militia wasn't patrolling the highway.

He was pretty sure Barnes wouldn't take that chance. He hoped not because he meant to find them and bring them back.

Shining the flashlight beam from side to side and moving cautiously so as not to tumble into a hidden crevice, Jack walked farther back into the cave, stooping slightly as the roof grew lower.

In the interior he saw some stalactites hanging from the ceiling. And about ten feet from where the ceiling lowered, it opened out again, and he saw some loose rock and a crevice in the floor. He stooped and slipped the bandages into the opening, using a rock to push them down, hoping they wouldn't be found anytime soon.

Ahead of him he saw dim light filtering in from above. He moved toward the light source, shining his flashlight beam upward. There was a natural chimney that went up from the roof of the cave. It was about three feet wide, but when he reached up, he found hand- and footholds that he could use to climb.

He wasn't sure if someone had put them there or if they were natural, but he was able to work his way slowly toward the top, being careful of his ankle. As he climbed, he felt cold air drifting down toward him. But the way wasn't totally clear. He reached a spot where a boulder partially blocked his upward progress. Moving to the side, he braced his back against the wall of the shaft and worked at the obstruction. It wasn't firmly in place, and he was able to wiggle it back and forth, thinking that he could ease it down.

Instead it slipped from his grasp, dropping downward and landing with a crash on the cave floor.

Below him he heard running feet, then saw the beam of a flashlight and heard Morgan's frantic voice as she called out to him.

"Jack? Are you all right? Jack."

"Stay back," he shouted down. The big rock had dislodged smaller ones, which were still coming down.

"Where are you?"

"I'm in a vertical tunnel above you." He switched on his light and shined it down into the cave. "There was a boulder blocking it, and I worked it out of the way. Sorry I scared you."

"I see it now."

"There's more stuff coming down. Stay back," he warned again.

"I thought something had happened to you."

"I'm fine. Can you see my flashlight beam?"

"Yes."

"Are you standing back?"

"Yes."

"I'm going farther up."

He worked his way upward again, the sensation of cold getting stronger as he climbed.

It took several more moments for his head to emerge into open air. In the gathering gloom, he couldn't tell much, but he thought he must be on a ledge above the cave. He wanted to investigate, but it was too dangerous to climb around out there now, especially with one bad leg. Instead he made his way down, wishing he was wearing a pair of pants as his bare legs emerged from the chimney.

As he suspected, Morgan was waiting below.

"I think there's a way out up there," he told her. "But I can't tell for certain until tomorrow where it actually goes."

"Okay."

"We'll stay here tonight and leave at first light."

They made their way back to the spot where they'd left their gear.

"Get back in the sleeping bag," he said.

"What about you?"

"I'll stay out here for now," he said. He carried both packs to the cave wall, emptied one, and used it for a cushion.

He saw Morgan watching him as he pulled out crackers and cheese from the other.

"Dinner," he said as he handed her some food and water. Then he took another water bottle for himself.

He found the fig bars he'd stuffed into the pack and handed her four, then took a bite himself.

"Nourishment?" Morgan asked.

"Dessert."

"First?"

"Yeah."

As they ate, Morgan eyed the man sitting across from her. A while ago they'd been in the sleeping bag together and that hadn't worked out too well. Now they were sitting facing each other, and she didn't think that was much better.

"That can't be very comfortable," she said in a low voice.

"I'll survive."

"Because you're tough?"

"Yeah."

"That's from your SEAL training?"

"When you grow up in the military culture, you learn the value of being tough early."

She nodded, wishing she could think of something they could talk about. Most people could talk about movies they'd seen or television programs. But she hadn't been to the movies in a long time, and television had little appeal for her.

She wasn't going to start a conversation about politics or religion. And she knew he didn't want to talk about anything that sounded like therapy.

She finally settled on a subject he'd probably enjoy. "What if we hadn't brought food from the house? What would we eat?"

"There's plenty of stuff around here. I saw wild strawberries along the wall. They don't taste great, but they're not poisonous."

"That's not much of a recommendation."

"Then there are mayapples, those plants that look like little umbrellas."

"Yes, I know which ones you mean."

"You're supposed to be able to eat the fruit, but the roots, stems, and leaves are poisonous."

"Oh goody."

"I could catch fish."

"You said we couldn't light a fire."

"Raw fish are a delicacy, don't you know that?"

She made a face. "I tried sushi a couple of times when I was in college. I never developed a taste for it."

"Well, there's wild garlic mustard. Also violet leaves. Of course, you've got to get the leaves while they're young and tender. Also fiddleheads of ferns. The young shoots that come up."

"Right. I know about them. And dandelion greens."

"And wild mushrooms."

"You know which ones are okay to eat?"

"Yes."

"You'll have to make me a salad with all that stuff."

"When we get out of here." The thick quality of his voice had her searching his face. It was in shadow. What was he thinking? That they might not escape? Or that maybe they could have a relationship when they got away? Or maybe not?

Her stomach knotted. A few days ago she couldn't have imagined a relationship with anyone besides

Glenn. Certainly not with a man like Jack Brandt. Now she was starting to imagine it.

She brought herself up short. It was probably like Stockholm syndrome. She wasn't exactly his captive, but she was thrown together with him in dangerous and intimate circumstances. And as soon as they were away from each other, her thinking would revert to normal.

Did she hope that was true? She was honestly too confused to know.

Dressed in plaid shirts, jeans, and baseball caps, Shane and Max loaded their Jeep Cherokee in the afternoon, partly with supplies they'd brought from home. Other equipment was from the office storage room. They had fishing rods and tackle boxes, but the boxes held handguns as well as tackle.

They waited until after rush hour, driving around the Capital Beltway, then south into Virginia, on Highway 66, heading for the town of Skyline, which advertised itself as the gateway to the beauty of Skyline Drive, a scenic highway that ran one hundred and fifty miles north and south along the crest of the Blue Ridge Mountains in Shenandoah National Park. The militia compound was on acreage near the edge of the park.

They arrived at the town near twilight. It was loaded with motels, and they stopped at the Red Bud, a rustic cabin-style establishment on the outskirts of the tourist community.

A plump woman with salt-and-pepper hair who was wearing a name tag that identified her as Mrs.

Sweeney greeted them with a friendly smile in the pine-paneled office.

"We're going fishing tomorrow," Shane told her as they registered.

"Nice weather for it," she commented.

"That's what we were thinking. Where's a good place for dinner?" Max asked.

"Hendley's Diner has good food and good prices."

"Appreciate the tip," Shane said.

"We had some excitement around here," Mrs. Sweeney volunteered.

"Oh yeah?"

"A house about five miles away burned down."

Shane's ears perked up. He was glad that she'd brought up the fire, and he didn't have to work his way around to it. "A propane accident?" he asked, thinking it was probably something else.

"The fire marshal said it was arson."

Shane made a clucking noise. Hoping to keep Mrs. Sweeney talking, he asked, "Who would do something like that? Is there a bad element in town?"

The woman shook her head. "There didn't used to be, but I hear there's some kind of military camp up in the hills."

"The government's doing something up there?"

"I think it's a private group. The Real Americans Militia or something like that."

"They're near the house that burned?"

She nodded. "It belonged to a widow lady. Mrs. Rains. She inherited the property from her parents."

"Uh huh," he answered, thinking that this woman was full of information.

"She's a professor at George Mason University. Hasn't been down here all that much since her husband died."

"He was a professor too?" Max asked.

"No, an aerospace engineer. The way I heard it, she was thinking of selling. Now she's got nothing to sell but the land. And a big mess to boot."

"They can probably bulldoze it under," Max said.

"Might be best," Mrs. Sweeney said. "Too bad, because it was built before the Civil War. Supposed to have been a stop on the Underground Railroad."

"You think she was at home when the place burned?"

"I heard her car's there."

"What about her?"

"She's missing. Could have burned up, of course."

Max nodded. "Did she have any enemies?"

Mrs. Sweeney looked at him. "What are you—a cop or something?"

"No. Just wondering," he answered.

"Well, you all be careful out in the woods. No telling what you can run into these days."

"We'll be careful," Shane answered.

"Here's the key to number fifteen. It's a right nice unit. The last one on the left down the road through our property."

"Thanks." He waited a beat. "We're probably leaving early. Can we pay now?"

"Sure."

Shane paid by credit card and took the key.

When they climbed back into the car, Max said, "Sorry about that last question. I got into it."

Shane shrugged. "It's done."

"But I called attention to us."

"It probably won't matter," Shane said as he drove over to their cabin.

Max was silent for several moments, then changed the subject. "It sounds like Professor Rains ran into Jack, and the militia attacked."

"That's making a big assumption."

"Why would someone firebomb the house of a widowed professor?"

"Some kid didn't like his grade?" Max asked.

Shane snorted. "Yeah, right. Kids weren't so violent in our day. Now I can almost believe that one would come hunting his teacher with a gun."

"More likely they'd gun her down in her office."

"We'll start at the house in the morning, then see if we can figure out where Jack and Rains went."

"You think they're together?"

"I'd bet on it. And there's some stuff we can do tonight."

"You mean a computer search on the professor?" Max asked.

"Yes."

Chapter 14

WADE TRAINER BROUGHT HIS MEN BACK TO THE compound. They were used to working hard, but the long day's activities had worn them out. They'd had plenty of training exercises, but this was their first real tactical mission, and they'd acquitted themselves pretty well.

When they reached headquarters, he decided to keep the routine as normal as possible.

"You did well today."

He saw his troops preen from the praise and thought about how easy it was to get men to follow his vision. You just had to be sure of your values and drum them into willing minds.

"Showers for everyone," he ordered. "Then clean uniforms. Be ready for inspection in forty-five minutes."

The men hopped to it, and he smiled in satisfaction as he noted their discipline.

He'd left ten men back here to guard the camp. Tomorrow he'd take all but five with him, because there was almost no chance of Barnes doubling back and attacking the compound.

He'd pick five from yesterday and use all of the fresh troops.

While they were getting ready for the inspection, he checked out the compound. It gave him considerable satisfaction to look at what he'd created here.

The old camp buildings were transformed into neat barracks, where his men slept eight to a room. And he had two buildings that hadn't even been used yet.

The new structures were steel buildings that he'd bought from a place that sold them online. The men had assembled them. They were sturdy enough to withstand an assault with conventional weapons, and he'd made sure that they had good locks. Not that he thought anyone here would dare to try and get into them. But now he had to worry about outside forces assaulting the compound.

The old dining room was the mess hall and the assembly area. The infirmary was also a holdover from the camp days, but he'd put in more modern equipment. He had an EMT named Philips and a male physician's assistant named Wentworth whom he'd recruited to man the facility. They'd X-rayed Chambers' leg and set it. He went over there to find out how the man was doing, then walked around the camp.

Finally, he gave himself twenty minutes to relax on his bunk. To tell the truth, all the running around had worn him out. He didn't like to think that he was losing his edge, but he found that he wasn't able to keep going all day the way he once had. Was there something that Wentworth, the physician's assistant, could give him? He didn't want to ask because that would show weakness.

He heaved himself up in time for the inspection, pleased that he didn't have to give any demerits. While the men were eating, he went back to his office.

He was surprised to find a voice mail message from the man who was bankrolling the militia operation.

Had he gotten wind of the day's activities? And if so, how?

Wishing he didn't have to call him back and give a report, Wade sat down at his desk.

He and his moneyman had met by chance at a rally in downtown D.C. where people had gathered to protest the war in Afghanistan. They'd gotten to talking and ended up leaving the rally together. Over sangria and tapas at a restaurant on Seventh Street, they'd kept up the conversation, both of them agreeing that the government was getting too big and ineffective and was using their tax dollars for the wrong things. That is, when it could get anything done at all.

Congress was dysfunctional, and the President was too weak to head the most important country on earth. It set his teeth on edge that the United States of America was losing its position in the world. The government needed to be jolted back into awareness, but one man acting on his own was bound to get caught.

Back then, Wade had been working as a security guard in a downtown office building. He was already in his late fifties and secretly disgusted with his life. He was divorced twice. With no children, thankfully. And his biggest career hope was that he'd get to be head of security in the company where he worked, which wasn't likely because the boss's son-in-law, a smug son of a bitch who thought he knew more than Wade, was probably going to get the job.

Wade had been entertaining secret fantasies about killing the guy. Until he connected with Mr. Money, and his fantasies changed dramatically. They met several more times, exchanging political views and then cautiously discussing what could be done to remedy the situation.

When Wade felt confident enough to finally venture that Timothy McVeigh had the right idea about teaching the government a lesson, his new friend had agreed.

"It would take a man with guts to pull off something like that in this climate," Mr. Money said. "Especially if they did it in D.C., not in the middle of the country."

Wade felt his excitement build. "It would take money too. One of McVeigh's problems was that he was trying to do it with a very small team. If he'd had the right financing and a disciplined organization behind him, he could have gotten away with it."

Mr. Money nodded. "You know anybody with the balls to attack the U.S. Government?"

Wade sat forward. "I've got the balls."

"Do you have an organization?"

"No, but I can build one."

"How long would it take?"

"I'd have something going in six months. It would take a year to have something effective."

"Let's talk about it some more. What do you think you'd need?"

Wade had been thinking about it. "A place where I could set up a military base and the money to outfit it."

"Maybe you should start looking."

He recalled that conversation as he reached for the phone to contact his benefactor. He'd have to ring twice and hang up—then wait for the other guy to get back to him. The man obviously didn't want anyone to know about his subversive activities. In fact, Wade was pretty sure he didn't even know the guy's real name. He was making it clear that he was invisible as far as reality was concerned, but not in terms of resources. He'd come through with money to buy the old camp that Wade was using. He'd bought equipment to go with it. They'd sat together for strategy sessions where they'd discussed Wade's first big attack. And most important, Mr. Money had been able to vet recruits before they joined the militia. That had given Wade confidence in each and every one of his men. But somehow Jack Barnes had slipped through the cracks. Which meant that Wade couldn't take all the blame for the fiasco with Barnes.

He squared his shoulders. Really, why should he take any of the blame? His money guy had access to a bunch of sophisticated databases, and Wade had relied on the man to make sure everybody was on the up-and-up.

Jack slept fitfully, with his legs alternately stretched out or drawn up to his chin and his back propped against the hard stone of the cave wall. Of course, he shouldn't be sleeping at all. He should be keeping watch, but he didn't think Trainer would send his men out at night.

After he and Morgan had both gone out for another call of nature, being careful not to trip the booby trap he'd set at the cave entrance, he'd returned to his place across from Morgan, leaning against the cave wall while she stayed in the sleeping bag, because he didn't want a repeat of the intimacy that had flared between them when they'd slept pressed together.

He kept drifting to the side and jerking awake, glad she couldn't see him in the blackness.

He woke with a start when he thought he heard the sound of a mountain lion in the darkness, but it was far off, and he relaxed again, glancing toward the sleeping bag. It was too dark to see Morgan, but he was very aware of her. He thought he could hear her even breathing in the darkness. He imagined her lying curled on her side. Imagined the curves of her body that had felt so tempting when they'd been pressed together. He could have made love with her. Maybe he should have. He could justify it as a bonding experience. Only he knew he was kidding himself. Afterward she'd think he had taken advantage of her, and that would be the truth.

He pushed thoughts of lovemaking away and focused on the practicalities of staying alive. Morgan had done well yesterday. He hoped she was up for a fast march through the woods to the road. They'd have to hitch a ride—and be careful that they didn't flag down the wrong driver. She'd brought money, which meant he could find a pay phone and contact Rockfort. He laughed softly. If there were any pay phones left in a world where everyone carried his own cell.

He felt himself teetering somewhere between sleep and waking. And as his mind swam in that twilight state, a name popped into his head. G. Washington.

G. Washington. That snapped him awake with a start.

George Washington. The man who had led the Continental Army against the British. The first President of the United States.

Why was he thinking about *him* now?

He had no real answer, yet he had the sudden sense that the name meant something else. Something important that he needed to remember.

He'd been half-asleep. If he let himself slip into that state again, would the meaning of the name come to him?

With a sigh, he tried it again, letting himself drift, trying to come up with some insights. But there was no way to force a connection.

Instead of coming up with anything, he slept.

———

As promised, Shane and Max were up before dawn and ate a quick breakfast of power bars and coffee in their room. They'd used Google to get the location of Morgan Rains' house, and they'd also searched for information on the professor. They found that she taught in the Psychology Department of George Mason University. She was a good-looking thirty-year-old woman with chin-length blond hair and blue eyes, the widow of an engineer who got shot in a robbery. There was a full account of the crime in an article in *The Washington Post*.

"Tough for her," Max had said. "And now it looks like she's in trouble again. Worse than before because this time she's the one who could get killed."

"I'd like to know how she got hooked up with Jack."

"Hopefully we'll find out."

Neither one of them said the other half of the thought. They'd find out—if she and Jack were still alive.

As they drew near the vicinity of the burned house, Shane slowed the Jeep.

"A lot of SUVs parked in the woods," Max commented. "You think they're from the militia?"

"Unless the fire department's back in force—with all the guys driving their own cars."

Shane swore under his breath. "Cunningham warned us not to tip Trainer off."

"Which is why this Cherokee is registered to my sister," Max said. He looked toward the SUVs, trying not to be obvious.

"Nobody's there. They must all be out looking for Jack and Ms. Rains."

Shane found a spot to turn around and headed in the other direction. He parked a quarter-mile down the road, and they trotted back, carrying their fishing poles and tackle boxes which contained their guns and other equipment that they might need.

They made their way cautiously through the woods and stopped short when they saw a squad of men dressed in fatigues walking smartly away from the ruined house. About a hundred yards from the house, the men split up, some going right, others left. A third group went straight ahead.

Hanging back, the Rockfort agents waited until the troops were out of sight.

"If they knew where to find Jack and Rains, they wouldn't have to split up," Max whispered.

"They probably have a better idea where to look than we do," Shane answered.

"Too bad we can't follow all of them."

Mentally flipping a coin, Shane answered, "You take the ones on the right. I'll take the middle group."

"I think it's better to stay together," Max answered.

Shane considered the problem as he scanned the surrounding area and the mountains beyond. "We could miss them entirely."

"But one of us can't take on the militia."

Shane nodded. "Okay. Let's head down the middle."

Gray light was filtering in through the cave mouth when Jack woke again and ran his hand through his hair. He was stiff from sleeping sitting up and from the activities of the day before, but he knew it had been the right thing to do. The good news was that he could see out of his left eye again and hadn't had any more flashbacks from the torture session. Instead he remembered the shreds of a dream. He'd been one of George Washington's troops in his Continental Army.

He snorted. Well, that was a great way to escape from his present circumstances. But before that, G. Washington had popped into his head, and he didn't think it was really a reference to the first President.

He'd planned to ask Morgan if the George Washington reference meant anything to her when he looked over at the sleeping bag and froze.

She wasn't there.

Had she done something stupid, like run away? Or had she just gone outside to relieve herself—and not wakened him to say where she was going?

Cursing under his breath, he scanned the area,

seeing that she'd left her pack—and everything else. Which meant she hadn't intended to take off, he hoped.

So he just had to worry about her getting into trouble outside on her own.

He stood, wincing at the sudden movement. Pulling up his shirt, he looked at his burns and decided they were healing, and when he inspected his arm, he found the bite marks had improved too. Luckily there seemed to be no infection.

As quickly as he could, he walked to the place where they'd left their wet jeans. Hers were gone. His were still there—and almost dry. He kicked off his shoes so he could pull the pants on, grimacing as the stiff fabric chafed against the burns on his thighs.

He shoved the shoes back on and headed for the cave mouth, wondering what the hell he was going to do now. When he spotted Morgan running back across the clearing, relief washed over him—until he saw the look of panic on her face.

Chapter 15

PAUSING AT THE CAVE MOUTH, MORGAN STEPPED carefully over the vine, then hurried inside. When she saw Jack, she dragged in a breath and let it out before starting to speak.

"Thank God you're up. I saw them."

He'd expected more time; now he began revising his timetable as he craned his neck toward the trees beyond the clearing. "I don't see anything."

"They're still in the woods. He must have a couple of search parties out. Two men are coming this way."

"They may not find the cave," he said, knowing that was a long shot. And either way, they had to be prepared, starting with removing the evidence that they'd been here.

"Come on." He ran back to the place where they'd camped out and scooped up the sleeping bag and one of the packs, looking around for more signs that someone had been here recently.

She stuffed the wrapper from a power bar into her pack and slung it over her shoulder.

Jack led her to the back of the cave, stopping to shove the sleeping bag into the crevice where he'd dropped the bandages the evening before. It was too bulky to go down easily, but he finally succeeded in cramming it through the wider part of the opening. Once freed, it dropped out of sight.

"Remember that natural chimney I found yesterday? I want you to take one of the packs and start climbing."

"What about you?" she asked, her voice rising slightly as she looked from him to the cave entrance and back again.

"I'll come after you as soon as I take care of them."

"Where does that thing go?"

"I'm not sure. It was too dark to see last night, but wherever it is, it's better than being caught in here."

She looked back toward the cave entrance. "There are two of them and only one of you."

He gave her a cocky grin. "One of me is better than two of them."

They had to hurry, but he spared a moment to pull Morgan into his arms and hold her tightly against the length of his body. She clung to him just as fiercely. He'd surprised himself by the impulse to gather her close, but it had felt entirely natural, like something fundamental had changed between them. Last night they'd been skittish around each other. Not now.

"It's going to be okay," he said.

"Be careful," she answered.

"You too. Now go on. There will be light coming down the shaft."

As he watched her run to the back of the cave, he thought about the change between them. Not just his feelings for her. Today they were working as a team, maybe because that was the only way to stay alive, he told himself.

—∽—

Morgan headed farther back into the cave, following the light coming down from above. When she reached the natural chimney, she hesitated. The idea of leaving Jack alone to face the militiamen made her stomach knot, but she knew he had to keep his total focus on them, and if she were still in the cave, his attention would be divided between them and her.

Knowing that climbing up the shaft was the best course, she tucked her gun into the waistband of her jeans and inspected the vertical tunnel. Craning her head up, she saw hand- and footholds that Jack had probably used to climb, but she was shorter than he was, and it was too much of a stretch to reach them. Standing on tiptoes, she fought to pull herself up. It was no good. She simply couldn't reach high enough.

Panic welled inside her. Now what? She could run farther back into the cave, but then Jack would have no idea where she'd gone.

Then she saw the rocks that had fallen onto the cave floor. The largest one was too big to carry, but she was able to roll it back and set it on the floor under the natural chimney. By standing on it, she could reach the first handhold. Breathing a sigh of relief, she pulled herself up, then braced her back and legs against opposite walls of the shaft, waiting a moment to catch her breath before she began to climb.

Finally, she started upward, knowing she was behind schedule and listening for any sound of trouble from below. She kept climbing, reaching for handholds, then pulling herself up and bracing her feet in the holes she'd previously used for her hands. The light grew brighter as she ascended. It was hard work for someone her size, but she kept going because she knew it was her only alternative.

Looking up blinded her with a shaft of sunlight, and she kept her head down. But she still missed a foothold, and she slipped, fighting not to cry out as she fell a couple of feet before she caught herself.

She'd torn the skin on her fingers, but she was sure she hadn't given herself away.

After catching her breath, she began to move upward again, this time being more cautious. When she reached the top, she stopped and allowed herself to rest again.

She'd done it!

Cautiously she poked her head out and saw that she was on a rock-scattered ledge above the front of the cliff. The view of the ground was blocked, and she carefully maneuvered herself around a boulder to look down. When she saw two militiamen approaching the cave entrance, she quickly ducked back down, hearing as they talked indistinctly.

They were out early. Presumably to capture or kill her and Jack.

She'd only caught a glimpse of them coming through the field, but she was pretty sure she recognized them as some of the men who had gathered around her burning house the day before. Both were young men in their mid-twenties, she judged. Both seemed wary of approaching the natural barrier of the rock wall.

As they came closer, she could hear their voices drifting toward her.

"This looks like a dead end. We can go back and report to Trainer."

The other man made a scoffing sound. "Come on! He doesn't want to hear we didn't find them. Could they have climbed up?"

There was a pause before the first voice answered, "Doubtful. Unless those vines are strong enough to hold them."

"But there could be caves."

"Okay, we'll poke around."

The sound of their footfalls told her they were moving along the wall the way Jack had done the day before, probably using their hands instead of a stick.

Jack waited several yards back in the cave. He was in shadow. The men out there were in the sunlight, which would make it difficult to see him.

As he stood with his pulse pounding, he listened to them talking. It was Jessup and Hamilton. Jessup thought they should turn back and contact the rest of the militia force. Hamilton wanted to investigate the cliff face. Too bad for them.

"Wait a second. There's something here," Hamilton called out.

Jack braced himself, waiting.

"Be careful. They could be in there. Or an animal."

They disappeared from his line of sight. Then Hamilton moved in front of the cave mouth, sweeping his left hand along the vines while he held a pistol in his right.

Hamilton moved in closer, his leg brushing against the vine that Jack had strung across the ground in front of the cave.

The rocks he'd positioned above the entrance fell, raining down around Hamilton and knocking him to the ground, but Jessup was too far back to get caught.

Knowing that he had to act before Jessup collected his wits, Jack raised his gun and fired, the report reverberating painfully in the confined space. But the light behind Jessup made it hard to see the man clearly, and Jack only got him in the arm, which wasn't enough to stop him.

Jessup fired, completely missing his target. But Jack got off a second round. This time it hit the man in the chest, and he dropped.

Jack rushed forward and checked Jessup. Blood spread across the front of his uniform shirt, darkening the camouflage pattern. The bullet had penetrated his heart and killed him. Moving on to Hamilton, Jack found the man stirring. Not wanting to risk another shot, he brought the butt of his gun down hard on the militiaman's head.

Then he pulled both men into the cave. The shots were unfortunate. They'd bring the rest of the militia running. The question was, where were they now and how fast could they get here?

~~~

Shane stopped in his tracks. "Shots."

Max nodded. "Coming from that direction." He pointed ahead of them.

In the next moment they heard one of the militia guys shouting, "Over this way!"

"Where are Jessup and Hamilton?" someone else called out.

"Maybe they're down."

"Hope that son of a bitch, Barnes, didn't get them."

Max and Shane exchanged glances. Barnes was the alias Jack had used when he'd approached Trainer. So he *was* on the loose.

Shane and Max followed the men, hanging back so as not to be spotted but staying close enough to keep tabs on the group.

They both heard men running through the underbrush. Ahead of them they saw a wall of rock.

"This is sure following Cunningham's directions. I mean staying out of the action," Max muttered.

"Yeah, but if Jack is in trouble, we're jumping in."

They saw the men close in on the wall of rock, fanning out, moving cautiously closer. Some stood back with their guns at the ready while others looked for something behind the vegetation that covered much of the surface.

The men were too close to see what Shane saw, a woman peeking out from behind a rock about thirty feet above ground level.

Her hair was blond. Her eyes were light, and she matched the picture of Professor Rains that they'd seen on the George Mason University Web page, only she looked like she'd been sleeping rough rather than getting prepped for a publicity photo.

Chapter 16

JACK DRAGGED THE TWO BODIES FARTHER BACK INTO the cave, around the bend where they couldn't be spotted from the entrance.

Then he ran farther back and found the shaft where he had climbed up the evening before. Craning his neck up, he looked for Morgan and didn't see her.

He'd told her to go up there, but had she been able to make it?

When he saw that the large rock on the cave floor had been pushed to the bottom of the shaft, he breathed out a small sigh. She must have had trouble reaching the first handhold and used the rock to give herself a little extra height.

Tucking his gun into the waistband of his jeans, he began to climb. Below him he heard footsteps in the cave, then shouts.

"It's Hamilton and Jessup."

"Jesus Christ, what happened to them?"

"Looks like they ran into Barnes and the woman."

"There's no evidence anyone was here."

"Except these two dead men. Go farther back. On the double." The order came from Trainer.

The men must have hesitated, because the militia leader barked, "I mean now."

"Yes, sir."

Jack had become a sitting duck. If anyone looked

up the natural chimney, they'd see him. He climbed faster, straining his ankle. He ignored the pain, knowing he had to get out of the shaft before anyone thought to consider it as an escape route.

He made it to the top and saw Morgan breathe out a sigh as he threw himself onto the ground beside her. Moments later he heard a voice from below again. She reached for his hand, her fingers clamping on his. Although he squeezed back reassuringly, he had no idea what was going to happen next.

Below them men were talking.

"The cave goes back for a long way. With low narrow tunnels. You could get lost back there easy."

"There's some kind of vertical passageway."

"They could have gotten out that way." The speaker was Trainer. "Preston, you climb up there and see."

"And if he's up there?"

"Shoot him."

"He's in a better position to shoot me than I am to shoot him," the troop protested.

The militia leader's voice turned dangerous. "Are you refusing a direct order?"

"No, sir."

The kid was right, of course. Well, not about getting shot. The minute he got to the top, Jack was going to kick him in the face and send him tumbling back down the shaft, hopefully onto Trainer's head. Nobody down there would be sure he hadn't lost his grip on the rock walls and fallen. Which would give them more time to get away. But to where exactly?

He moved his mouth to Morgan's ear. In a barely

audible whisper, he said, "Did you have a chance to check this place? Did you see a way out?"

She shook her head, then edged to the side of the ledge and looked over. When she gasped, he tensed.

"There are more guys down there. Maybe they're coming up here."

His chest tightened, until he lifted his head and followed her gaze. It was Shane and Max.

"My partners," he whispered, thankful and a little surprised that they had come. He hadn't expected it, since he'd known Cunningham didn't want any ties from the man known as Jack Barnes to Rockfort Security—or to himself.

He stood and waved to them and saw them zero in on him. But he had to duck back down when his attention was drawn from the shaft. The sound of heavy breathing told him that Preston was almost at their level.

Seconds later, the top of the man's head appeared.

Jack lunged for him, shoving him backward, into the shaft. He lost his grip on the rock and went hurtling down, landing on the stone below with a sickening thud.

"Christ!" someone gasped.

"Is he dead?"

"Did he fall?"

"I think he was pushed." The comment came from Trainer.

As he listened to the voices from below, Jack eased himself up again and waved his arm at Shane and Max, letting them know he was okay.

They gave him grins and A-OK signs before their

faces sobered again. They all knew Jack and Morgan weren't out of the woods yet.

From below Jack still heard men talking, but he couldn't make out much through the babble of voices.

Wade looked at the man sprawled on the cave floor. Preston was one of his most loyal recruits. He was holding perfectly still, breathing hard.

Wade came down beside him. "What hurts, son?"

"Everything," he answered in a barely audible voice. "Did you see Barnes up there?"

Preston didn't answer. He'd passed out, but he was moaning.

Wade looked at his gray face. Could he spare men to get him back to the medics at camp? He ruthlessly weighed the pros and cons and decided they'd have to deal with him as best they could here.

He asked for the medical kit he'd brought and gave the man a shot of morphine. It was the best he could do at the moment.

But what had happened to him, exactly? He could have fallen, or that bastard Barnes could have been up there and pushed him back. There was no way to know.

"We've got to find out what's happening up there," he said. This time he looked at Graves. "Go out to the front of the cave. You can get far enough away to see what's happening up there."

"Yes, sir."

Graves started toward the cave mouth. Before he could step into the sunlight, a shot rang out, and he jumped back.

Was Barnes already on the ground? And opening fire on the cave mouth?

How was that possible? Or was Barnes still above them and someone else was on the ground?

———ᴧᴧᴧ———

From his high perch, Jack heard a shot ring out. Looking toward his buddies, he saw that Shane had drawn his sidearm and fired toward the mouth of the cave. One of the troops must have tried to come out, and he'd given them a clue that it was a suicidal idea.

The men inside returned fire, but Shane had already joined Max behind a screen of boulders. They'd pinned down the guys inside, but there were more militia in the cave than there were Rockfort Security agents outside. Eventually the troops would break through. And the shaft was still a problem. Someone else could come up that way.

Looking around, Jack saw several boulders. "We have to block this exit," he told Morgan.

She followed his gaze and nodded uncertainly. "Can we move them?"

When he heard noises in the chimney again, he said, "We have to, or they'll keep coming."

He heaved at the closest boulder, bracing his legs and straining his upper body with the effort, but he barely moved the large chunk of rock.

Morgan joined him, and they both pushed, again having little effect.

Knowing that a person's leg muscles were stronger than his arm muscles, Jack turned around and braced his back against the rock wall behind him. Planting his feet against the boulder, he pushed with every ounce of determination he possessed, feeling the wounds on his thighs burn and his ankle protest.

Morgan sat beside him, imitating his maneuver. As they both shoved with their legs, the boulder teetered, then moved a few inches. Breathing hard and putting out a massive effort, they kept pushing, and it finally settled with a clunk into place over the chimney.

Someone below let out a loud curse. Jack would have cheered if he'd had the breath to spare.

With the top of the chimney blocked, the voices inside were less distinct now, but he knew they were angry that they couldn't get at him from that angle now.

He looked along the narrow strip where they were precariously perched. "Let's hope Shane and Max can keep them inside while we get down," he muttered.

He moved along the ledge, with Morgan following. Before they tried to climb down, they'd have to get farther from the cave entrance to avoid getting shot by the men inside.

As if to confirm his assessment, a barrage of bullets came from the interior, and Max and Shane returned fire. Jack hoped they had enough ammo to keep the militiamen inside until he and Morgan could get to safety.

He led her along the ledge, keeping one ear trained toward the mouth of the cave. The ledge got narrower, and he was starting to think that they might have to go back and try the other direction. But finally he came to a place where there were something like natural steps leading to the ground. Or perhaps someone had carved them long ago in the side of the cliff to give access to the ledge.

He pointed. "This way."

Morgan nodded.

He went first, making sure all the steps were solid. Still, there were several big gaps where he had to turn and help her.

When they came to a particularly long drop, he eased himself down, then held out his arms to Morgan, bracing himself against the side wall of the stairway.

"I can't make that."

"Yes, you can."

When she finally jumped into his arms, he held her for a long moment before turning back to the descent. As they made it to the ground, his relief was palpable, but he knew they weren't home free yet.

"I'm going to join Shane and Max."

"I'm coming too."

He might have said it was too dangerous, but it could be just as dangerous to leave her here. If someone got to the mouth of the cave and spotted her, they'd have too good a shot.

"Okay." He led her farther to the right along the cliff, stopping when he judged they were far enough from the cave.

"I don't like it, but we've got to cross the field and get into the trees. Then we can head back to the rocks they're using for cover."

She nodded

"I'll go first. If nobody fires at me, then you follow."

She looked torn.

"Wait for my signal."

He dragged in several breaths of air and let them out, then dashed across the open space, half-expecting bullets to pound into his back. But he made it safely, then gestured to Morgan.

She started her wild dash, and he stood with his heart pounding until she'd reached the shelter of the woods.

He gave her a considering look. "I don't suppose you'll stay here."

"I'm going with you."

With a firm nod, he started off, circling around toward the rocks where he could see Shane and Max pinning the militiamen down.

"Duck low."

They did, but Trainer must have spotted them because another barrage of shots rang out just before they threw themselves behind the barrier.

"You okay?" Max asked.

"I've been better."

Shane turned to Morgan. "And you're Morgan Rains?"

"How do you know?"

"We researched the owner of the burned house. Sorry we're meeting under these circumstances. I'm Shane Gallagher."

"Max Lyon. We're Jack's partners at Rockfort Security."

"I'm glad you're here," she answered. "How did you know where to find us?"

"We went to your place first, where we found the militia guys heading out," Shane answered. "We followed them. Then we followed the sound of gunfire."

"I assume they were trying to smoke you out of the house," Max said.

"Yes," Morgan answered. "When they realized Jack was in there with me."

"Sorry about the house," Max said.

"Better it than us."

Shane made a rough sound. "I'm thinking that we can give the bastards a dose of their own medicine."

"Like how?" Jack asked.

When Shane leaned forward and told the others what he had in mind, Jack laughed. "Poetic justice."

"I want you two to start back toward Morgan's house. We're in better shape to do this part," Shane said.

"The hell you say," Jack protested.

Shane gave him a sharp look. "Don't play hero. Get the hell out of here. You can get to my Cherokee. It's down the road from the house. Drive closer, and we'll join you as soon as we can."

Jack nodded. He hated to admit it, but he knew he'd slow them down if they all left together.

Shane handed him a set of car keys. "We'll be there as soon as we can."

Jack looked at Morgan. "Let's go. This time, we belly crawl across the field. At least until we get out of range."

They started off, making their slow way toward the woods and avoiding drawing fire.

Chapter 17

WHEN JACK AND MORGAN WERE GONE, SHANE turned to his partner, a hard look on his face.

"Did you see the cigarette burn on his arm?"

"Yeah."

"I wonder where else they burned him and what else they did to him."

"He'll tell us," Max said

"You think he'll talk about it?"

"We'll make him."

Shane wasn't sure, but he knew they had better put their current plan into motion. "Ready?"

Max nodded.

"You want to gather up brush first or return fire?" Shane asked.

"I'll gather brush."

"The dangerous part."

"You'll get your turn."

They alternated scooping up handfuls of the dry weeds, with one of them returning fire while the other worked. They also collected dry branches and small tree limbs, all the time exchanging fire with the militiamen in the cave.

"Persistent bunch," Max muttered. "You think we've got a big enough pile?"

"Depends. Do we want to roast them or keep them from coming out?"

"Good question. I think we can't gather enough for a militia barbecue. We'd better settle for pinning them inside while we get away."

"Agreed."

While Shane laid down a stream of gunfire, Max stood and hurled a smoke bomb at the cave mouth. It landed inside with a thud and went off, sending smoke into the cavern beyond.

They heard coughing and choking, which receded as the militiamen moved farther back from the entrance.

While they were away from the cave mouth, Shane and Max both rushed up. Shane carried the weeds. Max carried the branches. They threw them all into the cave, followed by a firebomb which they tossed onto the pile.

The weeds immediately caught fire, and the flames spread to the branches.

"Turnabout is fair play, don't you think?" Shane called out to the men inside the cave.

"Fuck you," somebody answered.

After that there was only coughing from the interior. The Rockfort men turned and dashed back across the field and into the woods, the sound of coughing and cursing following them as they hurried back toward Morgan's ruined house.

"What's Cunningham going to say when he hears about this?" Max asked.

"Is he going to hear about it?"

"I think he has another source inside the militia compound besides Jack," Shane answered as they slipped into the woods.

———ᴡᴠ———

Inside the cave, the troops began to cough and curse.

"Get down low. Get farther back," Wade shouted before a coughing fit seized him. He followed his own advice, sinking to his knees, then crawling to the back of the cave. His men followed.

When he saw Preston lying on the ground coughing, he grabbed the man's arm and started dragging him farther back. Another troop helped. In the smoke he wasn't sure exactly who it was.

The ceiling got lower as they moved farther back, but there was a piece of good news. There were several fissures in the floor, and the air coming up from below was uncontaminated.

"Lean over the cracks in the floor," he managed to gasp out, hoping that his men were in good enough shape to follow directions.

He lay on the cold stone, silently cursing Jack Barnes and his friends and wondering how they had happened to show up just in the nick of time.

It was obvious now that Barnes had never been working alone. Somehow the other guys had been alerted and come looking for him, maybe when he had missed a check-in date. After that, they'd stumbled onto the burned house. Or maybe they'd been monitoring the local news. In any case, he was going to find out who the hell they were. Like, for example, Jack Barnes couldn't be the traitor's real name. Wade wanted to know what it was and how to find the bastard.

A new thought occurred to him. He hadn't bothered to check the man's fingerprints because his moneyman had vetted him. Now he was damn well going to find a way to check them out.

And what if Barnes and his buddies were planning a raid on the camp? Another reason to move up his attack on D.C.

As he scrambled for a way out of this mess, he thought about using his cell phone to call back to camp. But what good would that do? They were too far away for a rescue operation. Either the smoke would get him and the men in the cave or it wouldn't.

He finally gave up trying to think about anything constructive and simply lay on the cold, hard floor of the cave, dragging air into his lungs and coughing. Maybe he passed out. He wasn't sure, but sometime later he felt one of his troops rousing him.

"Colonel? Are you all right, Colonel?" The man gave Wade's shoulder a tentative shake.

He blinked and rolled over, staring up into the troop's worried face. "I've been better." He laughed, and that triggered a coughing fit.

"The fire's died down a lot, and we were able to push the rest of the burning stuff away from the cave mouth."

"Good work."

"What are your orders, sir?"

He wanted to say they were going after Barnes and his friends, but probably they had too much of a head start.

"We're going back to headquarters and regroup," he said. "Then we'll get the bastards who did this to us."

—⁓—

Morgan was breathing hard by the time they reached her ruined house. She'd been thinking that Jack should be in worse shape because of his many injuries. But you wouldn't know it to look at him. He'd maintained a steady pace all the way back and stopped a couple of times when he saw she was having trouble keeping up.

He gave her a considering look. "We can rest again for a minute."

Her answer was immediate. "I don't feel safe anywhere around here."

"Yeah. Right."

Still, they walked more slowly as they continued up the road, looking for the SUV Shane had mentioned. Her relief was instantaneous when it came into view.

She leaned against the side of the vehicle, breathing hard, glad she couldn't see her ruined house from this vantage point. It was too vivid a reminder of how close she and Jack had come to death.

He unlocked the door, and she climbed in.

When he didn't move to the driver's side, she gave him a questioning look. "What are you doing?"

"I saw the militia vehicles back there. I want to give those guys another nasty surprise."

Instinctively she grabbed his arm. "Stay here."

He disengaged his sleeve. "Not until I disable their transportation."

"How?"

"Slash their tires. That should keep them busy for a while." As he spoke, he pulled a knife from the pack he'd carried with him.

She didn't like him staying in the open, but she

realized that he needed to exact some revenge on the men who'd tortured him and damn near burned them alive.

He handed her the keys. "If you hear any sounds of trouble, get the hell out of here."

She wanted to scream at him to just climb in the car and lock the doors, but she kept her lips pressed together as she watched him head for the militia's vehicles. Still, her heart leaped into her throat when he disappeared from view.

In a very short time she'd come to care what happened to Jack Brandt.

She sat with her pulse pounding, half-expecting men in camouflage uniforms to leap from the woods and surround the SUV. But apparently they were all back at the cave coping with the fire that Shane had said he was going to set. Or had he been able to pull that off? If he'd done what he said, why hadn't he come back with the other guy, Max?

Her tension mounted as she waited for Jack to reappear. When she heard the sound of breaking glass, she jumped. Did that mean trouble?

She fingered the keys where she'd stuck them in the ignition, watching and waiting.

Finally she spotted Jack, with his friends, Shane and Max. When she'd first spotted them, she'd thought they were very similar to Jack, tough-looking men who did what it took to finish a job. Now, to her surprise, all three men were grinning like little boys who had just raided the neighbor's watermelon patch.

Jack waved when he saw her staring at them. "I met Max and Shane on the way."

"What was that glass-breaking sound?"

"A rock through the window of one of the vehicles. I couldn't resist."

"And we got all the tires," Shane said.

"Good," she answered. She'd never been a party to destroying personal property, but in this case, it was more than justified if it kept the militia from coming after them.

The Rockfort men climbed into the SUV, with Shane slipping behind the wheel. Jack and Max climbed into the backseat.

Shane started the engine and glanced at her. "Put on your seat belt. We don't want anything to happen now."

She pulled the belt across her body and clicked the buckle into place as he drove up the road.

Shane turned around and looked over his shoulder at Jack. "I suggest we go to the Rockfort safe house."

"Agreed," Jack answered.

As they passed Morgan's house, she couldn't stop herself from turning in her seat, looking at what was left of the blackened structure, thinking that she would probably never see this place again. She'd gone there to bury memories of her husband and almost gotten buried herself. All because she'd tried to help a man who looked like he was in trouble. Of course, he'd ended up saving her.

"What happened to the militia?" she asked.

"We started with a smoke bomb to pin them down, then set a fire at the mouth of the cave like I planned," Shane answered.

"I mean, did it kill them?" she asked in a shaky voice.

"The fire wasn't going to burn long. I think they got out."

In the field outside the cave, Wade Trainer evaluated the men who sprawled around in the weeds looking like victims in a disaster practice drill. Only this was for real.

They'd all breathed in smoke, but they had all made it out of the cave under their own power.

"Report your condition," he ordered. "Starting with Salter and going clockwise."

One by one they sat up straighter and sounded off, each of them reporting, "Fit to travel." All except Preston, of course.

From the angle of his leg, it was clear it was broken. Probably some other bones as well. The morphine had worn off, and he was fighting pain.

Wade leaned down and spoke quietly to the injured man. "We'll get you back to camp, and you'll be as good as new."

He didn't know if that was true, but he was going to keep the guy's spirits up. That was the job of a commander.

He had his men improvise a stretcher out of two long poles and three uniform shirts tied by the sleeves across them to form a flat surface.

"We'll take turns carrying him back to the vehicles," he said.

He was gratified when several men volunteered to take the first shift.

They made reasonable time back to the place where

they'd left the SUVs, and he was feeling a measure of satisfaction until he saw the smashed windshield of the lead car.

Anger surged through him as he inspected the damage. The tires on every one were slashed, and the car with the windshield bashed in was his.

"The pricks." He wanted to unholster his sidearm and start shooting. But there was nothing that made an acceptable target. And he wasn't going to vent pointless rage in front of his men. He had to appear strong and confident. He had to make it clear that he was still in charge. Plus it could have been a lot worse. They'd all made it out of the cave. He should be thankful for that. He hadn't lost any of his loyal troops.

When he thought he could speak without shouting, he pulled out his cell phone and called the camp. DeStefano answered on the first ring.

"Are you all right, sir? We were worried when we didn't hear from you."

"We're all right. Only Preston needs immediate medical attention." He cleared his throat before continuing, "Send the troop-carrier truck to the burned house. On the double."

"What happened to your SUVs?" the man on the other end of the line asked.

"Don't question my orders. Just follow them," Wade snapped before clicking off.

He stood for a moment, struggling for control, aware that everyone was watching him, judging his reaction.

Again he focused on the positive.

He'd find Barnes and his friends, and he'd make them wish they'd never messed with Wade Trainer.

———

Morgan had never had more mixed feelings. Turning in her seat, she gave Jack a searching look, seeing the determination on his face. "If they got out, you have to stay away from them."

"I will, for now."

"You're not going into their camp again," she added for emphasis, knowing that she had no right to give him orders. Yet the words had simply tumbled out.

"Not without a lot of backup," he answered.

She sat with her heart thumping, afraid of what he was going to do. Could she keep him safe?

Not if he didn't want to be safe.

The three men in the car were talking, and she tried to follow what they were saying. But she was too worn out and perhaps too disoriented.

The events of the past few days seemed like an insane nightmare that Professor Morgan Rains had dreamed up—maybe when she was in the hospital after an auto accident or something. Yet she knew that they were true.

How was she going to get back to her normal life now? She didn't know, and she figured she was in no shape to think about it until she got some sleep. She'd go to their safe house with the men and deal with the rest later.

She leaned back in her seat as they rode through the Virginia countryside. Jack had said their offices were in Rockville, hadn't he?

It was difficult to keep her eyes open, and finally she lost the battle. She didn't wake until the car came to a stop.

Her eyes blinked open, and she saw they were in a circular gravel drive in front of what looked like an old farmhouse with a peaked tin roof and weathered siding.

Jack reached into the car and unbuckled her seat belt, then scooped her up in his arms.

One of the other men unlocked the door, and he carried her inside.

"I can stand up," she said stiffly.

He set her down, and she had to brace herself with a hand against his arm. When she was feeling more sure of her footing, she looked around. The exterior of the house looked like it hadn't been painted since before the turn of the last century. The interior had obviously been modified and modernized recently. Probably it had originally been broken up into a series of little rooms. Now there was a great room which incorporated the lounge, dining room, and kitchen area. The wide plank floor was polished, and the furniture was masculine overstuffed leather.

Jack led her up a flight of steps and into a room furnished with oak antiques—a double bed and a chest of drawers. There was also a comfortable chair, this one in a more feminine mode.

He leaned down to pull the spread and blanket aside, but she shook her head.

"I'm a mess. I can't get into that clean bed like this. Where can I take a shower?"

"There's an adjoining bathroom. And there are clothes in the drawers and closet that should fit you."

"Clothes that fit me? Where did they come from?"

"They weren't specifically for you. We've had

women here who needed a place to hide out. We keep clean clothing in the closet and new underwear in the dresser. There are several different sizes. There's also a toothbrush and other stuff you might want in the bathroom. I'll be here if you need me. "

She thanked him and waited until he'd walked out of the room before crossing to the closet and looking through the wardrobe.

Jack knew his partners wanted to talk to him about the events of the past few days, but he didn't want to talk to anyone at the moment about anything. Knowing the layout of the house, he continued down the hall to another bedroom, stepped inside, and locked the door behind him.

Almost everything inside the building had been modified, including the plumbing system. Because there was enough hot water for two people to take a shower at the same time, he headed directly for the bathroom. Inside he stripped off his filthy clothes and stuffed them into the trash can. Then he turned on the water and let it run hot before stepping under the spray and pulling the shower curtain closed.

The best he could say was that he had gotten out of Wade Trainer's clutches with his life. And he'd managed to take Morgan Rains along with him. But he knew he had failed in the basic mission. He could tell his partners about Wade Trainer's military organization, but he had no specific idea what the militia leader was planning.

Or had he?

A vague memory nagged at him. Something he couldn't quite pull into focus.

Where had he been, exactly, when Trainer had captured him? He didn't know. There was a hole in his memory that he needed to fill, but he simply couldn't do it.

Stop trying for now, he advised himself. Maybe it would come to him after he'd gotten some rest. Or maybe talking to Shane and Max about the mission would help jog his memory.

Chapter 18

MORGAN INSPECTED THE CLOTHING IN THE CLOSET. Some were too small for her. Others too large. But several looked like they would work, like the maroon running suit and white T-shirt. And the underwear he'd mentioned in the dresser.

She walked into the bathroom and pulled off her clothes. After looking at them for a few moments, she stuffed them into the trash. When the water was running hot, she stepped into the shower.

After mucking around in the woods and the cave for the past day and a half, she felt blessed to be standing under the pounding water and washing her hair and body. Finally, she stepped out and dried off before using the hair dryer she found in the cabinet and the new toothbrush on the counter. There was even moisturizer, which she used liberally on her face and hands.

By the time she finished, she was starting to feel unsteady on her feet again. She pulled on the T-shirt and pants to the running outfit and flopped into bed, wiggled under the covers—and closed her eyes. She dropped off to sleep, and for a while she was blissfully unconscious. Then suddenly she was somewhere else. Running through a tunnel. Climbing through a trapdoor. Dashing through the woods. Crawling around in a cave. Always alone and fleeing for her life.

She'd been alone for over eighteen months, and she'd

told herself she was handling it. But she didn't want to be alone now. There was someone who should be with her.

Glenn?

No, Glenn was dead.

Voices intruded on the dream, and her eyes snapped open. Men having an argument.

For a moment she had to think about where she was and who would be arguing. Then she remembered everything. Finding Jack in the woods, the escape from the burning house, the night in the cave, and the rescue by Jack's friends. Shane and Max.

The men had all seemed on the same wavelength back in Virginia. Now they sounded like they were in the middle of a bitter argument.

She pushed herself up, focusing on the dream to fix it in her mind before it evaporated. She'd relived the experiences of the past couple of days. Alone.

But someone should have been with her.

She made a snorting sound. She was no Freudian analyst, but she was pretty sure she knew what that meant. In her subconscious, she needed Jack Brandt, but she damn well wasn't going to allow herself to depend on him or anyone else, now that they were back in the real world.

She shook her head. The real world? Not quite.

With a sense of determination, she climbed out of bed and straightened the covers, then headed for the bathroom. She wanted to go find out what the fuss was downstairs, but the dream stopped her.

Leaning over the sink, she peered at herself in the mirror. Her face was flushed, and she splashed it with cold water before using the facilities. Next she took a look at the bite marks on her arm. The wound was healing.

Back in the bedroom, she found some socks in the drawer and running shoes that were only a half size too big in the closet.

As she got ready, her mind kept circling around the dream and what it meant, because she knew it was about Jack, not Glenn.

Had she finally come to the realization that there was no future in calling up the ghost of her dead husband? But could there be any future for her with a man like Jack Brandt?

Too bad her subconscious hadn't caught up with her waking self. She dragged in a breath and let it out, trying to sort through her feelings. In her own mind, she was ready to admit that she was attracted to him, and she knew he cared about her—at least on some level. But now that he'd gotten her away from the militia, where did that leave them?

They had been in a pressure cooker of danger together. All that had changed. She wanted to talk to him in private, but she suspected that wasn't going to happen. Not with his friends around. And what if he was planning to use them as a shield to keep her at arm's length?

She could stay up here and silently dither about their relationship. Or she could go down and see how he reacted to her.

That was the better course, unless she wanted to keep making guesses about the two of them and everything else about this situation.

By the time she got to the stairs, the sound level of the conversation had gone down considerably, and perhaps she could get some information by eavesdropping on the men. That wasn't her usual style, but in this situation she felt justified.

Reaching the ground floor, she listened to the men's voices.

"They beat you up pretty bad," the one named Shane said.

"It could have been worse." Jack switched the subject abruptly. "You talked to Cunningham?"

"Not since we got back."

"When?"

"Yesterday. After you didn't report in," Shane said.

"You called him, or he called you?"

"The latter."

"What did he say?"

"He told us not to interfere with the situation because he didn't want Trainer to know you weren't acting alone," Max answered.

Jack laughed. "You sure obeyed orders." Then his voice turned sober. "I guess when push came to shove, he was willing to sacrifice me."

"Maybe *he* was, but we weren't going to leave you there."

She heard Jack drag in a breath. "Yeah, thanks for saving my life."

"You were doing pretty well."

"We would have had a tough time making a clean getaway on our own."

"Which brings us to the subject of Ms. Rains," Shane said.

"What about her?"

"How did you hook up with her?"

"After Trainer and his men tortured me, one of

them was stupid enough to think I was harmless. He leaned over, and I head butted him. Then I got the hell out of there. I made it out of the compound in one of their SUVs but ended up in a ditch. Then I hoofed it as far as Morgan's house, when I passed out. She found me in the woods and somehow dragged me inside."

"Lucky for you."

"But not lucky for her. You know we can't let her go."

The stark words propelled Morgan into the great room to confront the men. They were sitting around on the comfortable leather furniture. A tray of sandwiches was on the round table in the middle of the seating arrangement, along with coffee mugs and beer bottles.

"What do you mean you can't let me go?" she asked. "You're planning to hold me captive?"

Jack turned and ran his gaze over her, and she saw a mixture of emotions on his face that made her chest tighten. He looked glad to see her. Relieved that she was okay. And regretful. That she'd heard them talking about her?

"How are you?" he asked.

"I'm fine. Physically." She swallowed, fighting to keep her own emotions off her face. She needed to talk to him, but not in front of these two other men.

She took in his appearance. He still looked battered, but his bad eye was fully open. And he'd shaved.

"You look better," she murmured.

"Yeah."

"No infections from those bites?"

"No. And yours?"

"They're healing."

Satisfied that he was on the mend, she went back

to her original question. "What do you mean that you can't let me go?"

He shook his head. "Wade Trainer probably already knows who you are. He'll be looking for you. If you go back to your house in Falls Church, he may have someone waiting to kidnap you."

"I didn't tell you I live in Falls Church."

"No. We found it on the Web, and so can he."

"People will worry about me. They'll think I burned up in the house."

"Yeah. That's a good thing. For now."

She wanted to shake off the assessment, but the way he said it made her pay attention.

"Why would this Wade Trainer guy want me? I don't know anything."

"He can't be sure of that. To his paranoid way of thinking, you could have been in the Skyline house, hanging around waiting to help me out if I got into trouble."

"I just happened to be there that weekend."

Jack kept looking straight at her. "You don't want to mess with him. Or more to the point—you don't want him messing with you. You saw what he did to me. He won't give you special consideration because you're a woman. Or maybe he will—if you take my meaning."

She caught her breath.

"It's a lot safer for you to stay here until we can wind up the operation."

"Which is when?"

"We don't know," Max said.

"I'm sorry," Jack added.

"So am I," she answered.

Shane gestured toward the food on the table.

"When's the last time you ate? Why don't you sit down and have something?"

She wanted to be stubborn, but she'd had nothing but power bars, cheese and crackers, and some fig cookies in the past twenty-four hours. The sandwiches looked tempting.

"We've got ham and cheese, roast beef, and we thought you might like chicken salad," Max said.

"Yes. Thanks."

"There's tea, coffee, sodas, and most anything you want to drink."

"Coffee's fine. With milk and sugar," she added.

Max got up to get the coffee, and she put a chicken salad sandwich on a plate and started to eat.

"This place isn't so bad," Max said. "We've got a full gym in the basement. We have a ton of DVDs. We can get you any book you want to read. And if you get really bored, we can take you for a helicopter ride over the Maryland countryside."

"You have a helicopter?"

"In the barn out back. It's really a hangar."

She absorbed that. Apparently Rockfort Security had technology she hadn't thought possible for a private company.

Still, she wasn't going to just sit there and let them dictate what she could and couldn't do. "But not computer access, I'm betting."

"We'll have to talk about that," Shane said.

So they were willing to save her life, but they didn't exactly trust her.

She put down her half-eaten sandwich and turned to Jack. "Why don't you explain what's going on."

He looked at the other two men, who both nodded.

"You understand none of this can go any farther?"

"Yes," she answered, because that's what they expected. She'd reserve judgment about what she was ultimately going to say and do.

"Taking this assignment seemed like a good idea at the time. Now it sounds kind of crazy when you try to explain it."

When she kept her gaze on his, he cleared his throat and began.

"A guy we call Deep Throat came to Rockfort Security with a job offer. He wanted one of us to infiltrate Wade Trainer's homegrown militia and find out what he's up to. Trainer thinks of himself as a real American, in the same vein as Timothy McVeigh. He thinks the U.S. Government needs shaking up, and he's the guy with the balls to do it."

"Like how?"

"We don't know exactly. We assume he's planning an attack on Washington, D.C. But we don't know where, when, or how. That's what I was trying to find out."

"The Deep Throat guy, does he have a name?"

"He calls himself Arthur Cunningham."

"Calls himself? You're saying that's not his real name?"

Jack sighed. "There's actually no record of him working for the government."

"You think he's with some private company?" Morgan asked.

"No," all three men said.

"We think—the CIA," Jack clarified.

"Why?"

"Because that agency isn't tasked with operations inside the United States. Because he considered Trainer a threat, he contracted out the work."

"Something too dangerous or too controversial for the government to admit they were doing?" she asked.

"That's what we assumed," Max answered.

"What if he's really working for a foreign power? Did you check that out?"

"No. Looking back, we should have tried to get his real name. But if he was working for a foreign power, why would he be trying to prevent an attack on the U.S.?"

"You're asking *me?*" She set down her coffee mug on the table with a thunk. Since she'd met Jack Brandt under highly unusual circumstances, she'd felt like her world was spinning out of control. The past fifteen minutes hadn't helped.

"So now I'm deep into some kind of mess that you can't really explain, and you're working for a guy who hid his identity. Which means I have to stay here until you figure out what's going on—at some undisclosed time in the future."

She was angry with them. Angry with herself for going out and taking Jack into her home, although she knew that her thinking was irrational. She couldn't have left a human being in need out there. Moreover, she knew they were coping with a situation they had come to detest.

They were all looking at her, and she hated that as much as anything else. Standing, she marched out of the room, back up the stairs, and into the room they'd assigned her, slamming the door in her wake.

Chapter 19

MORGAN PACED FROM THE WINDOW TO THE BED AND back, longing to get out of this house. Away from these men who were trying to dictate her life. What if it hadn't been the end of the semester? What if she'd been expected back in class after the weekend? Then what? She was just supposed to blow off her job at George Mason University?

She'd had a very normal life up until she'd found Jack Brandt in the woods. Well, normal if you conveniently forgot the part about her husband getting shot and killed by a burglar. She'd been sure Glenn's violent death was the worst thing that could ever happen to her. Now she was caught in a situation where she had no control. Not over the circumstances and not over her feelings.

When Morgan heard a car start outside, she ran to the window in time to see the SUV they'd come in pull away.

Were they simply leaving her to rattle around in this house by herself? What if she made a phone call and told someone where she was?

That thought was driven from her mind seconds later by a knock on the door. Without waiting for an invitation, the door opened and Jack stepped inside.

She challenged him with a defiant look. "What are you doing here?"

"I need to talk to you."

She'd had that exact thought before. Now she heard herself say, "About what?"

"Keeping you safe."

"I'm tired of hearing your bullshit." She had always thought of herself as a rational person. It seemed her roiling emotions had moved her beyond rationality. Without considering the consequences of her actions, she flew across the distance between them and raised her hand to pound on his chest.

The blows rained onto a solid wall of muscle.

"Don't."

Maybe he meant to restrain her because he grabbed her by the shoulders, his gaze locking with hers. For a charged moment, neither of them moved, and then everything changed, as though the world had suddenly turned the wrong way on its axis.

"Morgan." The look of desperation in his eyes tore at her. They had only known each other for a matter of days. But the danger swirling around them had forged a bond that cut through months of an ordinary relationship. Tension thrummed in the air around them, tension that seemed to pull them together.

Did she move first, or did he?

All she knew was that he lowered his head, and she raised hers, and she understood that this moment had been in the making for a long time.

Their lips met, and she held on to him, because he felt like the only point of stability in a wildly tilting universe.

His lips settled on hers, then began to feast on her, with hunger and passion and need.

The invitation and the question in the kiss made

her heart beat faster. And faster still when his hands began to move restlessly across her back, touching her with a sensuality that she'd thought might be buried so deeply inside him that he could never reach it.

Earlier she'd questioned herself. Now she didn't want to think about what she was doing and why. She only wanted to be in this moment, with this man.

With her arms around him, she reached under the hem of his shirt and pressed her palm against the naked skin of his back, sliding fingers over his warm flesh, feeling the ripples of sensation that skittered across his skin.

When she slid over a burn mark, he went still.

"Am I hurting you?"

"No."

Those were the only words they had spoken since she'd stopped hitting him. It seemed that words were unnecessary.

He did the same thing she had done, reaching under the back of her shirt and stroking his fingers across her naked flesh.

Closing her eyes, she marveled at the way his touch made her feel hot and cold at the same time. And marveling at the wonderful taste of him as she brought her mouth back to his for another heated kiss. When it finally broke, they were both breathless. Yet she sensed that he could turn away and walk out of the room. Not because he didn't want her but because he thought this was wrong for her.

She wasn't going to let his warped judgment or anything else come between them.

Her hands abandoned his back and went to the

front of his shirt, pushing it up so that she could stroke her hands over his chest, avoiding the burn marks and drawing a sigh from him.

She leaned forward and pressed a gentle kiss to one of them, then found his nipples and circled them with her fingers, drawing a gasp from him.

She'd touched him intimately to tend his wounds. This was so different, and it seemed like a miracle that they were finally doing what they both wanted.

Closing her eyes, she murmured his name as she caressed him.

His hands stroked over her shoulders, down her back, up her spine, then back down again, to cup her bottom. She held her breath when he pulled her more tightly against himself, and she felt his erection pressing against her middle.

She stayed where she was, clinging to him, knowing that she was making a conscious decision.

When he stepped away, a tremor went through her, but he was only setting his pistol on the bedside table before yanking his arms out of his sleeves and tossing the shirt on the floor.

While he was doing that, she made herself busy taking off her own shirt and reaching around to her back, so she could unhook her bra, pull it off, and drop it on the floor, along with the shirt.

She saw his gaze go to her breasts. Saw him swallow.

"Lord, you are so beautiful."

"So are you."

He gathered her into his arms, a needy sound rising in his throat as her breasts pressed against his chest.

It was difficult to take a full breath, difficult to

keep her balance as he swayed her in his arms so that her breasts moved back and forth against his broad body, drawing a small sobbing sound from her.

He hooked his fingers into the elastic at the top of her running pants, so that he could drag them down her legs along with her panties. She kicked both away and stood naked in his arms.

It felt wonderful when he slid his hands over the curve of her bottom, her hips, the indentation at her waist, all the places where she'd longed to be touched.

When he eased a little away, her hands went to his belt buckle, fumbling with unsteady fingers as she opened it. Next she undid the button at the top of his jeans and finally lowered his zipper.

Seeing him naked had felt intimate. This was so much more powerful. Reaching inside his undershorts, she closed her hand around his erection, feeling the length and girth of him, gratified by the way he caught his breath when she squeezed and stroked.

She wanted to keep touching him, but she knew that might bring their lovemaking to a conclusion too quickly. Withdrawing her hand, she knitted her fingers with his and led him to the bed where she pulled down the covers that she'd straightened so recently.

When she held out her arms, they climbed into bed together, rolling to their sides, facing each other.

His gaze was on her face as he cupped her breasts, shaping them to his touch, then played his thumbs over the throbbing tips.

She closed her eyes, her breath catching as he bent to take one hard peak into his mouth, drawing on her as he used his thumb and finger on the other side.

"That's so good," she whispered.

"Oh yeah."

When he slid one hand down her body, into her hot, moist folds, she cried out with the pleasure of it, then found out quickly that he wasn't going to rush this encounter.

As he touched her and kissed her, she did the same, thrilled by the tenderness and the sensuality between them.

She felt passion molded on her features, felt her hips lift restlessly against his fingers as he stroked her most intimate flesh.

And finally she knew that the time was right.

"Now," she whispered as she rolled to her back and opened her legs. She kept her gaze on his face, seeing the intensity written there as he shifted his body on top of hers.

His eyes met hers, and everything inside her clenched.

Taking him in her hand again, she guided him to her, crying out as he filled her.

He kept his gaze on her as he began to move inside her. She matched his rhythm, her hands kneading his buttocks as she climbed toward orgasm with him.

She could feel him holding back, feel him waiting for her to reach her peak. It had been a long time since she had done this, but it was so natural with Jack. She felt herself contracting around him as pleasure flooded through her. As she climaxed, he let go, his whole body shuddering as his own pleasure claimed him.

When the storm had passed, he looked down at her for a long moment, and she smiled up at him.

He rolled to his side, lying on his back beside her.

Reaching for his hand, she twined her fingers with his.

"Thank you," she whispered.

"I think that's my line," he answered with a smile in his voice.

She breathed out a small sigh, closing her eyes and letting herself relax as she snuggled next to him.

His next words tore at her feeling of contentment. "You know I'm not the right man for you."

Chapter 20

WADE TRAINER SAW TO HIS MEN FIRST. HE SENT everyone who had come back from the burning cave to the infirmary. While they were being checked out, he flopped onto his bed and ordered himself to relax. But he couldn't stop his heart from pounding as he went over and over in his mind what had happened—starting with his man discovering Barnes in the office, proceeding through the interrogation, and the rest of it.

Had he made a fatal mistake by leaving the interrogation room when he thought Jack Barnes was unconscious? Was that his only mistake? Well, in retrospect, he knew he should have tied the man to the iron bed, but he'd been confident that he and two of his men could handle the guy when he was in shit shape. Wrong.

He knew for damn sure that he'd locked his office door. He always did. Or had he somehow slipped up that one time—and given Barnes an opportunity he shouldn't have had?

Finally he was rescued from his dark thoughts by the vibrating of his cell phone.

Wentworth, the male physician's assistant who served as his chief medic, was on the other end of the line. "You should come in to be checked out."

He wanted to stay by himself in his room, but he

muttered his agreement, then heaved himself off the bed and stopped in the bathroom to wash his face and dry it before walking smartly to the infirmary.

Only Wentworth and Philips were there, along with Preston, good news if you considered that they'd discharged the rest of the troops. Even Chambers was out and about with his leg in a walking cast.

He stepped into the small room and saw the injured man lying pale and unmoving on the bed.

"How is he?"

"He appears to have slipped into a coma."

"Is he going to make it?"

"He'd have a better chance in a hospital. This is a well-equipped facility, but we don't have a real intensive care unit."

"That's too bad," Wade said with genuine regret. He hated losing any man, and he knew others would die when they made their attack on D.C. "We can't take him to a hospital and have him talk about what happened to him."

"Understood."

"Do the best you can for him. If he doesn't make it, we'll give him a hero's burial."

"I will. Now let me check you out."

When Wentworth had given him a clean bill of health, he went back to his office and pulled up his phone book on the computer. He'd made lots of contacts in the D.C. area while he was working security. He'd done favors for a number of men, and he thought about which one would be best to approach now.

He finally settled on Bob Davenport, a cop who worked for the National Park Service, which was big in the Washington area because of all the monuments and other showy wastes of money in the city. Davenport likely wouldn't approve of Wade's current enterprise, but he had a cover story he could use. The guy was black and normally Wade didn't trust blacks. But he'd known Davenport for a long time and was sure he could rely on him—as much as he was willing to rely on anyone who wasn't a part of the militia.

He was just about to call when the phone on his desk rang. As he looked at the number, a sick feeling rose in his throat. It was his money guy again. For a moment he thought about not answering, but he knew that wasn't a good idea.

"Trainer here," he said.

"What the hell happened?" the voice on the other end of the line demanded, the tone somewhere between annoyed and angry.

"I got my men back to camp safely."

"And did you apprehend Barnes?"

"He and the Rains woman got away."

"Perhaps you'd better fill me in on your adventures," the voice said with a trace of sarcasm.

Wade began explaining what had happened.

"Wait a minute," the other man stopped him. "You say that Barnes had help getting away?"

"Yeah. From two other guys who showed up outside the cave."

"Who were they?"

"I don't know yet, but I'm going to find out."

"You'd better, or your whole operation could be compromised."

Did that mean Mr. Money was going to withdraw

his funding? Wade didn't want to ask, but he knew he had to get back on track.

As soon as he could get off the phone, he pushed back his chair and stood up. His fists clenched and unclenched as he left his office and walked across the compound to one of the steel buildings that his troops had erected on the militia compound.

The two windowless structures with barrel-vaulted roofs held the neatly stored conventional armament his troops used for practice—and what they'd taken with them on the recent missions. He had enough weapons and ammo to supply a small country.

He stepped into the building on the right and switched on the lights, looking around at his neatly arranged military might. He was especially proud of his stash of AR-15 rifles, adapted for semi-automatic, three-round bursts and full-automatic fire. They were the civilian version of the army's M-16, but just as effective.

The building didn't just contain small arms. He had everything from mortar launchers to a troop carrier. And he kept some of his big earth-moving and construction equipment in here too. Like the front-end loader and the steamroller.

The treasure trove of high-tech guns and other military toys never failed to make his chest tighten with pride. Look what he'd done in such a short time!

The weapons also gave him a sense of security. But it wasn't what really counted. At the back of the building was a second smaller structure, a steel-reinforced cube.

Stepping up to the keypad, he punched in the code that unlocked the door. When the mechanism clicked, he entered, switched on the overhead light, and closed the door behind him.

Inside, everything was quiet and still. He could have been in the tomb of an ancient king, if the ancients had had modern ways to protect their bodies and the valuables they hoped to take with them to the afterlife.

This place always gave him a mystical feeling, as though he was in church or something. He was like a priest who had been ordained by God to carry out a sacred mission, and this sanctuary was where he kept the means to that end.

Inside was a long metal table and rows of cabinets with small, locked drawers. Ten rows across, stacked four high. Forty drawers in all.

Most of them were only there to confuse anyone who managed to break into the room. Only one held anything of importance.

Make that of vital importance. He walked to the row of boxes, touching them lovingly in the ritual he'd developed. He thought of it as a way of insuring the success of his mission, but he had another purpose as well. If anyone was going to try and find his treasure by checking for traces of the oil from his fingers, they still wouldn't know which drawer was the right one.

But he did.

It was the one labeled number twenty-one. Three times seven. A magic number. Third row down, first on the left.

Not that he believed in magic, of course, but he knew there must be something to the old ways. And he was willing to use anything he could to insure his success.

He opened the drawer and peered in at the metal box. A vessel that held the seeds of destruction of the U.S. Congress and much of Washington, D.C. Chosen men would deliver it. They would die, but they would be martyrs in the cause of righteousness.

He murmured a few lines from the Twenty-third Psalm. Of course God wouldn't protect those men on earth, but he would give them a special place in heaven for their sacrifice.

And when Wade made the ultimate sacrifice himself, they would be waiting to greet him. And they would thank him for what he had done for them.

Morgan turned to Jack, her mouth so dry that she could barely speak. "Are you saying you're sorry you made love to me?"

She saw a quick succession of expressions cross his face. Denial. Doubt. Regret.

He dragged in a breath and let it out. "Part of me is angry at myself for giving in to temptation."

"And the other part?"

"We needed something from each other."

She'd had her own doubts. Now she wanted to say that making love had been the beginning of something, not the end. But she wasn't sure how to make him believe it.

Jack shifted toward her. "I'm not prime relationship material."

"What are you?"

"A hard-bitten former Navy SEAL who's lost his edge."

She'd been angry with him when she came upstairs. Now she was quick to defend him. "Lost your edge? Of course not."

"I let Wade Trainer figure out I was a ringer."

"That's not your fault."

"Whose fault would it be? I was the man who infiltrated his camp."

"Why don't you blame that Deep Throat guy for dishing out an assignment you couldn't possibly fulfill?"

He ignored the first part of the question and focused on the second part. "I could have done it if I'd had more time."

"You looked through his computer?"

He hesitated.

"Did you or didn't you?"

"I'm not sure." He swallowed hard. "I think someone hit me over the head, and I lost a piece of my memory."

"What piece?"

"Whatever happened just before I woke up in the interrogation room."

That was interesting information that she wanted to pursue, but Jack didn't let her.

"The point is, I got caught. And in the process I put you in great danger."

"And you got me out of it."

"With help from Shane and Max. And as we pointed out downstairs, you're not safe until we find out what he's doing and end his operation."

Before she could answer, he plowed ahead. "And there's something else you don't know about me. My

SEAL team was on a mission in Afghanistan, looking for insurgents in a village in the hills. I'm the only man who came back."

She felt a shudder go through her. Maybe he misinterpreted the reaction, because his face darkened. Rolling toward him, she slung her arm across his chest and held tight to him.

"I'm so sorry. That must have been horrible for you."

He lay without moving as she stroked her hands through his hair and over his back.

"What happened to them wasn't your fault."

"I try to tell myself that."

The explanation helped her understand him better. Coming back alive from Afghanistan was probably the reason he'd taken that risky assignment, infiltrating Wade Trainer's militia.

"I understand better than you think," she murmured.

"Oh yeah?"

"Something similar happened to me. It didn't come out as badly—no fault of my own."

He was staring intensely at her as she sat up, dragging the sheet with her to cover her breasts.

"A lot of people who teach psychology are also in clinical practice," she said, almost wishing she hadn't introduced the subject. "I'm not."

"And you're going to tell me why."

"I was doing an internship at Springfield State Hospital. One of my patients was a severely depressed man. I thought I was handling him correctly. He hanged himself in the shower."

Jack winced. "That must have been hard to deal with. But you said it came out okay. I guess he didn't die."

"That's right. But not because I saved him. An orderly found him and cut him down in time." She kept her gaze fixed on him. "After that I didn't take a chance on working with patients again."

He nodded.

She'd wanted him to understand that she "got it" about Afghanistan. Message sent, she changed the subject.

"What are your plans for Trainer?"

He breathed out a little sigh, probably relieved that she'd switched back to business. "We have to find his moneyman and make him tell us what Trainer's up to."

"Then let's work together to find the guy."

He gave her a quizzical look. "You?"

"Yes. I'm trained in research. There's no reason I can't apply my research methods to helping find your guy."

He thought about that, then nodded. "Okay. We could use the extra help."

Was he going to give her real work? Or was he trying to keep her busy while she was confined here? She guessed she'd find out soon enough. And find out where the two of them really stood. She felt like Jack could walk away from her at any time. At least anytime after they solved the Wade Trainer problem. Meanwhile, she knew they were stuck with each other. Maybe that gave her an advantage—force him to deal with her.

She wanted to ask what he was thinking; instead she made another suggestion. "You said you didn't remember what had happened before you ended up in Trainer's torture chamber. Maybe I could help you recover those memories."

"How?"

Before she could answer, a car pulled up outside the house, and they both jumped.

Jack reached for the gun he'd set on the bedside table. Naked, he leaped out of bed and ran to the window.

Wade knew he had to solve the Jack Barnes problem as soon as possible. Immediately after hanging up with Mr. Money he picked up the phone to call the Park Police guy, Davenport.

He was prepared to leave a message, but he got the man on his cell phone.

"This is Wade Trainer."

"Long time no see."

"I've been busy with that home security business I told you about."

"Right. How's it going?"

"I've got a little problem. A guy I hired might be stealing from me. I'm hoping you can run his prints for me."

Davenport hesitated for a moment.

"I'm willing to pay for the service," Wade said. "How does five hundred sound?"

"Sounds pretty good," Davenport allowed.

"I can bring you some stuff with his prints. Where do you want to meet?"

"At that bar we used to go to up on Capitol Hill."

"Perfect. Can we do it tonight?"

"Yeah."

———

Jack turned from the window, raising his arm against the glare of the setting sun.

"Nothing to worry about," he reported. "It's Shane and Max coming back. With groceries."

After returning to the center of the room, he found his clothing where they'd dropped it and started getting dressed.

"I'll go down," he said.

And pretend this never even happened? She didn't say that out loud, of course.

She wasn't quite so comfortable walking around in front of him with no clothes on, and he must have realized that because he turned away from her as he pulled on his pants. She scooped up her clothing and carried it into the bathroom where she could look at her face in the mirror the way she had when she'd woken up. Did her eyes look brighter? She hoped not, because she didn't want any comments from Shane or Max.

Well, they probably weren't going to make any teasing remarks, even if they realized what she and Jack had been doing.

She heard him descend the stairs and was grateful that they weren't going to show up together like they'd just climbed out of the same bed. While she was alone she took the time for a quick wash, then dressed, brushed her hair, and put on a little bit of blusher that she found in the bathroom.

As she dealt with her appearance, she thought about her emotional temperature.

The question was, had making love with Jack changed her in some fundamental way? After eighteen months of widowhood, she'd thought she would never get over the loss of her husband. But Jack Brandt had swept into her life and changed everything. She could imagine a future with him. The trouble was, he didn't see it that way. Or to be more clear, he didn't think he deserved a future with anyone. And if she wanted him, she'd have to change his mind about that.

With a show of confidence, she walked out of the bathroom and downstairs.

Jack was in the front hall. "There you are," he said, like they hadn't been together a few minutes earlier. "I should show you how the alarm system works."

"Okay."

He led her down the hall to a small office. "The control panel is in here. It's not just for the house. There's no fence around the place because that would be conspicuous, but we have sensors set up all around the property. If anyone approaches, we know."

"What about animals?"

"We do have a deer fence. A low voltage system that keeps them away. Anything smaller could get under, but we figure anything smaller isn't going to be a threat."

"Unless someone sends in a cat with a bomb strapped to its back," Max said as he entered the room.

"Very funny."

When he gave her a studied look, she fought to keep her features neutral.

"I see you're feeling better."

"Maybe you can call it adjusting to reality," she answered.

"Okay," Max said.

Jack went back to showing her how to arm the system and how to disarm it.

"If you have to disarm it, how did you get inside?" she asked Max.

"We all have a remote."

"And we all go armed here. That includes you, unless you're not willing to do it."

"I'm willing."

"Jack told us you know how to use a gun. We have a firing range set up on the property. You can have some sessions with the rest of us."

Before she could answer, the alarm on the console went off, and they all froze.

Chapter 21

THE THREE MEN PULLED OUT THEIR WEAPONS AND turned toward the driveway.

"I want you in the safe room," Jack said to Morgan, his voice low and urgent.

As he had done upstairs, he went to the window and looked out. Just visible in the fading light, a dark Mercedes was pulling up in front of the house. It stopped abruptly, and a man got out.

In the illumination from the security lights, Jack saw a man in his mid-fifties, with straight blond hair that was shot with gray, a broad face, and light eyes.

"Who is it?" Morgan asked.

"Cunningham," Jack answered as he put his weapon away. "Turn off the alarm," he said to Max.

As the other agent hurried out of the room, Jack turned to Morgan. "He's the guy who hired Rockfort to infiltrate Trainer's organization."

He saw her face contort. "The man who gave you an impossible assignment?"

Jack shrugged. "We'll meet him in the great room."

He and Morgan went down the hall while Shane hurried to answer the door.

They heard Cunningham barrel inside. Shane and Max trailed behind him.

As soon as they all stopped walking, he rounded on the two agents. "I gave you direct orders not to interfere in this situation, and it looks like you ignored me."

"We weren't going to leave Jack twisting in the wind."

"Tell me how you got there. How you found him. And what you did," he growled.

"Tell me how you know about it," Jack shot back.

"Satellite photography."

Was that plausible? Maybe, if you were using the resources of the CIA.

"We might as well sit down." Jack sighed.

Cunningham glared at Jack as he sat.

The others followed suit until the newcomer was the only one standing. Finally he sat, his expression stony.

Shane began to tell what had happened, starting with their idea of outfitting themselves for a fake fishing trip, through their conversation with the motel clerk and their arriving at the burned house as the militiamen were leaving to look for Jack and Morgan.

"And you engaged them?" Cunningham demanded.

"Jack and Ms. Rains had taken refuge in a cave and were under attack. We did what we could to help them escape alive."

"Let's hear the rest of it."

Max continued with the remainder of the story.

When he was finished, Cunningham made a snorting sound and flapped his arm. "And now Trainer knows that Jack is working with well-trained men capable of pulling off that operation."

Max nodded.

"Which is going to make him jumpy." His head

swung toward Jack. "Did you figure out what kind of attack he's planning on Washington?"

"He confides his plans to no one. And as far as I could tell, there's nothing written down."

Morgan's head jerked toward him. Apparently he no longer trusted this guy, and he wasn't going to talk about his memory gap in front of him.

"Just great," Cunningham muttered. "But there's one thing we can be sure of. Trainer's moving up his timetable. And he's going to have guards patrolling the compound."

"There's no point in attacking the compound," Jack said. "He's not doing anything illegal in there."

"Wasn't it illegal to burn down my house?" Morgan asked. "Or to chase us to that cave and try to kill us?"

"We don't have any proof that it was him," Jack answered. "Our word against his."

"Exactly," Cunningham agreed. "Someone's backing him. My guess is it's someone in the private sector with power. We need proof of his activities. I want to capture him on the move toward Washington with a bomb or something in his van."

"Risky," Morgan murmured.

"It's the only way we can nail him, which is why I wanted to know when he made his move."

"We're going to attack the problem from another angle," Jack said.

Cunningham's gaze swung toward him.

Morgan waited for him to talk about her plan to dig out his memories.

Instead he said, "We're going to see if we can

figure out who's funding him. That might give us a clue."

The government man looked thoughtful. "I suppose it's worth a try."

"We can monitor traffic in and out of there," Shane said.

"If you can do it from a location where he won't know he's being watched." Cunningham stood. "I want daily reports of your progress."

"Fine," Jack said.

"And if I want to have a face-to-face, I'd like to be able to get in here without setting off an alarm. Do you have a spare remote?"

Max also stood. "I'll get you one."

Jack and Morgan remained in the living room. When they heard the front door close, she turned to him. "I don't like him."

"He's not very likable."

"Do you trust him?"

"We did at first."

"But you didn't tell him about your memory loss."

"That wouldn't have been productive," Jack answered.

Morgan had offered him a technique that might or might not work to get those memories back, but he wanted time to think about it before he committed himself. And they did have other business that he considered urgent after Cunningham's surprise visit.

Standing up, he said, "Before we do anything else, let me show you the safe room, in case there's any real trouble around here."

"Where is it?"

"It's in the basement." He led her over to a

bookcase near the entrance to the kitchen area and pressed about halfway up along one of the vertical supports. A click sounded, and the shelves glided open, revealing a set of stairs.

"Like something out of a spy movie," she murmured.

"But this is for real." He turned on a light, then descended a few steps. She followed.

"You close the bookcase here," he said, like a real estate agent giving a house tour. When he flipped another switch, the shelves swung back into place, sealing them off.

He led Morgan the rest of the way down the steps into an unfinished basement. Pointing toward a shelf of canned goods, he said, "There's another hidden entrance over here."

"If someone gets this far, won't they suspect the shelves?" she asked.

"We did this one first, then thought the ones on top would be more effective."

He pushed a switch on the wall and the shelves swung aside to reveal a metal door, where he turned a handle to swing the barrier open.

"It's not locked?" she asked.

"You lock it from the inside." He walked in, and she followed. The basement had been cold. It was several degrees warmer in the little room where she found herself. It was furnished with two sets of bunk beds, a small table and four chairs, and shelves with rows of supplies.

"It's bulletproof and fireproof," Jack said, struggling to be matter-of-fact. He didn't like to think about Morgan having to lock herself in here.

He heard her swallow. "Fireproof—that's important."

"Yeah. We don't have an escape tunnel, but we've got this." He gestured toward the shelves. "There's plenty of water and food. Not gourmet, but high in protein."

The weapons were on another set of shelves. Handguns and Uzis. He turned toward another small table by the door. "This is the wireless communications equipment."

"Why are you telling me all this?" she murmured. "Won't you be with me?"

"First, we may not be at the house all the time. And even if we are, if we're under attack, no telling what could happen. You may have to get yourself down here."

Her expression turned stark. "Okay, show me how to call for help."

He crossed to the table and pointed to the broadcaster and receiver. "You just flip this switch. The instructions are written on this plastic card. I'll show you how to turn on the generator."

Pivoting away, he almost bumped into Morgan who was standing right behind him.

"Jack." She reached out and pulled her arms around him, holding tight.

He had told himself that making love with her had been a mistake. He'd told himself that there was no future for the two of them, but when she hugged him to her, he brought his own arms up and pulled her more tightly against himself.

He wanted to keep holding her. Hell, he wanted to make love to her again, but he finally forced himself to ease away. What he'd said in bed was still true. He wasn't good for her.

"We should go back up," he said.

"We should talk. This might be a good place to do it."

He met her questioning gaze. "There's nothing much to talk about—until we take care of Trainer."

"If that's the way you want it."

"It's the way it has to be."

"What about my memory suggestion?"

He thought about it, wondering if he was going to like what he found out if they tried it.

They came up the stairs to find Shane waiting for them with a scowl on his face.

"What?" Jack asked.

"I did something we should have tried months ago. I ran the plates on Cunningham's car."

"And you know who he really is?"

"No. The car's registered to a rental company."

"And they don't give out the names of clients?"

"They did when I told them the car had been in an accident. The name on the rental is Arthur Cunningham, the same name he gave us."

"So that leaves us nowhere with finding out who he really is."

—␣—

Maybe he should have run the fingerprints on all his men, Wade Trainer thought as he considered the personal possessions Jack Barnes had left in the compound. He decided his toothbrush would be good. To be on the safe side, he also included his comb and his billfold. He put each into a separate paper bag because he remembered that paper was better than plastic for fingerprints. All the little bags went into a canvas carry bag, along with the five hundred dollars he was paying for Davenport's services.

After placing Emerson in charge, he left the compound that evening and headed for the bar where he'd arranged to meet the Park Service officer.

He had a bad twenty minutes while he sipped a beer and waited for the man, but finally the guy showed up, dressed in civilian clothes.

"Sorry I'm late," he said as he slid into the booth across from Wade. "There was an accident on North Capitol Street that blocked both lanes."

"No problem."

"You got that stuff for me?"

"Right here." Wade handed over the bag with the items Barnes had handled and also the cash.

The big black man counted that first, then looked at the objects Wade had assembled. "This is a good selection."

"How soon can you give me his name?"

"Tomorrow, if he's in the system."

"That's great," Wade answered. "You can just email me the results." Wade gave one of his email addresses.

"So buy me a beer," Davenport said.

Wade ordered another Dos Equis for himself and one for Davenport, although he wanted the cop to leap up and deal with the fingerprints. Not only that, he was nervous about being away from camp when the situation was so unsettled.

All of that made it hard to sit and chat with the

man, but he forced himself to be sociable. He wanted this information—badly.

But he also wanted to stay on this guy's good side, in case he needed his services again.

"How's that security company of yours going?" Davenport asked.

"Fine."

"Any chance of my getting some part-time work? The wife wants a new car, and I need some money to pay for it."

"I'm pretty full right now," Wade answered.

When Davenport's face fell, he said quickly, "But I'll put you at the top of my list for new hires."

"Thanks."

Wade shifted in his seat. The conversation had made him nervous. He didn't like sitting here and lying to the man's face. But that was part of what you needed to do in his position, Wade told himself.

There were no jobs available in his "security firm." He only took recruits who were willing to dedicate their lives to his cause. But he couldn't explain that to Davenport. And in the end, he wouldn't need to. Davenport would likely buy the farm, along with everyone else who was close to ground zero.

Chapter 22

"Max and I will alternate taking care of pending business at Rockfort," Shane said.

"Okay."

"You'll both stay here," he added, looking from Jack to Morgan and back again.

"Okay," they both answered.

"Actually, it's probably safest if we all sleep here."

Jack agreed, thinking that having the other guys around would help keep him and Morgan from getting into anything heavy.

He cleared his throat. "I told you when I was hit on the head that I lost the memory of what happened right before Trainer's men captured me."

Shane nodded.

Jack kept his voice even. "Morgan wants to try a technique that might help me recover the memory."

Shane studied her. "Like what, exactly?"

"Hypnosis," she said.

"I thought that kind of thing was discredited," Shane said, sounding scornful.

She wanted to answer in the same tone, but she kept her voice even.

"To a certain extent it is, when a therapist is trying to dig up long-term memories of abuse. But this is different. It's something that happened to Jack a few days ago. And there's no downside. Either he can recall the incident, or he can't."

"You're qualified as a hypnotherapist?" Shane asked.

She opened her hands. "I took a course in it and had some practical experience with volunteers. But if you wanted, we could call someone else in."

"Not a good idea from a security standpoint," Shane answered.

Jack nodded in agreement.

Shane gave him a searching look. "But you want to try it?"

"Like she says, what do I have to lose?" He glanced at Morgan. "If we're going to do it, let's go ahead."

"And you're not going to poke into any of his other memories?" Shane asked.

"Of course not," Morgan answered promptly. "If you want to be there, you can."

"Won't that be distracting?"

"Yes, but I'm willing to do it if you don't trust me."

"I trust her," Jack broke in.

"Then go for it," Shane said.

She looked toward the great room. "We need a quiet place."

"We can use one of the bedrooms," Jack said.

"We'll need two comfortable chairs," Morgan answered.

"They all have one. I just have to bring another one in."

<hr/>

Morgan had made herself sound confident as she'd told Jack and Shane what she had in mind, but she was less sure of herself than she pretended. The class she'd taken in hypnosis techniques had been a couple of years ago, and she hadn't practiced since then. But she wanted Jack to get those memories back, for more than one reason. Whatever he'd found out might speed up the process of putting the militia leader out of business, but more important to her was Jack's attitude toward himself. She knew he felt like he'd failed in his mission. If he'd discovered something, and she could help him recover the memory, that would help his attitude.

And help their relationship? She hoped that would be true too.

Her heart was pounding as she followed Jack upstairs. There was a lot riding on this session.

He hesitated in the hallway. "Maybe a room that's not being used is best."

"Sure."

He opened another door and ushered her into a chamber that was similar to the one where she was sleeping, only the decor was more masculine than in hers.

Jack gestured her to the easy chair in the corner. "Be right back."

She sat and felt her heart start to pound even harder. This was her idea, but now she was nervous.

When Jack stepped out of the room, she clutched the chair arms in a death grip, then eased her hands into her lap and did some deep breathing exercises to calm herself.

Jack was back all too soon, carrying another large chair which he set down a few feet from her. "Now what?"

"Push that chair over toward the bed so that you can look at the far wall. Then sit down."

He did as she asked, leaning back in the chair.

"Are you comfortable?"

"Yes."

She could see he was nervous. She hoped she wasn't projecting the same tension.

"The usual procedure would be to spend at least a session discussing your background before we got into hypnosis."

"I thought you didn't do clinical work," he snapped, revealing his anxiety.

"I don't. But I know the procedures."

She heard him drag in a breath and let it out.

"Maybe what we can do is have a practice hypnosis session where we only get into relaxation techniques."

"Okay," he answered, and she heard some of the tension ease out of him.

In the next second, he came up with an objection. "We don't have a whole lot of time."

She struggled to keep her voice even. "So which do you prefer? Getting right to the main event or doing a trial run?"

He considered the question. "Maybe a trial run."

"Then let me tell you a little about the technique we'll employ. I used it in the class I took. Really, it's self-hypnosis. And I'm just there to guide you back to an earlier time you want to remember and help you control the experience. The best part is that you're perfectly safe. Nothing can harm you while you're there." After giving him a fuller explanation, she asked, "Any questions?"

"No."

"Then make yourself comfortable."

He stretched out his long legs, crossing his booted feet at the ankles.

Morgan leaned forward slightly in her chair. "The technique will be the same this time and next. Breathe deeply, raise your eyes just a little, and look up at the line where the wall meets the ceiling."

Jack did as he was asked.

"Now I'm just going to help you relax. Relax. Relax now." Morgan continued in a soothing voice. "If you could get away from your problems and go on vacation—where would you go?"

He laughed. "I wish."

"We can do it here."

He shrugged. "I don't know. A beach, I guess."

"You like the beach?"

"I did when I was a kid. Not much time to lie around since then."

"Well, you can now. Imagine you're in a sling chair staring out at a beautiful blue ocean. The waves are rolling in, breaking on a horseshoe stretch of white sand."

She saw the tension ease out of Jack's face.

"It's nice, isn't it?"

"Um."

"Can you talk to me?"

"Yeah," he answered in a slow, drowsy voice.

"When I tell you to wake up, you'll come right back to this room."

"Uh huh."

She looked at his relaxed posture, pleased with her

success. It was tempting to ask him questions that had nothing to do with recovering his memories of the time before Trainer's men had captured him, but she wasn't going to bait and switch on him.

"Let's just stay here for a while, enjoying the sun and the surf."

"Okay."

"Do you see any dolphins?"

"Uh, yeah."

"Are there any sailboats out on the water?"

He smiled. "Um hum."

"Wiggle your toes in the sand."

She spent another ten minutes with him on the beach, then said, "The next time I say, 'wake up now,' you will wake. Now or anytime you are in the trance state. Do you understand?"

"Yes."

"Wake up now."

His eyes blinked open, and he stared at her. "I guess it worked."

"How do you feel?"

"Better than before we started."

"Refreshed?"

"Rested."

"Good." She was feeling pleased that it had gone so well and gave him an encouraging smile.

"Next time we'll start the same way, then I'll take you back to Trainer's camp."

That sent a small wave of doubt across his face, and she suspected that the last place he wanted to visit was the training camp. Perhaps she should give him a little time before they started in again.

"Maybe we should have a snack, then come back up here and try it again," she said.

He nodded in agreement.

---~~~---

Wade felt his tension mount as he drove back to the militia camp. He'd rushed off to meet Davenport because it was important, but now he was thinking about what Barnes might do.

Although Wade had put a few extra men on guard duty, there had been no problems. Everything was the way he had left it, including in the infirmary.

"No change in Preston?" he asked.

"Sorry."

"Do your best," he answered, wondering how long they were going to keep the man lying in a hospital bed. Would Wentworth cooperate if he suggested giving the troop an overdose of painkiller? Or would Wade have to do that himself?

He made a quick inspection of the camp. A few men were still in the recreation area shooting the breeze, but most of them were already in bed because the RAM days started early.

After he was satisfied with the camp, he went back to his office and checked his email, relieved that there were no communications from Mr. Money.

While he was sitting at the computer, a message came in from Davenport with the subject header, "Bad News."

Wade felt his stomach clench. Was the guy going to tell him he couldn't get the information on Jack Barnes after all?

His finger hovered over the mouse button. Then he remembered his cover story—that a man named Jack Barnes was stealing from him.

He opened the message and quickly read:

"You wanted to know if your employee, Jack Barnes, was legit. It wasn't hard to run those prints. They came right up. His real name isn't Jack Barnes like he told you. It's Jack Brandt. It looks like he's working for a security company in Rockville called Rockfort. Weird. Is he stalking you or something?"

Wade's heart was pounding as he hit the reply button. "Thanks for the info. I owe you one, buddy."

Chapter 23

Shane joined Morgan and Jack in the kitchen when he heard the refrigerator open.

"How did it go?"

"The test run was fine," Jack answered with more animation than he'd displayed when they'd been alone together. "It left me feeling good. We're going to have something to eat and get to the real deal."

Morgan turned away from the two men and took out the tray of sandwiches they'd served earlier, glad that there was prepared food at hand. She didn't want to get stuck being the cook for three guys at the safe house. Or should she impress them with her chicken cacciatore? The thought brought a wave of emotions surging through her. It had been a long time since she'd thought about cooking in any way besides providing herself with the essentials. Maybe while she was here she *could* play around in the kitchen. For her own amusement, of course. Not because she wanted to impress Jack and the rest of the Rockfort men.

In addition to sandwiches, she pulled out coleslaw and potato salad that they hadn't served earlier.

They all helped themselves and carried plates to the kitchen table, along with coffee.

"I'm checking into Trainer's finances," Shane said after he'd chewed and swallowed a bite of roast beef sandwich.

"How do you do that?" Morgan asked.

"We have a program that can look at bank records."

Morgan kept her gaze on him. "Isn't that illegal?"

He laughed. "You could say it was illegal for him to torture Jack. Or burn your house down. I'm not losing any sleep over how we nail him."

"I guess that's right."

"What did you find out?"

"That he's getting regular infusions of cash that's being transferred from an account in the Cayman Islands."

"Where people like to hide money that might not have come from legitimate sources."

"It could be from legitimate sources too, but it could be there to avoid paying taxes."

She nodded.

Jack set down his sandwich. "And you haven't found out who owns the account?"

"Not unless I can find someone who has better access to the banking system. But there is some other information I might be able to get."

"Like what?"

"Like when the account was established."

"You think Trainer owns the account?" Morgan asked.

"I'm betting it's someone else," Shane said.

He explained something of Wade Trainer's background to Morgan. "He's never had nearly enough cash to finance an operation like his militia. We've always thought the funds were coming from a third party."

Morgan nodded. They discussed the problem while

they ate, but she saw Jack getting more and more rest-
less. Finally he set down the unfinished part of his
sandwich. "I get the feeling I'll have a better appetite
after the session. Let's go up and get it over with."

"You sound like you're anticipating an unpleasant
medical procedure," Morgan answered.

He shrugged. "Whatever. The sooner we start, the
sooner we'll finish."

Excitement coursed through Wade Trainer. He had
the bastard now. His first impulse was to wake the
men immediately. Then he reminded himself not to
go off half-cocked. Barnes—no, Jack Brandt—had
put one over on him before. The guy was tricky, and
Wade had better have his ducks in a row before he
went over there.

Starting with scoping out Rockfort Security.
He Googled them and found the firm's address in
Rockville, Maryland. Not so far away, which made
sense. There were three partners: Jack Brandt, Shane
Gallagher, and Max Lyon. Those other two must be
the bastards who'd pinned Wade and his men down
in the cave and set the fire at the mouth while they got
away. He confirmed the assumption by finding their
pictures on the Web site, along with a head shot of the
super-prick, Jack Brandt.

He had to keep himself from throwing a glass
paperweight against the wall before continuing.

When he was more in control of his anger, he read
Jack Brandt's biography. In a lot of ways, it followed
the general pattern of what Brandt had told him. But

he was definitely a former Navy SEAL, unless he was lying about that on the Web site.

Switching to the other two guys, he found out that Shane Gallagher had been a cop, and Max Lyon had been an officer in the Army MPs. They'd formed the Rockfort Security Agency about a year ago. How the hell had the three of them hooked up?

Well, that wasn't important. The important thing was making them wish they'd never tangled with the Real Americans Militia.

Various scenarios ran through his mind as he called up a map, checking the exact location of the agency. It was in an industrial park a little north of downtown Rockville.

Would they be stupid enough to be in the office now? And was the woman, Morgan Rains, with them? That would be a nice bonus, if he could capture her.

While he was at it, he put her name into the Web too and found that she taught at a local university. As he stared at her self-confident face, he imagined stripping her and strapping her to his torture table. The idea aroused him. He got up and locked the office door, then unzipped his fly, grabbed a handful of tissues, and let himself enjoy the fantasy of what he would do to her.

Morgan and Jack returned to the bedroom where they'd had the first session.

"As I said, we'll start the same way," she said to Jack as she sat down in the chair she'd occupied earlier. "Then I'll take you back to Trainer's office—in a safe way."

"How?" he asked as he took the opposite chair.

"I'll distance you. You won't actually be there, but you'll see it on TV."

"TV?" he asked, sounding confused.

"Well, an imaginary TV over there." She gestured toward the far wall.

She saw his hands gripping the chair arms and knew he was forcing himself to do this.

"Comfortable?" she asked.

"Yes."

"Then we'll start. Like before, look up to the line where the ceiling meets the wall."

When he'd directed his gaze to the line, she said, "Relax now. Relax now. We're going back to that beach."

She saw his features soften.

"Are you there?"

"Yes."

"That's good. What do you see?"

"Sailboat. Dolphins," he answered in a dreamy voice.

"Okay, now you're going to get up from your chair and come inside the beach house."

She saw him shift in his seat.

"Come on inside, and take the chair across from the big television screen on the wall. Are you sitting across from the TV now?"

"Yes."

"Use the remote to turn it on. We're going to watch the Wade Trainer militia program. Three days ago. That's the day that somebody caught you sneaking around the compound. You won't actually be there, but you can see everything that's happening. Just like it happened before. But you'll be at the beach house. Nothing you see can hurt you."

He grunted.

"There's no threat to you. Do you understand?"

"Yes."

"Do you see yourself in the picture?"

"Yes."

"What are you doing?"

"Peeing."

She made a low sound. "I don't need to know about that. Skip to breakfast."

"Okay. I'm eating breakfast in the mess hall. They've got pancakes today. They're pretty decent. But I always make sure I have protein. Scrambled eggs."

"Then what?"

"Inspection. Trainer's going over my stuff with a fine-tooth comb. I think he wants to find something wrong. But he ends up giving me a superior rating."

"After that?"

"We're supposed to go to the firing range." He paused.

"What?"

"I start walking with the rest of the men, but I tell Trainer I have a bad stomach. He lets me go back. Lucky he doesn't make me shit in the woods. I go back to the main compound. I go into the bathroom and stay there for a while. When I come out I make sure nobody's around. Then I go to Trainer's office."

"Have you been in the office before?"

"Yes. He's called me in for talks on his theories about why the U.S. Government has gone bad. I always nod and agree like I think he's a master of philosophy."

"Have you been there alone before?"

"Yes, I've used my lock picks to open the door and slipped in to poke around." He laughs. "I figured out his password. McVeigh. His hero, apparently. Not very imaginative."

"What do you do now?"

"I check again for a tail. Nobody's there. Then I sit down at the computer. I get into his email account. I've been there before. He's on the mailing list for a lot of nut groups. And one guy in Delaware. Someone who calls himself G. Washington." He stopped short. "Wait a minute. I guess that's why I thought of George Washington in the cave. But I couldn't make it make sense."

"What?" Morgan asked.

"Never mind. Hasn't happened yet. I'm coming in in the middle of Trainer's conversation with the guy. Could G. Washington be his moneyman? I fix that address in my head. Must report that to Rockfort. There's also a message from someone named Yarborough. I read it. Then I scroll through his mail looking for messages from either one of them. Both have been talking to him a lot. I'm memorizing the Yarborough guy's address too. I want to read more of what they have to say, but I think I've been in the office long enough. Also, I can't stay away from the firing range forever, so I get back out of the mail and onto his desktop. Then I hear a stealthy noise in back of me. I'm starting to turn, when thump…"

He gasped and slumped to the side.

Morgan hadn't been prepared for that. She'd told him he was safe here with her. Apparently she'd been wrong.

Leaping out of her chair, she crossed to him, kneeling at his side.

"Jack, wake up now."

Nothing happened.

"Jack, wake up now," she ordered, hearing the panic in her voice as she gave the command. She'd been sure she could bring him out of the trance with the suggestion, but it was like they weren't even in the same room.

"Jack. Jack!"

His face had turned pale, and he had stopped breathing. Morgan's heart was in her throat as she leaned over him.

Chapter 24

THE DOOR SLAMMED OPEN WITH THE FORCE OF A gunshot, and Shane Gallagher barreled into the room, his gaze zeroing in on Jack.

"What the hell?"

Morgan looked at him in panic. "He stopped breathing."

Shane pushed her out of the way and leaned over his friend.

"What the hell did you do to him?"

"Nothing. He was in a trance; he was fine until just now."

Shane gave her a look that could have killed. Drawing back his hand, he slapped Jack across the face, then slapped him again.

Morgan gasped as she watched his shock treatment. She wanted to scream at Shane to stop, but she didn't know what else to do.

It felt like eternity hung in the balance. Probably it was only seconds. Finally, Jack coughed, and his eyes blinked open. He focused on Shane, who had drawn back his arm for another slap but dropped his hand to his side when he saw Jack's eyes open.

Jack's gaze swung to Morgan. "What happened?"

She was too choked to speak. Reaching for him, she pulled him close, not caring what Shane Gallagher thought. For a moment she clung to him, and she felt his arm come up and rest against her side.

"Are you okay?" she asked urgently.

"Yes."

The response sounded automatic, and she thought maybe she should give him air. Reluctantly she backed away again.

"I'm so sorry," she murmured as she searched his face.

"What happened exactly?' he asked again.

"What do you remember?" she countered.

His gaze turned inward. "You and I were doing another session. I was on the beach like before. Then we went into the beach house and turned on the television set like you suggested. You told me I could see the day that they captured me, but that nothing would happen to me." He gave her a questioning look. "What went wrong?"

"I don't know. I hope we can figure it out."

"What I do know is that you're not doing that to him again," Shane broke in, his voice hard-edged.

"What—were you lurking around outside like you didn't trust me?" she asked as she picked up on the hostility in his voice. It was bad enough feeling like she'd made a serious mistake. It was worse having someone look at her with accusing eyes.

"My ex-wife taught me it's dangerous to trust women."

"All women?"

He sighed. "Okay. Forget I said that. I thought somebody should be on duty in case you screwed up."

"I didn't screw up."

"How would you put it?"

Jack dragged in a breath and let it out. "Mind if I come up with a theory?"

"Let's hear it," Shane answered.

"The session took me back to Trainer's office, where I was trolling through his email." He looked at Shane. "I'd already gotten his password. I'd decided I'd better get back to the rifle range. Then everything went blank. Later—I mean in real life—I woke up in his interrogation room. I must have been out cold. Whoever came up behind me must have whacked me on the head, and I guess I repeated that experience in the hypnosis session."

"That could be it," Morgan mused.

Shane jumped back into the conversation. "Yeah, well, whatever happened, it wasn't worth it."

Jack straightened in his chair. "Yes, it was."

Shane gave him a questioning look.

"I got two names we need to check out ASAP. One's a guy who calls himself G. Washington. Obviously not his real name." He looked at Morgan. "Actually, I remembered that name in the cave, but I didn't know what it meant. Then we got busy."

"What's the other one?" Shane demanded.

"Yarborough."

"Yeah, that sounds phony too."

"Why?" Morgan asked.

"Because it means a bridge hand with no card higher than a nine, the implication being that it's a name with no real reference."

She nodded.

"But I have the email address for both of them," Jack continued. "Yarborough is yarborough@

slicknet.com. And the other guy is commander@
gmail.com. We can see who they really are."

"Maybe."

Jack ignored him and plowed ahead. "You said
you were checking into electronic funds transfers.
Maybe we can link one of them to the Cayman
Islands account."

"If they use the same email for banking business
as for subversive chatting." Shane looked from Jack
to Morgan and back again. "Maybe I'll get on that,"
he said.

And despite the crack about not trusting women,
maybe he'd figured out that he should leave her and
Jack alone, Morgan thought as she watched him leave
the room and close the door behind him.

She'd wanted to talk to Jack in private. Now that
she had the chance, her mouth was so dry she could
hardly speak, but she managed to say, "I'm glad
you're okay." Then, to her horror, she started to cry.
Trying to hide her tears, she turned away.

But not before Jack saw. He heaved himself out
of the chair and reached for her. Folding her close,
he lifted her into his arms, then sat back down in the
chair, cradling her against himself.

"It's okay," he murmured as he stroked her.

"No, it's not," she managed to say before the tears
came harder and faster. "My... idea almost killed you."

"I'm fine."

"Because Shane woke you up."

She leaned in to him, struggling to contain her
sobs. She knew why this was happening. She was in
a fragile emotional shape, and seeing him pale and

lifeless had made her insides knot. Maybe it was because she'd watched her husband die. And then when Jack had stopped breathing, the horror of those terrible moments had come flashing back to her.

A few days ago, her dead husband had been the most important man in her life. Now she knew that everything had changed for her. She still wasn't willing to put a name to her feelings for Jack Brandt, but she understood that they were deep and powerful.

Jack closed his eyes and cradled Morgan against his chest. Lowering his head, he stroked his lips against her hair. He was a man who'd guarded his emotions for years, but this woman had brought out tender feelings that he'd thought were long dead, and he wished he could wipe them away. He was wondering what he could say to her that would distance the two of them.

What would she think, for example, if he told her about his mother? To make extra money, she'd taken jobs cleaning the houses of officers on the bases where they'd lived. Until his father had found out she was also making arrangements to sleep with some of the officers—also for a little extra money. His father had kicked her out of their quarters before getting a divorce. That was when Jack had been fourteen. He'd kept that dark secret to himself all these years. He hadn't even told Shane and Max.

And Morgan? He suspected that it wouldn't matter to her. She'd say it was something his mother had done—not him.

He smiled as he continued to stroke his lips against her hair, loving the texture.

He'd told himself that making love with her was a mistake. He'd told himself that he was bad for her. He'd told himself a lot of things, but all he could think of now was the look of panic—and then relief—he'd seen in her eyes after Shane had slapped him and he'd come back to himself.

"I did that... to you. I'm so... sorry," she said between sobs.

"You didn't do it," he answered as he stroked his hands up and down her arms.

"Of...course I did. Shane..."

"Forget about Shane. He was upset."

"Because he wants to protect you from me."

"I don't need protecting."

He knew she was going to argue with him again, and the only way he could think of stopping her was to tip her face up and lower his lips.

She went very still as his mouth touched hers. Maybe he had intended the kiss to be comforting, but the moment their lips met, he knew he'd been kidding himself.

He wanted her. More than just physically.

He couldn't admit the emotional part, and at the same time, he couldn't deny the physical component.

He focused on that.

He liked the taste of her. The texture of her lips. The heat of her body, the way her arms crept up to circle his neck. In response, he gathered her closer as he turned his head first one way and then the other to change the angle of the kiss, then change it again, feasting from her.

His tongue played with the seam of her lips, asking her to open for him, and she did, so that he could explore the line of her teeth, then stroke the sensitive tissue on the inside of her lips.

His heart leaped when he heard her make a small sound deep in her throat. Accepting the invitation, he dipped farther into her mouth, his tongue doing a slow dance with hers.

He was beyond caring what the right thing to do was. If they'd been sitting in a chair without arms, he would have shifted her in his lap with her legs draped on either side of his. Instead, he stood and carried her to the bed, lying down with her in his arms, settling her on top of himself so that his erection was pressed intimately to the cleft at the top of her legs.

Even through their layers of clothing, her body seemed to melt into his. She lifted her head and looked down at him. Their gazes locked for long moments before she lowered her head so that she could bring her mouth back to his.

He felt urgency building inside himself, and at the same time he felt as though they had all the time in the world to make her understand that he didn't fault her for what had happened a while ago.

"You gave me a gift," he whispered.

"Of what?"

"Of knowledge. I'd lost important memories, and you gave them back to me. And don't tell me it was the wrong thing to do. We both know it was right."

They stopped talking, and he let sensations flow through him, building to a steady, insistent passion.

Dizzy with it, unable to speak of what he was feeling, he used his hands and mouth to show her.

They clung together, swaying on the bed, and he knew that if he'd been standing he wouldn't have been able to keep his balance.

When his fingers found the hem of her T-shirt and pulled upward, she lifted her torso away from him so that he could pull the shirt over her head and toss it away. Then he worked the catch at the back of her bra, sending that garment after the shirt.

She kept her position, offering her breasts to him. When he took their weight in his hands, she threw back her head and dragged in a quick, gasping breath. As his fingers began to tug on the distended tips, the breath turned into a sob.

He was caught in a dilemma of his own making now. He'd pulled her on top of himself when he was still dressed.

Gently he rolled her to her side, so that he could climb off the bed. He pulled off his shirt, then his jeans and briefs in one quick motion, his erection springing free.

When he turned back to Morgan, he saw that she'd also kicked away her pants. Now she lay naked on the bed, her ivory skin luminous in the dim light and her eyes focused on him.

"You are so beautiful," she whispered.

He laughed softly. "I think that's my line."

"It depends on your point of view. Come here."

When she held out her arms, he came back to her, rolling to his side so that he could hold her as he devoured her mouth, then slid lower to kiss her neck and shoulders.

They'd made love a few hours ago. It had no effect on his desire. He needed her more than he had ever needed a woman.

He forgot everything but the piercing ecstasy of being with her.

When his fingers stroked down her body and slipped into the hot, slick core of her, she sobbed as she arched into the caress.

He was stunned by the way she responded to him. Silently he pushed her higher and higher still until she was quivering in his arms.

Reaching down, she closed her fingers around his erection, squeezing as she moved her hand up and down, driving him toward the edge, the way he was driving her.

"Jack. Please. Now."

It was a plea he was helpless to deny.

"God, yes."

As he slipped inside her, he made a hoarse sound deep in his chest—unable to express in words what he was feeling. How much he was feeling.

All he could do was whisper her name.

She gazed up at him, reached to gently touch her fingertips to his cheek, his lips.

He went still above her, the two of them joined and absorbing the moment—until the longing to move his hips became more than he could bear. As he thrust into her, their mutual need flared.

Sexual need. Emotional need that was more than he had a right to expect.

Heat surged through him. Not just the heat of erotic contact—but heat that burned through his brain, hotter than any fire he could imagine.

Intense pleasure combined with a kind of peace he had never felt in his life.

He quickened the rhythm, taking Morgan with him to a high desert plateau where the air was almost too thin to breathe. She clung to him, her body trembling as she approached the summit. He fought the need to let himself go, waiting for her to reach her climax. And when he felt the inner contractions take her, he allowed his own control to slip.

She called his name as his own climax shook him, a giant whirlwind plowing through his body and soul.

When he could move again, he rolled to his side, holding her in his arms.

She snuggled against him, and when he looked down, he saw the smile on her face.

As he started to speak, she pressed her fingers to his mouth. "Don't make any decisions about us," she murmured. "Just enjoy what we have now. I know we can't talk about the future until you get Trainer. But we will."

He dragged in a breath and let it out. She wasn't putting any pressure on him to make a decision. She was giving him space, and that was a gift he wouldn't deny.

"Thank you," he whispered against her fingers.

She relaxed against him. "I need to sleep."

"Good idea. Too bad we have to move to get under the covers."

"And maybe put on some pants and a bra in case someone comes in."

"I don't need a bra."

"Funny."

He watched her slide out of bed and collect her

underwear. For good measure, she also put her T-shirt back on.

While she was out of bed, he straightened the covers but didn't bother with any clothing. When she came back into his arms, he let himself drift off, more content than he had ever remembered. He thought he should go back to his own room, but sleeping with Morgan was too tempting.

Sometime later, the loud ringing of the secure line woke him, and he wished he'd bothered to put on some clothing.

———⁄⁓⁄———

Early the next morning, Wade Trainer called four of his most trusted men—Rayburn, Chambers, Salter, and Porter—into his office.

"We're going on a covert recon mission," he told them. "In Rockville, Maryland. We'll dress like good old boys. T-shirts. Baseball caps. Jeans. But we'll have weaponry with us, in case we get the chance for some action."

He led the way to the wardrobe room, where he kept outfits for various occasions. He started off personally picking clothing for each of them. Boots and a Redskins T-shirt for Porter. A similar outfit with a John Deere T-shirt for Salter.

Chambers gave him a glance then turned back to the rack of clothing. "Sir, can I have a Hooters shirt?"

Wade was in an expansive mood. He'd been burned, and now he was striking back. Maybe not with an attack right away, but he was definitely going to get the lay of the land at Rockfort Security.

"That will be fine," he allowed, then let himself have some fun as well. He took a fierce-looking dragon shirt for himself along with worn blue jeans and hiking boots.

Selecting the clothing helped relax the guys. When they were dressed in the outfits, he gave them a quick inspection, pleased with the effect. Nobody would know they were seasoned troops on a vital mission unless they got out of the vehicles and snapped to attention.

"We'll take two SUVs," he said. He was about to order everyone into the vehicles when another thought struck him. "Chambers and Porter, go to the supply shed and get a couple of sets of Maryland license plates. No use giving ourselves away with ones from Virginia. Chambers will change the plates on the tan vehicle. Porter will take the dark blue."

"Yes, sir," the two men answered, then hurried off to carry out the orders.

The plates were stolen from vehicles that he'd figured nobody was going to drive again. Using them would mean that they'd have to strictly obey all traffic regulations.

"You get the SUVs ready while I personally select the weapons and other armaments."

He left Hamilton in charge at the compound, then got on the road.

Chapter 25

WHEN THE LOUD RINGING OF THE SECURE LINE WOKE Jack, he climbed out of bed and pulled on a pair of pants, then dashed down the hall to the phone at the top of the stairs.

Shane and Max were already talking when he picked up the receiver. He was aware of Morgan following him. She had also pulled on pants to go with the clothes she'd been sleeping in and leaned in close to him to hear the conversation.

"What?" Jack demanded.

Max, who had ended up staying at the office, was speaking. "There's been some activity here. A few minutes ago, the security cameras picked up two SUVs with guys driving in."

The office was located in an industrial park, but the Rockfort men had tapped into the park security system. The cameras that scanned the exterior of the strip of warehouses gave them a visual check on the whole complex.

"What guys?"

"They're all dressed like rednecks, with baseball caps pulled down low to hide their faces, and T-shirts, but I suspect it's Trainer and some of his men."

"The vehicles have Virginia tags?"

"No, Maryland, but they could be stolen."

"You want us over there?" Jack asked.

Morgan grabbed his arm.

"No," Max said. "I'll keep an eye on the situation. They can't get in here without heavy arms. And that would draw the attention of the Montgomery County cops."

Morgan's grip tightened on Jack's arm. "How did they find your offices?" she asked. "I mean, they didn't know who you were when you were at the camp, did they?"

"No," Jack answered, not liking the implications. There'd been no indication that Trainer knew who he was during the interrogation. It seemed that had suddenly changed.

He swore under his breath. "Maybe through my fingerprints. Unless he ran back to camp and burned everything I'd touched, he's got them."

"Didn't he check them before?" Morgan pressed.

"Apparently not."

"And how did he check them now?" she asked.

"I don't think he's sophisticated enough to tap into law enforcement databases. He must have a contact who can do it for him."

"Now what's the plan?" Shane asked.

"I'll stay here for the time being," Max answered. "And if I come back there, I'll make damn sure nobody follows me."

Jack and Shane murmured their agreement.

"What are they doing there?" Morgan asked.

"We have to assume they're thinking about getting even."

"As in taking us down," Jack growled. "But it ain't gonna happen."

"Well, they've tipped their hand," Max said.

Morgan sucked in a sharp breath, and Jack slung his arm around her.

"Keep us in the loop," Shane said. "And let us know if you need us there."

"It's probably better if you stay away," Max answered.

They hung up, and Jack looked at Morgan's worried face.

"If they know who you are, don't you have to *do* something?" she asked.

"Nothing's changed at our end. If we move on them now, we lose the opportunity to find out their plans."

"But…"

"We can't attack them without proof of what they're up to."

He reached for Morgan and wrapped his arms around her. "I know this seems scary, but it's going to be okay," he said.

"I don't like it that they found Rockfort so fast."

"Neither do I, if you want to know the truth."

She raised her face so she could meet his gaze. "Promise you won't keep anything from me."

He hesitated.

"Promise."

"I don't make all the decisions here."

"But anything involving the militia also involves me."

"Yeah."

Maybe she realized that was all she was going to get out of him because she said, "I think we'd better get to work investigating those names on the emails."

"Uh huh." He was thinking they should have

already been working on that last night, but he didn't say it. Maybe she was thinking the same thing and keeping it to herself.

"Which one do you want to take?" he asked.

"I can take the G. Washington guy. You do the other one. Yarborough."

They went back to the bedroom, finished getting dressed, and came downstairs.

Shane was in the office. He gave them a long look when they entered but said nothing about where they had spent the night. Jack was grateful for that. He was sure Morgan wouldn't like any remarks about their personal relationship.

"Any progress on the money trail?" Jack asked.

"I know that the account in the Cayman Islands was established about two years ago."

"A year before Trainer actually got the militia going," Jack said. "But he would have needed prep time. He's got a very complete setup there, even considering that he used an old camp."

"Let's see if we can get any clues that tie the money to either of the men Trainer was emailing," Morgan said. "Do you have a computer that I can use?"

Shane got up, took a laptop off the shelf over the desk, and handed it to her.

"Do I need a password?"

"All the computers here are connected to the house's internal network. When you turn it on, you're in."

—◦◦◦—

Wade was circling around for another look at the Rockfort Security offices when his cell phone rang.

Jesus, what now?

When he saw the name on the caller ID, he gritted his teeth. It was his moneyman. The last person he wanted to hear from. He considered not answering, then decided that might be a bad idea.

"Trainer here," he said, then pulled over to the shoulder of the access road that wound through the industrial complex. No use getting pulled over by a cop for talking on his cell phone while driving.

"Where are you?" the voice on the other end of the line demanded.

"Why are you asking?"

"Because I want to make sure this Jack Barnes thing doesn't blow up in your face."

"It won't." Wade glanced at his men. "Give me a minute," he said. He pulled to the side of the road and motioned for the other SUV to pull over. When both vehicles had stopped, he turned to his men. "Wait here for me. I'll be right back."

He climbed out of the car, closed the door, and walked a few yards away.

"I have the situation under control," he said. "I found out that Jack Barnes is really a guy named Jack Brandt, who works for the Rockfort Security Agency."

"How did you find that out?"

"I had a law enforcement contact check his fingerprints."

"And the contact has no idea why?"

"Right. I gave him a story he bought."

"I advise not making a move on the Rockfort agency—yet."

"I've got heavy arms with me."

"Do not attack them now."

"Why not?"

"You want to get all of them, right?"

"Damn straight."

"Give me a minute to think."

There were several moments of silence during which Wade felt his stomach knot. Finally his money-man began to talk. "How about this?"

Soon Wade was grinning.

"That's perfect," he said.

"I thought you'd like it."

"Are you sure you can pull it off?"

"Absolutely."

After securing Wade's approval, Mr. Money seemed to relax. "I never did tell you why your mission was so important to me," he said.

"That's right."

"My only son was a West Point graduate. The Army sent him to Afghanistan. And he died in one of those damn Humvees that didn't have enough armor. His death could have been prevented, if only Congress had authorized the money for the right equipment. But they didn't do it. And I want them to go down for it. Understand?"

"I'm sorry. I didn't know about your son. Why didn't you tell me?"

Wade had always assumed that Mr. Money was simply a super patriot who wanted to teach the U.S. Government a lesson. Now it seemed that he had personal motives for financing the Real Americans Militia.

"I didn't want my personal story to get in the way

of our business relationship, but now I want you to know why your attack is important to me."

"I understand. We're only days away," Wade assured him.

"But you have to neutralize Rockfort first. If they're all dead, they can't interfere."

"Yeah."

The phone clicked off, and he went back to his men. When he was behind the wheel again, he turned to the troops and said, "Change of plans. We're going back to prepare for an attack tomorrow." He looked at Salter. "Convey my orders to the men in the other vehicle."

"Yes, sir."

—⁓—

Morgan took the laptop from Shane. "I can work in the great room," she said.

"Fine."

She slipped out of the room, glad to get away from the two men. She didn't much like her personal life on display, and she knew it was. She'd like to know what Shane Gallagher really thought about her.

Dragging in a breath, she tried to stop focusing on herself. She wasn't important right now. At the moment her mission was finding out as much as she could about Trainer's buddy, G. Washington.

She grabbed a sandwich for breakfast and a cup of coffee and sat down and booted the computer. She'd grandly told Jack that she was a researcher and could use those skills in any field, but now that she was considering the problem of researching someone who called himself G. Washington, she realized it wasn't going to be so easy. And what if he was using a different name for the Web?

She started with a Google search. Among the many references to the first president, she found a couple of people who might be right and started clicking on the name. After a few tries, she hit something that looked promising. It was a guy replying to a post from one of the online news Web sites. He was complaining about the government's heavy-handed interference in matters that should be left to the states. It sounded like it could be the right man, but that didn't help in coming up with his real identity.

Well, she wasn't going to give up that easily. She checked a couple more sites until he finally mentioned where he lived. Delaware.

Okay, good. That was something she could use.

She opened a notepad in another window and copied the text of his post before she went searching again. This time she used G. Washington and Delaware and came up with a hit that gave her more complaints about government regulations.

Looking up, she saw Jack watching her.

"How are you doing?"

"I'm getting somewhere, but I don't have enough to make any judgments yet."

He went into the kitchen and came out a few minutes later with a mug of coffee. She might have asked if he wanted to sit in the great room with her, but she figured that she'd get more done if she didn't have to think about the two of them while she worked.

So what were the cities in Delaware? The only one she could think of off the top of her head was

Wilmington, but she found more on the Web. Dover. Newark, Milford, Lewes, Rehoboth Beach. She put G. Washington back into the search engine, paired with each of the cities, and came up with nothing. Frustrated, she went back through the earlier references and found that he was complaining about gas prices and highway regulations. And also unfair taxes on new cars.

Which gave her an idea. She returned to the cities and called up a list of car dealerships. In Wilmington, she found a Chevrolet and Cadillac dealer named G. Washburn. Not Washington, but close.

Focusing on him, she found that he was prominent in the chamber of commerce, in the First Methodist Church, the Rotary Club. He also sponsored a couple of youth sports teams and gave to the local SPCA. He looked like an upstanding member of the community.

Digging into his personal life, she discovered that he was married, belonged to the most prominent country club in the area, and owned a condo on Longboat Key in south Florida, where he and his wife spent the winter months.

"Found anything?" Jack asked.

She looked up and saw him standing nearby. She'd been so intent on her assignment that she hadn't even heard him come in.

When she searched his face, she saw that he looked frustrated and tired.

"You're not making much progress?" she asked.

He raised an arm and let it drop back to his side. "I wish I were." He walked over to the couch and lowered himself to the seat beside her. "What do you have to cheer me up?"

"Well, I've got a lot of information on G. Washington. I know who he is."

His face brightened. "You're sure?"

"Pretty sure." When she explained her search process, he nodded. "And he's got money, although I'm not sure if it's enough to outfit a militia organization." She started telling him the facts she'd uncovered.

He looked impressed. "You said you were good at research."

She laughed. "Well, some of my research was tracking down plagiarized term papers."

"You get a lot of that?"

"More than I used to. Or—now there are methods for seeing who's cheating." She switched back to G. Washington. "I think GW wasn't as good at hiding his identity as your guy." She turned her head toward him. "What about Yarborough?"

"He doesn't have any kind of personal persona that I can tie to him."

"Too bad."

"It means he's going to great lengths to hide his real name. I did trace his email account, though. It goes through a server in Romania."

Morgan moved so that her shoulder was pressed to Jack's, reassured by his rock-solid body.

He gave her a measured look. "You're doing great," he said. "And I'm not just talking about research. You're holding up under stress."

"I wish I were doing better," she answered. There were so many things she wanted to talk about, and she didn't know where to begin.

"I guess you've been under pressure like this a lot," she murmured.

"It's not as bad as sitting around waiting to go into combat. At least we've got something to focus on."

"True." She reached for his hand and held on.

He knitted his fingers with hers.

"My experience is different from yours," he said in a low voice.

"What's that supposed to mean?"

"I went right from high school into the Navy."

"And worked your way up."

He ignored that and said, "You kept on in school. A BS. An MS. A PhD."

"You've heard the old joke. Bullshit. More shit, and piled higher and deeper."

He laughed, then sobered again. "You're smart, and you can apply your brainpower to many types of problems."

"So can you. But you have a wider background. I've never been out of the U.S. There are a lot of things we can teach each other."

He was saved from a comeback by the sound of footsteps. They glanced up to see Shane come into the room, a satisfied smirk on his face. "Even more interesting—information on the Cayman Islands account is coming through a server in Romania."

"Then it's him!" Morgan exclaimed.

"We can't be absolutely sure, but that's sugges-tive," Shane allowed. He looked at Morgan. "But we still have to keep going with your guy. It would be nice if you could uncover some information that he's kept hidden."

"Like what?"

"Other affiliations. Or maybe something through his wife."

"I'll get on that," Morgan said.

"And we'll keep trying to find a link between the Yarborough guy and the money."

"Will he know you are poking around in his banking business?"

"Maybe. That might get him to do something rash. Like cut off Trainer's funding."

"Trainer could keep going for a while, couldn't he?"

"Probably. But cutting him off from his cash might make him panic."

Chapter 26

MORGAN DID SOME MORE RESEARCH ON G. WASHINGTON and couldn't find anything that he'd tried to keep under cover. Which didn't mean there wasn't anything to find. Knowing she needed a break, she got up, wandered into the kitchen, and started looking through the refrigerator and the pantry.

She had sworn she wasn't going to cook, but when she found the ingredients for a classic dessert she liked, she decided to go ahead and make it.

The aroma of cooking apples and cinnamon brought both men into the kitchen.

"What's that?" Jack asked.

"Apple pie."

"It smells wonderful."

"It will be ready soon. We can have some before dinner."

"Isn't that the wrong order?" Jack teased.

"You mean like cookies before cheese and crackers in the cave?"

"I guess you're right."

Forty minutes later, she called them into the kitchen to eat the pie with ice cream she found in the freezer.

Shane had been standoffish with her, but the treat seemed to thaw him considerably.

"This is wonderful," he told her as he finished his first bite. "You didn't even have a recipe, did you?"

"I like to cook, and pie is something I can do without a cookbook." She looked at Jack. "What have you found out about Yarborough?"

"Not much. He's in deep cover, which leads me to believe he's Trainer's moneyman—not G. Washington."

"Does that do us any good?"

"It will if we can figure out who he really is."

The conversation was interrupted when Max called. Shane put him on the speakerphone so that everyone at the safe house could hear. "I've been monitoring the video feeds. Trainer and his guys seem to have gone away."

"I wish I could be sure that was good news," Jack answered. "I can't believe they're not planning *something*."

"None of them actually came near the building. What do you think I should do?" Max asked.

"Stay there," Shane answered. "That's probably safest—from the point of view of not revealing this location."

Jack nodded, but Morgan picked up on his uneasy expression.

"What are you thinking?" she asked him.

"That I made Wade Trainer insanely angry by proving to be a traitor in his eyes—then getting away. I'm pretty sure he's not going to rest until he's figured out a way to get even."

"But not today, apparently," she answered.

"Does that make you feel better?" he shot back.

"I guess not."

They discussed possible scenarios before hanging up.

"I've got one more thing I can try," Shane said. "When I was still doing criminal investigations for the Army, I worked with a banking expert named Hank Bernstein. Maybe he's willing to look into the Cayman Islands account for us."

They had more of the sandwiches for supper, then another small slice of pie apiece.

"We'll save the rest for Max," Jack said.

"Good idea," Morgan agreed. "How do you keep from gaining weight—sitting around here?" she asked.

"I told you, there's a gym in the basement."

"I only saw the safe room."

"You go down a different stairway."

"Let me put on shorts and a T-shirt."

"I'll come down with you."

They met in the great room again, both dressed for the gym. Jack took her down what looked like the main basement stairway, which landed in the weight room.

She opted for the elliptical trainer while he started on the weight machines.

"Tell me some stuff about Trainer," she said as she moved her arms and legs back and forth.

Jack kept up his motion on the leg press. "Like what?"

"I want to get a handle on his personality."

Jack kept pressing with his legs. She couldn't see what weight he was using, but she suspected it was double what she could do.

"He needs to be in charge, and he's highly organized, also highly disciplined. He put together the militia compound on his own."

"He built the whole thing?"

"No. It was an old camp, and he modified the

buildings to suit his purposes. He keeps his armament in steel buildings." He paused. "And I think there's something special in one of them."

"Special?"

"Just a hunch, from the way he acts around it."

She nodded as she kept up her aerobic workout.

"He doesn't listen to the opinions of others. He's sure of his mission." Jack paused for a moment while he switched to the leg curl machine and adjusted the weights. "That's putting it mildly. I sometimes had the feeling that he thinks he's got some kind of divine sanction."

"That makes him more dangerous."

"He doesn't talk about it a lot. I guess he figures he'd be revealing too much."

"Good insights." She climbed off the machine, walked to the case of water bottles, and unscrewed the cap on one. After taking a long pull, she asked, "He never mentioned his family?"

"No. But we did some research on him. His family was lower middle class. His dad supplemented the family larder by hunting, sometimes illegally. Probably he was into corporal punishment, and Wade grew up with a healthy disrespect for law and order. His dad worked in a lumber mill and was killed in an accident there—leaving the family in bad shape. Wade was sixteen when it happened, and he had to quit school and get a job at a local convenience store to help his mom make ends meet."

Morgan nodded. "All that would have formed some of his attitudes. It sounds like he was a responsible kid—helping to support the family."

"Yeah, but he's broken with them completely. He has two sisters and a brother, and he never sees any of them now."

"Did something happen to cause the break?"

"Well, his brother did get arrested for auto theft and other crimes."

"Maybe he was ashamed of that. Or disgusted."

Jack joined her and got a bottle of water for himself. "I guess we can only speculate about that."

"Yes. And other stuff. But interestingly, the parents' behavior can cause kids in the same family to go in different directions. His father's corporal punishment could be a factor in his brother's going bad. And it could have had the opposite effect on Wade. It could have made him big on harsh discipline," she said.

Jack's eyes took on a faraway look. "I'd say he enjoyed meting out punishment."

"What kind?"

"He liked to gather the troops to watch offenders getting whipped."

She dragged in a sharp breath. "Nice."

"And we know he likes harsh torture methods." He gave her a quick look. "Methods that were painful but wouldn't kill me. I guess he's studied those techniques."

"Nasty."

"He wanted information. He was going to kill me later."

"But you got away."

"Which has made him angry as hell. Not just at me, but at Shane and Max, now that he knows about them. Cunningham was right on that score."

"Well, Trainer's angry with me too," she added.

His gaze shot to her again. "Another reason why we need to put him out of commission."

She asked a question she'd never thought she'd consider. "Can you do a preemptive strike?"

"We may end up having to do that." He kept his gaze on her. "You didn't like it when I set up that accident for Gibson. How will you like it if we make it look like his men started a revolution?"

She sucked in a breath and let it out. "I guess my attitude has changed, now that I understand the realities of the situation."

He answered with a clipped nod.

They both worked out for an hour, with Morgan switching to the machines and lowering the weights considerably from the positions Jack had used.

Both of them were sweating by the time they called it quits. Upstairs, they both grabbed bottles of water and drank thirstily.

As they stood by the kitchen counter, she could feel the heat coming off Jack.

"Something we have in common," she said. "We both like to work out."

"Yeah." He was looking at her like he was thinking about pulling her sweat-slick body against his, and she felt a jolt of awareness. Instead he said, "We should both take a shower and get some sleep."

She wanted to make a different suggestion, but she knew he was right.

"Shane and I will alternate guard duty," he said.

"You think we need a guard?"

"I hope not. Trainer doesn't know this location, but under the circumstances, it's a good idea."

She nodded, wishing she could take Jack up to her bedroom. Not necessarily to make love but to lie in his arms for a while.

After her shower, they had dinner, then turned in early. She lay awake for a long time, mulling over the conversation with Jack in the gym.

Did she really think it was okay to attack Trainer's compound? And what did that say about her?

She'd like more information about the militia leader. Maybe they had a file on him that she could read.

The ringing of the phone woke her, and she heard running feet in the hall.

Jack must have switched on the speaker upstairs, because she heard Max Lyon's voice.

"The troops are back. I'm under attack."

"We'll be right there," Jack answered, then ran into her room. "We're going to help Max. You will stay here."

She wanted to protest, but she knew that Jack wasn't going to allow her to come with them.

"Okay." Climbing out of bed, she ran to him and dragged him close, holding him tightly. "Be careful."

"I will."

She reached up and pulled his head down for a fierce kiss, which was over all too quickly.

"Call me when you know something."

"I will."

Then he and Shane left the house. She ran to the window, watching them drive away, feeling a sense of foreboding.

She put on another running suit, then went down to the great room and looked at the time. She was surprised to see it was only 11:00 p.m. Unable to sit still, she paced back and forth, her glance sometimes going to the window as she peered out into the darkness.

———

Max Lyon kept in touch with the other men as they drove toward the Rockfort offices.

"I'm alternating camera views. They're holding in formations around the front and back entrances," he reported.

"How many?"

"Six at each door."

"They can't get in," Jack said.

"Unless they use a mortar or something big."

"We're still fifteen minutes out," Jack said. "We've got the firepower to chase them away."

"And alert the Montgomery County Police."

"Trainer started it, not us."

"Either way, the cops may be pissed about a gun battle at an industrial park in the county."

"I guess we'll worry about that later. If we're attacked, we have the right to defend ourselves."

———

About a half-hour after the men had left, the phone rang, and Morgan leaped toward it, hoping for news from Jack.

The voice on the other end of the line said, "This is Arthur Cunningham."

It was the man who'd hired Rockfort Security to keep tabs on the militia leader.

"Yes."

"Jack wanted me to stay with you. I have the remote for the alarm system. I'm coming in."

She hesitated. "Why didn't Jack tell me?"

"He's busy."

Before she could answer, she saw headlights in the driveway. Then a car came into view through the darkness. As it pulled up in front of the house, floodlights came on. When the vehicle stopped, a man got out, and she could see him clearly. It was the same man she'd met the day before. Earlier he'd been dressed in a business suit. Now he was wearing cargo pants and a windbreaker over a knit shirt.

He strode up to the house. When she didn't immediately open the door, he knocked.

"If you don't let me in, Jack's going to be angry," he said.

She still hesitated. Something about this didn't feel right. "I'm going to call Jack," she said.

Turning away from the door, she started for the phone.

Behind her, the door blasted open like it had been hit with a guided missile. Morgan was knocked to the floor, where she lay stunned for a moment, but she knew she couldn't stay there. She had to get to the safe room.

She was pushing herself up when Cunningham leaped on her. She hit at him with her fists, but he ignored the blows as he fumbled with something under his jacket.

She was still fighting him when she felt the prick of a needle through the fabric of her pants. It plunged into her thigh, and Cunningham pushed himself off of her.

"You'll take a nice nap now," he said.

She was already feeling woozy, but she managed to ask, "Why?"

"I need your help," he said.

She wanted to ask why again, but blackness was already closing in on her.

"Wait a second," Max said.

"What?"

"Every one of them is pulling back."

"They realize they can't get in?"

"I don't know," Max answered.

He kept watching on the video screens as the militiamen raced back to their cars, climbed in, and sped away, leaving the area around the offices as it had been before the start of the attack.

Max waited tensely as more headlights swung into the parking area. This time he recognized the vehicle. It was Jack and Shane.

They stayed in their car, and he knew they were evaluating the situation.

"Did you see them leave anything?" Jack asked.

"Negative."

"Then what the hell is going on?"

"I have a bad feeling about this," Jack said.

Chapter 27

Jack pulled out his cell phone and called the safe house. The phone rang. He waited through ten rings before hanging up.

"Morgan's not answering," he said, then looked at Shane. "We'd better go back there."

"Should I stay here?" Max asked.

"For the time being. In case they're going for a double tricky play."

Jack's chest was so tight that he could barely breathe as he turned the vehicle around and started back to the safe house, driving above the speed limit and praying that they didn't get stopped by a cop.

They made it back in twenty minutes. As soon as they got out of the SUV, his worst fears were confirmed.

The front door had been locked, but now it was standing wide open, and the house appeared empty.

He and Shane both pounded inside, both of them calling Morgan's name. Shane ran down to the safe room.

"Unlocked and empty," he called out.

Jack took the second floor, not knowing what to hope for. He didn't want to find Morgan lying dead on the floor, but he didn't want to find her missing either.

The latter was true. She wasn't hiding in any of the closets or under any beds.

They both headed for the office, where Jack rewound the security tapes to the past forty minutes.

They saw Morgan inside the house pacing back and forth and occasionally looking out the window.

Then another camera showed a car pulling into the driveway.

"How did they get in?" Shane asked.

"Oh fuck," Jack answered as he saw Cunningham get out of the vehicle and approach the front door. "What the hell is he doing?"

Switching to the inside view, he saw Morgan heading for the phone. She never reached it.

The door blew open, and Cunningham leaped toward her. She tried to run, then tried to fight him off.

He brought her down to the floor, where they fought.

Jack watched the monitor in horror as the man who had hired them to keep tabs on Trainer pulled a hypodermic from under his windbreaker and plunged it into her leg.

He pushed himself off of Morgan, watching her as she tried to say something before her eyelids drifted closed.

Jack didn't realize he was screaming, until he felt Shane put a hand on his arm and murmur, "Take it easy."

He whirled toward Shane, ready to lash out until he saw the concern on his friend's face.

"What the hell is going on?" Shane asked.

"Oh Jesus. I have a feeling that I know," Jack answered, and he didn't much like it.

Jack strode into the computer room and checked the mail that had come in.

"You have a message from that guy who was checking out the bank account in the Cayman Islands."

Shane sat down at the computer and scanned the

text. "He doesn't have a name, but he gave me the account number." He pointed to the screen.

Jack stared at it. "Check the number of the account where Cunningham is sending us our monthly checks."

Shane compared the two numbers and dragged in a startled breath. "It's the same number."

"Yeah. Fucking surprise," Jack said. He looked at the time stamp on the email. "It came in after we left, but we probably wouldn't have stopped to check the mail."

He was sick inside. Sick that Morgan was gone and sick that they'd been tricked.

"It looks like Arthur Cunningham and the guy named Yarborough are one and the same. And neither one of them is his real name."

When the phone rang, they looked at each other. It was Max. "I have a call from Wade Trainer on the office public line."

"Put him through."

The voice of the militia leader came over the speaker. "Is Jack Brandt there?"

"Yes," Jack growled.

"I guess you're not so smug now."

"I never was smug. Get to the point."

"I have your girlfriend."

"She's not my girlfriend."

"She's got twenty-four hours to live, unless you and the rest of your gang surrender to me."

Jack glanced at Shane as his hand tightened on the receiver. "Is Morgan all right?" he shouted.

"For now."

"You'd better not hurt her."

"You're not in a position to make demands."

The line went dead and Jack was left with a feeling of horror so profound that he wanted to start screaming again. He would have, if he'd thought it would do any good.

He'd gotten Morgan into this. All she'd done was rescue him, and that had set Wade Trainer after her.

Jack closed his eyes for a moment, picturing her sweet face. He'd been fighting what he felt for her. Now it was as clear as the warmth of her smile: He loved her, and if he couldn't get her back, he saw no reason for continuing his miserable existence.

He spoke aloud, his voice anguished but strong. "Maybe he'll trade her for me."

An answer came from the other end of the phone line as Max spoke. "Unlikely. And if you decide this is going to be a suicide mission for you, then she'll end up dead too."

"Okay, smart guy, what the hell are we going to do?" Jack shouted, unable to deal with his out-of-control emotions.

"We all go after her," Shane said. "We were thinking about raiding the place. Now we have a reason."

"That's what he wants. So he can kill us all. And her too."

"We're not going in there on his terms. There wouldn't be any point to it," Shane said. "We're going to figure out something tricky that he can't anticipate."

Jack answered with a dip of his head.

"Sit down," Shane said, "and we'll do some planning."

"I'm coming in," Max said.

"Might as well," Shane answered. "It won't matter if he burns down our offices now."

"Yeah, we've got insurance," Max said.

They hung up, and Jack kicked his foot against the desk.

"Cunningham pulled one over on us," Shane said, ignoring the outburst. "But why?"

"He said he wanted to catch Trainer doing something illegal. I have the feeling he had me in there reporting back to him so he could make sure Trainer was going to carry out his attack."

"How does that make sense?"

"He was willing to give him buckets of money, but he didn't trust him," Jack suggested. "Having me there was a check on what was happening."

"So fucking with the government was important to him," Shane said. "I'd like to know why."

"Maybe we can figure that out later. What matters is saving Morgan," Jack shot back. "Trainer said she's got twenty-four hours. And God knows what that bastard might do to her in the meantime." He dragged in a breath and let it out. "And like you said, we'd better come up with a plan he's not expecting. If he sees us coming, he could kill her anyway."

Shane nodded in agreement. "We'll make sure that doesn't happen."

Jack felt his stomach knot again as he wondered if they could pull that off. It wasn't like they had days to plan. More like hours.

———

Morgan woke but kept her eyes closed as she recalled what had happened to her.

The man who had called himself Arthur Cunningham

had captured her, and she had no idea what he wanted with her. But she knew at once that her hands and feet were tied. Each wrist and ankle was secured to the corners of the metal bed where she lay.

She'd been dressed in a running suit and a T-shirt. Now the cold air on her body told her she was wearing only her bra and panties. But at least she had those on.

The position in which she was tied was frightening, but she knew that was the point. It made her totally vulnerable and defenseless.

"I know you're awake," a sharp voice said.

She didn't move. The man who had spoken was not the same one who had drugged her.

"Open your eyes, or I will punish you." The way he said it made her think he was looking forward to the prospect.

Her eyes blinked open. In the dim light from a single overhead bulb, she zeroed in on the man sitting in the comfortable leather chair across from her uncomfortable bed.

"That's better," he said, his voice full of satisfaction.

"Who are you?"

"Wade Trainer."

She'd suspected as much. Now she fought to maintain her composure as she tested her bonds. The ropes that held her down were tight, and it seemed there was no way she could get free.

"What do you want with me?"

"I want to lure Jack Brandt and his friends here so I can kill them."

"Why do you think he cares about me?"

"He cared enough to hustle you out of that burning house and take you somewhere he thought you'd be safe."

She didn't bother explaining that she was the one who'd gotten them out of the burning house.

"You won't get him," she said in a steady voice, then wondered if that had been the wrong thing to say.

"I think he and his buddies will come to rescue you. I told him I'd kill you in twenty-four hours if he didn't."

She felt a wave of cold sweep over her. Twenty-four hours. That wasn't much time to live. Or maybe it was—depending on what the man planned to do to her.

"And if that's not good enough to get him here, I can email him a video of my torturing you," he answered calmly, sweeping his hand toward the wall where she saw racks of whips, knives, mallets, and other implements she didn't want to examine too closely.

The harsh words delivered in such a matter-of-fact tone and the equipment in the room made her heart skip a beat, then start to pound, but she warned herself it was dangerous to let her fear show. That's what he wanted.

"You don't have to keep me trussed up like this," she said, struggling to keep her voice even.

"I'm afraid I do. I didn't have Jack Brandt secured, and he got away."

"I don't have his skills."

"Too bad for you. And he's not as good as you think. One of my men caught him in my office and clunked him over the head. He wasn't breathing, and my medic had to revive him. How's that for screwing up?"

She caught her breath. Jack had thought he might have been hit on the head by one of Trainer's men, and the militia leader was describing that scene. Now she knew for sure why he'd stopped breathing during the hypnosis session. That was what had really happened to him.

Trainer had given her an important piece of information, but she wasn't going to tell him she'd brought back Jack's memories.

In fact, she'd better consider carefully how she was going to proceed with this man. She thought about what Jack had said about the militia leader. It had been an interesting conversation. Now she wished she had pressed him for every scrap of information he could dredge up.

But there were things she knew from that discussion and from Trainer's behavior now. The man was self-centered. He pretended to be sure of himself, but deep down he had doubts. Maybe that was why he never talked about his plans. He was afraid they would blow up in his face.

And maybe her best strategy was to hold his attention so that he couldn't focus too much on what the Rockfort men might be doing. That made sense, but she knew it was also dangerous. She'd be walking a fine line. She had to keep his attention focused on her but not make him angry enough to harm her.

Jack and Shane looked up as Max burst into the room. He zeroed in on Jack. "I feel like a jerk for luring you away from here," he said.

"We all thought it was a legitimate attack," Jack answered. "Trainer wanted us to think so."

He quickly filled in Max on how Morgan had been snatched by Cunningham.

"That bastard," Max muttered. "Where is he now, do you think?"

"No way of knowing. Either he's at the militia compound or he's gone to ground somewhere."

"I'd like to know his real identity," Shane said.

"We can work on that after we rescue Morgan," Jack answered, then looked at his two partners. "I think I figured out how we can get in there."

The two other men turned to him expectantly.

He was thinking aloud as he spoke. "It's got to be by air. And it's got to be before the sun comes up, because after that he'll spot us." He looked at his watch. "Which means we have five hours to get this whole deal in place."

"He'll hear us miles away if we come in by helo," Max said.

"I know. That's why we're going in by glider."

"You can't fly a glider from the ground. You've got to be towed up."

"I know," he said again. "There's an airport near Skyline that we can use. A small plane will tow us up and stay far enough from the compound so nobody down there thinks it's got anything to do with the rescue. Then we'll glide in and land on the firing range."

"Two small planes," Shane said. "I went for a glider ride once. We can get two men in one of them, and the third will go in solo."

"You ever piloted a glider?" Max asked Jack.

"Yeah."

Shane looked at Max. "I haven't. You?"

"I'm a quick learner," Max said. "I can handle the other one."

Shane looked like his friend had ordered up the impossible.

"You got a better idea?" Jack asked.

"No. But I have a lot of questions. Starting with, how are we going to land in the dark without plowing into any of the camp buildings?"

"Like I said, we land on the firing range. He has lights on the perimeter at night.

"Okay," Shane answered.

"I know where we can get Navy surplus gliders in a hurry," Jack continued. "I'll get on that. Then I'll make arrangements for the planes."

"You can do all that in five hours?"

"If I pay enough."

When Jack had exited the room, Shane and Max exchanged glances. "You think it will work?" Max asked.

"It has to."

"I'd like to go in there with gas masks and poison gas," Max said. "Exterminate all the rats."

"Only we'd kill Morgan too."

"What about that stuff they used in Russia to rescue the people being held hostage in that school?"

"Risky. A lot of the hostages died," Shane said. "We can't take a chance on that."

"Might work on a limited basis. We're going to

have to kill or disable as many of them as possible without making any noise."

"Maybe we should stop making plans until Jack comes back."

Max looked toward the monitor. "Okay, show me the picture of Cunningham capturing Morgan. Let's see it in slow motion."

Shane scrolled back through the tape to the point where the car arrived in the doorway and slowed the speed.

"Not yet. When he goes after Morgan."

Shane speeded up to the part where Cunningham was leaping inside and heading for Morgan, bringing her down.

As they rolled together on the floor, Max shouted, "Stop the tape."

Shane paused the video. "What?"

"See that?" Max asked, pointing toward the picture.

"Jesus," Shane said as he examined the frame. "I missed that. His hand is pressed against the floor."

"Which means we've got his prints," Max said.

"Didn't Jack say he thought that was the way Trainer discovered his identity?"

"Yeah. Poetic justice, as I said when we set that fire in the cave." Shane went to the supply cabinet. "We're going to use old-fashioned fingerprint powder."

They were down on their knees in the hall, dusting for fingerprints, when Jack came back.

"What the hell are you doing? We're supposed to be getting ready to raid Trainer's camp."

"Giving you a nice surprise before it got wiped away by the cleaning lady," Shane answered. He held up the sheet of contact paper. "Max had me go back over the tape of Cunningham capturing Morgan. He pressed his hand to the floor, and we have his prints."

"Good news," Jack said. "But we'll have to deal with him later."

"Agreed."

"I've arranged for our transportation." He gave each of his partners a long look. "There's no armor on the gliders. If they see us and shoot, we're dead."

Chapter 28

WHEN MAX AND SHANE BOTH SAID, "UNDERSTOOD," Jack breathed out a small sigh. It was one thing for him to risk his life to save Morgan; it was quite another to ask his friends. But from the moment he'd met these men, he'd known he could rely on them.

"I've got to take care of something," Shane said, and headed for the door. Before he left, he looked at Max. "Fill him in on what we've been talking about."

"Sure," Max said as though they were about to discuss strategy for a football game. "We've got to kill or disable as many of them as possible without making any noise."

"Maybe with guns that fire tranc darts," Jack said. "And knives."

They made their preparations quickly, because their window of opportunity was growing short. After dressing in black stealth outfits, they went out to the firm's helo hangar and started loading equipment in the helicopter. All of them were certified to pilot the craft, but Jack took the controls because he'd had the most flight time. Less than two hours after they'd gotten the phone call from Trainer, they were in the air.

A knock at the door of her cell startled Morgan.

"Come," Trainer called out.

One of his militiamen, decked out in full combat gear, including a wicked-looking assault rifle, stepped smartly into the room.

"You asked for a face-to-face report, sir."

Trainer nodded.

"All troops are in position. There has been no sighting of the Rockfort men."

"Probably because they haven't had time to get here," the militia leader said. He climbed to his feet. "I'm going to inspect the positions."

He looked at Morgan and grinned. "Wait here for me."

She wanted to say something sarcastic, but she knew it was better to act like she was completely pacified.

Without giving her another look, he marched out of the torture chamber.

Outside, Wade took a deep breath, relieved to be out of that small room. This wasn't going exactly the way he'd anticipated. He liked having Morgan Rains in his power, but for now she was a means to an end. He couldn't focus on her the way he'd like to. He'd gotten excited when he'd thought about raping her. The same was true when he'd thought about what he could do to her with his implements. But to be brutally honest, he knew he couldn't enjoy any of those activities right now. He had to stay focused on the Rockfort men. A major distraction would be a serious mistake.

The security agents were coming to rescue the woman, and he had to be ready for them.

When they were all dead, he'd give himself some

quality time to make Morgan Rains scream for mercy. And he'd finally give it to her with a bullet in the brain.

Of course, he wasn't going to let her know his state of mind. Right now, he had her where he wanted her, and if need be, he could go ahead and kill her. Then he wouldn't have to worry about the bitch at all.

Putting her out of his mind for the moment, he followed Salter around the camp, inspecting the preparations for the invasion.

———◆◆◆———

The moment Trainer was gone, Morgan dragged in a breath and let it out. Now that she was alone, it was almost impossible to keep from weeping. Or cursing. But neither of those would do her any good. She had to keep her head and figure out how she could help herself. She started by giving the room a closer inspection. It was about thirteen feet square, she judged, with gray walls that looked like they were made of cinder block and a cement floor with a drain in the middle.

Nice! Was that to get rid of the blood?

And was this where Trainer had tortured Jack? She shuddered.

"Jack. Oh, Jack," she whispered. They hadn't had much time together, but that time had completely changed her life. She'd been going through the motions of existence before he'd stumbled into the woods near her mountain retreat.

Every moment with him had made her feel more alive than she ever had. It was like that Hemingway short story she'd read in a lit course in college. "The

Short Happy Life of Francis Macomber," about a miserable little man who comes alive on a big-game hunting expedition in Africa, and then his wife shoots him.

She shuddered. No, this was nothing like that story. It was only the title that was gnawing at her. She was going to survive. And so was Jack. She didn't know how it was going to happen, but she wouldn't let everything end now—not when she was so close to happiness.

After taking a couple of deep, cleansing breaths, she began testing her bonds. Her wrists were circled with leather cuffs, but they were held to the bed with ropes. She pulled on them and found very little give. Moving as much as she could, she felt along the edge of the metal bed and found a place where the rough, flat end of a screw stuck out from the frame. Could she use it to saw through the rope? It seemed unlikely— and impossible when Trainer was in the room. But he was somewhere else now, and she wasn't going to simply lie here and wait for him to kill her. Or do anything else he wanted.

Grimly she began moving her hand, dragging the rope back and forth across the screw head. Every time she moved, the manacle chafed against her wrist, but she kept working on the rope anyway.

There was no way to judge time in this little room. She worked for what she thought might be twenty minutes, then turned her head and inspected her efforts. It looked like she was making some progress. Some of the strands of the rope had now parted, but she'd barely scratched the surface. It was going to take a lot more sawing to get through the rope. The question was, did she have the time?

The door opened abruptly, and she went instantly still.

Trainer was back. "Everything's ready for your new best friends," he said in a cheerful voice. "I don't think they're getting onto the militia compound, but if they do, my fierce troops will cut them down. And even if they get to this room, if they open the door, they'll get blown to smithereens."

When Morgan couldn't hold back a gasp, Trainer grinned at her.

Above the noise of the rotors, Jack, Shane, and Max used the comms units on the helicopter to discuss their plans as they flew toward the airport outside Skyline, Virginia. They'd all studied aerial maps of the compound before Jack had approached Trainer, but now he reminded the other two men of the layout.

"The living quarters, infirmary, mess hall, and Trainer's office are all grouped together. Behind them are the storage buildings. And behind them are the firing ranges, obstacle course, and other training grounds. Look for the lights, and you'll see a big open area."

"Where do you think he'll be holding Morgan?"

"Maybe the place where he tortured me," Jack answered, keeping his voice even.

"Which is where?"

"An annex to the infirmary. With no windows," Jack answered. "We'll rendezvous at the edge of the firing range closest to the building complex."

After the others had asked some questions, Jack

continued, "Trainer will have his main force at the front gate."

"No other way in?" Shane asked.

"There's a high-voltage electric fence. And there's no back exit."

"Some men will be patrolling the grounds."

"They'll probably be our main problem. The guys at the gates will be behind barricades, but facing the wrong way."

It helped Jack to discuss the plans, but he knew there was no way they could come up with firm tactics until they were inside the compound.

His heart was pounding as they approached the airport and scanned the tarmac. He'd said he could guarantee the transportation, but it was a relief to see the gliders waiting in the shadows on the ground.

They were shaped like small planes, with a transparent canopy that resembled the top of a fighter plane, only this was made of a much lighter material. Everything about the gliders was light because they had no engines to keep them aloft.

Aside from that, they had many of the same components as ordinary aircraft, but on a much smaller scale and in somewhat different proportions. The wings were longer and narrower. The fuselage was also narrow because there was no engine. And the landing gear consisted of a single wheel.

Jack set the chopper down near one of the hangars and cut the engine, then hurried over to the pilots of the small planes, both single-engine Cessnas.

"I appreciate your coming on such short notice," he said to the pilots.

One was a short, middle-aged man dressed in jeans and a plaid shirt. The other was a taller, younger guy wearing a running suit. "I wasn't going to turn down the kind of money you're paying." The man inclined his head toward the gliders. "You sure you want to leave before dawn? Riding those things in the dark is dangerous."

Max had joined them. "We're thrill seekers," he said with an easy confidence.

The guy looked them up and down. "Your funeral," he answered.

"We'd better get going," Jack said as he gave the pilots the coordinates of where he wanted the gliders to be released.

They divided up the gear, with Max taking more of it to compensate for the weight of the two men in the other glider.

All of the Rockfort agents were experienced pilots, which made it easy for Jack to give Max a quick lesson on steering and landing the craft.

"You good to go?" Jack asked.

Max stroked the smooth fiberglass skin of the little craft. "As ready as you are."

The pilots of the Cessnas hooked towropes to the gliders.

Jack and Shane slipped into the first one, with Shane in front and Jack in back with the steering mechanism. Both stretched out their legs on the deck in front of them and leaned against the backrests before pulling the canopy into place.

The small plane towing Shane and Jack's glider took off, and he felt a surge of elation as they went airborne. Finally they were doing something!

As they lifted into the air, he spoke to Morgan in a barely audible whisper, making promises he hoped he could keep. "Hang on until we get there. Just hang on. Just stay alive until I can get you out of there."

When they reached the agreed-upon coordinates, Shane released the towrope, and the glider went free. Jack worked the foot pedals to control the rudder, circling above the second plane, watching in the gray light that comes before dawn as the other glider also detached. When he was sure Max was with him, he pointed the nose toward the militia compound.

They were maintaining radio silence in case Trainer was listening to find out when they were coming in for a rescue attempt, so Jack couldn't communicate with Max. But he could see the silvery shadow of the other glider plane behind him.

Jack checked the altimeter and the airspeed indicator, then worked the rudder to point the nose toward the right. Below him he could see trees and mountains and occasional lights from widely scattered homes.

The gray light before sunrise helped him see where he was headed. At the same time, the approaching dawn increased the risk of being discovered by the militiamen on the ground.

But they wouldn't be expecting a silent attack from the sky, and they wouldn't be looking up, Jack told himself, hoping that was true.

Morgan breathed out a sigh. Trainer was gone again, obviously nervous about his defenses and anxious to check them again. She went back to frantically working on the rope that tied her right wrist to the iron bed. She'd sawed partway through the rope, and maybe she could free herself. But then what?

When she'd first awakened, she'd been frightened and at the same time full of hope—knowing that Jack would be coming to rescue her. Now she didn't know what to pray for. The idea of his getting killed trying to get to her made her chest tighten so painfully that she could barely breathe.

Could she free herself and somehow disable Trainer? Maybe that was her only option. And she knew her chances were slim. But she had to try because she wasn't simply going to lie here and let him kill her—and Jack, too.

Clenching her teeth against the pain in her wrists, she redoubled her efforts, sawing at the rope on her right arm with all the energy she had, telling herself she was making progress.

Stopping, she pulled at the rope, but not enough fibers had been cut for her to sever the rest of the cord.

She bit back a sob of frustration. This was going to take forever. But what else did she have to do?

Doggedly she went back to work, until she heard the doorknob turn again.

Her heart leaped into her throat. She could feel sweat beading her brow. Did she look like she'd been working hard at something?

She turned her face away when he came in, hoping she was looking fearful instead of flushed from sawing at the bonds. Still, she could see him from the corner of her eye standing over her.

She lay perfectly still on the uncomfortable bed,

praying that he wasn't going to bend down and examine the ropes.

When he walked a few feet away, she let the breath she'd been holding trickle out of her lungs.

In her mind she was making desperate calculations, weighing advantages and disadvantages of her next move.

Trainer made the decision for her. "Maybe your boyfriend isn't coming for you."

"I hope he's not."

"You don't mean that."

She turned her head toward him.

"If you're going to kill me, I don't want him dead too."

"It's not a question of if."

Instead of responding to the taunt, she asked, "How do you think I got here?"

"My moneyman came up with a scheme to get Jack and his friend away from the safe house. We attacked their offices, and while they were rushing to the rescue, he swooped in and got you."

"And how did he do it?" she pressed.

"He gave you a knockout shot."

"I mean, how did he tell you he was getting past the safe house defenses?"

"What does that matter?"

"Did you know he's the man who hired Jack to spy on you?"

Trainer reared back, looking like she'd slapped him across the face. "Liar."

"What's his name?"

"What does that matter to you?"

"I'd like to know."

He waited for a beat before answering, "I suppose it doesn't matter, since you're never going to tell anyone. It's Yarborough. But that's obviously not his real name."

"Uh huh." She dragged in a breath and let it out. They'd gotten that far with the man's name themselves. "Rockfort Security was hired to infiltrate your organization by a man who called himself Arthur Cunningham."

"So?"

"He happens to be the same man who's financing you."

"That's a lie."

She kept her gaze even. "He got past the alarm system at the safe house because he had a remote that turned it off. The Rockfort men gave it to him when he visited—after they got back from Virginia."

"You're lying," he said again.

"Why would I bother?"

"To throw me off my stride."

Yes, that was exactly what she hoped she was doing, but she certainly wasn't going to admit it. "I'm telling you so you can consider what's been going on and act accordingly."

"Oh, thanks," he answered in a sarcastic voice.

Ignoring him, she continued, "This Cunningham/ Yarborough guy obviously doesn't trust you. He hired Rockfort to keep tabs on you."

Trainer went from sarcasm to full-out anger. "No," he bellowed.

"So what's his game now? Is he going to stop you from carrying out your main mission?"

"He wouldn't do that."

"Are you so sure of that? Did you think he'd arrange to have a plant in your militia?" She kept speaking, working on his emotions. "And while we're asking leading questions, how come you let Jack trick you into taking him on? Did Yarborough vet him?"

She saw Trainer swallow hard.

"Shut up. Just shut the fuck up. I'm not going to listen to any more of this." He stood up, glaring down at her, and for a few frightening seconds she thought she had gone too far and that he was going to grab one of the whips from the rack on the wall and flay her.

Somehow she managed to keep her voice even as she said, "I've already told you what you need to know."

Before she had finished speaking, the man turned and stalked out of the room, and she knew she had seriously disturbed him.

She allowed herself a few moments to savor her victory. Then she went back to working on the rope that tied her right wrist to the bed.

———

Wade felt the blood pounding in his temples. But he waited until he had carefully closed the door before starting to curse. The bitch was messing with his head. He knew it. She was lying through her teeth. Yet he couldn't stop himself from wondering if she could possibly be right. Like how *had* Yarborough gotten into the safe house? How did he even know where it was? He hadn't shared those details with Wade.

He was stalking to his office when one of his men

stepped into his line of sight. It was Simmons, the man who had been with him the longest. His blond hair was cropped so short that he looked almost bald.

"Sir?"

"What is it?" he asked, struggling not to yell at the worried-looking young man.

"Why haven't they attacked?"

Why indeed. He had no answer for the man.

"Just keep up the vigilance," he advised as he hurried his steps again.

He was going to call Yarborough, but he decided he couldn't spare the time now. He had to make sure that everything on the compound was as it should be, that the Rockfort men hadn't somehow gotten past his defenses. The only way to assure himself of that was to personally inspect every position.

—⁓—

As Jack glided through the darkness toward the militia compound, he was aware of Max keeping pace with him, following his moves. His friend was doing a great job of piloting the other glider, considering that this was his first experience with this kind of craft.

They were getting to the crucial part of the flight, and he wanted to call out directions for the final approach, but there was no way Max could hear him without radio communications.

Jack peered through the darkness, concentrating on his own descent, hoping the other pilot could follow his example. When he saw the lights surrounding the shooting range, he let out the breath he'd been unconsciously holding.

Pulling back on the stick and at the same manipulating the foot pedals, he kept the glider moving in a lazy circle as he continued to descend, keeping his gaze on the center of the lights that Trainer had so thoughtfully provided.

The sight of the camp spread out below him made his stomach clench. He'd barely escaped with his life from this place, and coming back made his heart pound and sweat pop out on his forehead. But he had to return here. He had to rescue Morgan. He'd gotten her into this mess, and he was going to damn well get her out. This wasn't like Afghanistan where he was the only guy on the team who'd survived. He wouldn't let it be.

Teeth gritted, he eased his way toward the ground. As the buildings grew larger he fought the sick feeling tightening his chest. He thought he saw men in positions at the perimeter of the property. Praying that none of them would look up as he passed over, he glided silently toward the ground, knowing there was no room for a mistake. In a plane with an engine, you could always pull up again if your descent wasn't quite right. But he had no engine. If he overshot the field, he was in bad trouble.

He knew Max was coming in behind him, and he prayed his friend could bring the craft down in the field as well.

He executed one more circle, then lined up with the firing range as he made his final descent. Something shot past him, and he realized it was Max, who was making his first landing in a glider.

"Shit!"

Jack watched in dismay as Max kept going into the woods, his craft finally coming to rest as the wings were caught by two tree trunks. Not exactly a crash landing, but not the kind of return to terra firma that he would wish on anyone.

From the seat in front of him he heard Shane curse, and he knew the other man had seen the mishap as well.

He could only imagine the effects of the rough landing, but there was nothing he could do until he was on the ground and could get out of his plane.

He'd been anticipating his return with a kind of leaden dread. Now he had no time for his own emotions—only for action.

As he applied the brakes, he saw three of Trainer's men rushing toward Max's glider.

"Christ." Even before the craft had come to a stop, Shane was lifting the canopy and grabbing one of the equipment packs.

Jack followed him, yanking a knife from his pack as he raced toward the trees.

Chapter 29

JACK COULD HEAR THE RAM TROOPS TALKING excitedly as they surrounded the disabled glider.

When Max didn't emerge, Jack's stomach knotted. Was he hurt? Dazed? What?

The good news was that the men were entirely focused on the disabled glider plane, giving Jack and Shane an opportunity to get closer before they engaged the troops. Silently, Jack readied himself for an attack.

Three militiamen were trying to lift the plastic canopy over the pilot's seat, but were having trouble doing it from the outside.

Although Jack was unable to see Max, he knew his friend was in a dangerous position.

When Rayburn raised his AR-15 to demolish the canopy and the man inside the craft, Jack leaped forward, slashing out with his knife as he took the man down, feeling the blade slice through flesh.

Rayburn screamed, but the wound didn't knock the fight out of him. He dropped his weapon, trying to keep himself from getting cut again as they rolled across the brush on the forest floor.

Déjà vu all over again. Hadn't he been through this with Gibson a couple of days ago outside the burning house?

When Rayburn made a desperate grab for the

knife, Jack tried to thrust the blade forward, but the other man reared back.

As he and Rayburn struggled for position, the militiaman suddenly made a strange gurgling sound and went slack.

Jack blinked, trying to figure out what had happened. He hadn't cut him again, had he?

He rolled the guy to his back and stayed down behind the limp body, trying not to make himself a target in case the other militiamen turned and fired.

There were no shots. Looking toward the glider, he saw that the canopy was open, and Max stood on the seat, a tranquilizer dart gun in each hand. While the militia guys had turned their attention to Jack and Shane, Max had emerged and fired at Rayburn and Harmon, taking them down.

Shane was still grappling with the third guy.

If Jack could have shot the troop, he would have done it. But he couldn't take the chance. Instead he leaped toward the two struggling men and brought the barrel of Rayburn's assault rifle down on the militiaman's head. The guy went slack, and Shane pushed him to the ground.

"Thanks."

"No problem," Jack answered.

They both looked toward Max.

"You okay?" Jack asked.

"I've been better. Wish I hadn't plowed into the woods."

"You seem to have made it okay," Shane answered. "Thanks for the darts."

"What happened when those guys surrounded the glider?" Jack asked.

"I played dead while I got the weapons ready. I was going to shoot them as soon as they opened the canopy, but then you distracted them."

Jack didn't bother pointing out that he could only have shot two of them.

He looked at Rayburn, Walsh, and Harmon sprawled on the ground. Blood spread across the right sleeve of Rayburn's uniform shirt, but it was obviously not an arterial cut. Aside from that, he was a fit young man like his fellow grunts. Jack had avoided getting to know them well. But he sensed that Rayburn was young and confused. Walsh and Harmon were angry with their lot in life and eager to take out their frustrations on any convenient target. Being in the militia gave them a feeling of power and control that they probably couldn't have gotten any other way.

Too bad all of them had fallen under the sway of a leader who'd filled their heads with the wrong nonsense.

"We'll tie them up, just in case," he said as he looked from their uniforms to the black outfits he and his friends were wearing. "But maybe we put on their cammies first. That way, we'll blend in with the rest of the troops."

"Good idea," Max agreed. "And we'd better take their weapons to complete the charade."

He climbed out of the glider and stood for a moment with his hand on the smooth skin of the craft, which was now cracked on the left side. In fact, as Jack looked more closely, he saw that the impact with the tree had split the right wing where it joined the body.

"Sorry about that," Max said as he followed Jack's gaze.

"It's insured. The important part is that you got out okay."

"Flying is easier than landing," Max said, as he tested his left leg against the ground.

"Did you lose consciousness when you crashed?" Jack asked.

"No." Max turned and pulled plastic handcuffs out of his pack.

Jack watched, thinking it would be easier to just slit these guys' throats, the way his Navy SEAL training had taught him to deal with the enemy. Then he thought about Morgan's reaction when he had faked Gibson's fatal accident. She'd been repulsed by the role of Jack Brandt as cold-blooded killer. He had done what he knew was necessary to save their lives. Now he knew he'd changed because of Morgan.

He shuddered.

"What?" Shane asked.

"Nothing. Let's secure these guys and get out of here."

He and the other men started stripping the camouflage gear off of the men they'd disabled. Jack pulled off Rayburn's T-shirt and slit it in half. He used part of it to bind the knife wound on the man's arm—and the other half for a gag.

As they were stripping the clothing off Harmon, a radio in his pocket chattered.

"Position three, report," a voice demanded.

The three Rockfort men glanced at each other.

Jack pulled out the radio.

"Position three, report," the voice said again.

Jack clicked the send button. "This is Harmon."

"Anything to report?"

"Negative," he answered.

"Your voice sounds funny."

Jack coughed. "Sore throat."

"Take care of yourself."

"I will."

"And watch out for those bastards that are coming in."

"If they have the guts," Jack answered.

When the radio went dead again, he breathed out a sigh, then looked over his shoulder at the glider sitting in the middle of the firing range.

"We'd better move that thing," he said, jerking his shoulder toward the aircraft.

They quickly finished stripping the militiamen to their undershorts and cuffed their hands and feet. Then they gagged them with their undershirts and pulled them into the woods where they'd be less likely to be discovered.

Next they took off their own outfits and pulled on the ones the troops weren't going to need anytime soon.

Jack took the bloody shirt, making a low sound as he thrust his arm through the sticky sleeve.

When they had donned the uniforms, Jack and Shane trotted out to the field and pulled the glider into the woods, tipping it to its side to slip it between the trees.

"What next?" Max asked.

"I'd like to head right for the place where I think they're holding Morgan, but we could be trapping ourselves."

The other two men nodded.

"I assume Trainer stationed the largest force at the entrance to the compound. If we take them out, there's less chance of our running into trouble."

The comment drew nods of agreement.

"One more thing," he said. "If we can do it, we need to find out what's in the steel building where he's keeping something special."

Shane gave him a questioning look. "You'd risk Morgan to do that?"

"I hope not. But I get the feeling we're risking a lot more if we don't go in there." He dragged in a breath. "Let's get Morgan, and then make a decision."

Morgan's arm ached and her wrist was raw as she kept sawing at the rope, but she allowed herself only short periods to rest. Trainer could come back at any time, and she wanted to be free when he did.

And then what? She didn't know, but she was going to give herself every chance she could.

As she worked, her thoughts zinged back to Jack. If only she could send him a telepathic message to warn him that Trainer had some kind of booby trap waiting for him.

She bit back a sob of frustration.

"Oh, Jack," she whispered. When he got here, she didn't want to be tied to this bed. He'd escaped from this place once. She knew that coming back must be the worst thing he could imagine. Yet she knew he'd do it—to rescue her. She had no doubt about that whatsoever. And when he did, she had to be ready to help him.

She stopped sawing and pulled at the cord. She thought she felt some give in the rope, and her hope surged.

"Just a little more," she whispered to herself. "Just a little more."

She turned her head, looking at the rope, seeing how much she'd already cut. That gave her the will to work harder, and she redoubled her efforts, stopping the sawing after a couple of minutes to pull on the rope again. To her astonishment it parted, and her arm jerked upward, wrenching her shoulder.

She managed to keep from crying out, then lay panting on the bed. She had one arm free. Now she only had to get the other arm and her feet before Trainer came back.

Forcing down the fear that leaped inside her, she rolled as far to the side as she could and pulled at the knot that held her left arm in place.

The three Rockfort men moved quietly across the militia compound as though they were patrolling the area under Trainer's orders. Each of them had two of the dart guns, ready to fire at anyone else who was moving around.

Jack was thinking that he'd like to meet up with Trainer and finish this thing off. If he killed the head of the snake, he knew that discipline would fall apart. But he couldn't be sure where to find Trainer, and if he made a mistake, he was risking Morgan's life.

"This is a hell of a place," Shane whispered as they rounded one of the former camp cabins that had been converted into barracks.

"Cunningham made sure Trainer was—" His

answer cut off as a militiaman named Cooper stepped around the corner.

"You're off your post," he said, not recognizing the three fakes.

"Special assignment," Shane said.

The guy gave Shane a sharp look, but Jack was already in back of him. He jabbed the rifle into the man's back, and he went still.

They marched him into the barracks, and Shane started tying him up.

Cooper shot them dagger looks. "You won't get out of here alive."

"Let us worry about that," Jack said. "How many men are on duty?"

"You think I'm going to tell you?"

"Yeah, because if you don't, I'm going to cut your balls off." He reached for the guy's zipper and yanked it down.

The militiaman would have screamed if Max hadn't clamped a hand over his mouth.

"How many?" Jack asked again, as Max moved his hand enough so the troop could speak.

His frightened eyes darted from man to man.

"How many?" Jack pressed.

"Nineteen."

"Including you?"

"Yes." He swallowed. "How did you get back in here?"

"Trade secret." He gave the guy a shake. "If you're lying, we'll be back to finish the job." For emphasis Jack yanked the man's pants down, along with his shorts so that his privates were hanging out.

Cooper whimpered, until Shane shot him with one of the tranc darts, and his eyes went out of focus, then closed.

Shane gave Jack a shocked look. "Were you really going to cut off his balls?"

"He never demonstrated much in the way of guts. I think a nick from the knife would have had him talking. He doesn't love Trainer enough to lose his manhood for the guy," Jack said as he took off the bloody shirt he was wearing and tossed it onto the floor before pulling another one out of a nearby footlocker.

Shane nodded.

When Jack had exchanged his ruined shirt for a clean one, they all stepped out into the still morning air and stood close to the cabin where they had a good view of the compound.

"We've taken down four of the troops including that guy," Jack said, jerking his shoulder toward the cabin. "If there are ten at the gate, then that leaves five loose cannons, plus the medic, his assistant, and Trainer."

"Still good odds," Max said. "Let's go get the gatekeepers. "

Jack led the way toward the entrance, stopping in the shadow of some trees as he looked at the men who were stationed behind concrete barriers with their guns at the ready, and all of them with their backs toward the interlopers. It reminded him of the famous Maginot Line that France had built after World War I. The line was a series of gun emplacements pointed toward Germany. The only trouble was that all the artillery were in fixed positions. When the Germans broke through and got behind the line, the guns were pointing in the wrong direction.

———

Morgan got her other hand free and shifted the cuffs so that she could rub her wrists. Leaning over, she began working on her ankles, unbuckling the leather cuffs.

She allowed herself a moment of elation. She'd done it! Against all odds, she'd done it.

Moving carefully, she climbed off the bed. After being tied in such an awkward position for hours, she was shaky on her feet and had to steady herself with a hand against the wall. When she was feeling surer of herself, she started doing stretching exercises, trying to get the circulation back into her hands and feet. Now that she was out of the bed, she wished she could find some clothing, but there was nothing in the room she could wear. At least she wasn't naked.

She looked toward the door, wondering if she dared open it. Trainer had said it had some kind of explosive charges. He could be lying since he'd certainly come in and out without doing anything special that she noticed.

———

Wade was walking briskly back to the interrogation room when his comms unit crackled.

He looked at the call signal. It said Big Dog, which meant it was for him.

"Sir?"

"What is it?"

"Cooper and I are patrolling the grounds. I was supposed to meet up with him at the mess hall five minutes ago. He hasn't shown up."

"Does he answer his call signal?"

"His comms unit was on the fritz when we started the patrol."

Wade repressed a curse. Damn incompetent men. Couldn't they get anything right? "Why wasn't I informed?" Trainer snapped.

"I was gonna meet him every twenty minutes."

"Search back over his patrol route."

"Yes, sir."

Trainer quickened his pace. First thing he'd better do was go back and check the prisoner.

Morgan eyed the door as she continued stretching, trying to get her body into fighting shape. The good news was that she worked out regularly, which meant that the awkward posture on the bed hadn't been as debilitating as it could have been.

As she stretched, she eyed the rack of torture implements, trying to decide what she would use to defend herself. She'd dated a guy once who was into bullwhips, and she'd tried them out a few times. Maybe that was the way to go. Taking a large whip off the rack, she cracked it experimentally a few times, getting the feel of it, making it coil and snap. Then she laid it on the bed with the grip facing toward her.

Still working out the kinks in her body, she licked her dry lips, wishing there was something to drink in here. Or maybe that wouldn't be such a good idea. Maybe anything in here would be drugged.

She tested her balance, making sure she was steady on her feet. But she never stopped watching and listening. Trainer would be coming back, but he would think she was still tied up. That gave her an advantage. She hoped.

Knitting her fingers together, she raised her arms above her head, doing a couple of yoga stretches, then leaning forward to stretch her back. She had just started down to touch the floor with her hands when she heard the doorknob turn.

Out of time. But not out of luck, she hoped.

Leaping for the bed, she grabbed the bullwhip and pressed her shoulders against the wall behind the door where Trainer wouldn't see her immediately.

He stepped smartly into the room. She saw he was taking no chances. His gun was in his hand. As soon as he saw the empty bed, his eyes bugged out.

"What the hell? Where are you?" he shouted, turning in all directions as he tried to figure out where she had gone.

Morgan waited with her heart pounding until she had a clear shot at him. Teeth gritted, she lashed out with the whip, striking him on the hand.

He screamed in surprise and pain and dropped the weapon. As he zeroed in on her, his eyes turned murderous.

Chapter 30

Jack, Shane, and Max crept quietly into position behind the militiamen, who had all their attention on the gate. One of them had a walking cast on his leg. He'd apparently gotten hurt, but that didn't excuse him from duty in an emergency.

Each of the Rockfort agents held two tranc guns. They held their fire until they were ten feet away—when one of the troops became aware of something behind him and started to turn.

Jack shot him with a tranquilizer dart, then took down the man next to him. Max and Shane fired at the same time, taking out more troops.

Six of the defenders went down immediately. Which meant they still had to deal with four armed and dangerous militiamen.

As their buddies slumped to the ground, two of them looked toward the gate in confusion, trying to figure out what had happened.

But two of them realized the attack had come from behind. Ducking for cover behind the fallen men, they turned and raised their rifles in firing position.

The Rockfort men's only option was to fire the weapons they'd liberated earlier. They dropped the remaining men at the gate, then whirled as they heard the sound of running feet. Three more men were converging on them, shooting as they ran. Jack, Shane, and Max returned fire, cutting down two of them. The third turned and ran.

"Shit," Shane growled.

"It's Duffy. He may run for the hills. But keep a lookout for him. I'm going to look for Morgan."

———

Trainer's expression was murderous as he grabbed the end of the whip and pulled it out of Morgan's hands. She was close enough to the rack of torture equipment to reach one of the implements on the wall. Her fingers closed around a mace, which she smacked into Trainer's forehead.

He kept coming after her until the sound of automatic weapon fire outside made him look toward the door.

"Shit."

Leaving her where she stood, he turned and ran out of the room.

———

Wade ducked out of the building where he had been holding Morgan Rains. Somehow she'd gotten loose. Could she have had help? And from whom? Another traitor in his midst?

The thought made his skin crawl, but he told himself it couldn't be true. Somehow she'd freed herself, but now what was happening?

When he cautiously stuck his head out the door, he was greeted by eerie silence.

Then he saw three figures crossing the parade grounds. He thought it was three of his troops, and he was about to shout to them. Then he did a double take. It was the three Rockfort men, wearing uniforms that they must have stolen.

He pressed the button on his comms unit, calling for a report. Every man he tried failed to respond. The only answer he got was from Duffy—who said he was hiding from the attackers after seeing the men at the gate cut down.

"Go after them," Trainer screamed, sure Duffy and the medics couldn't stop the invaders. But maybe they could hold them up.

Somehow while he'd been occupied with Rains, the Rockfort operatives had gotten the rest of his men. And now they were coming for the woman.

But Wade wasn't going to let them leave with her. He'd been cautious, letting his men precede him into danger. Now he was the only one who could stop the Rockfort bastards. At least he could do that.

He didn't think about his own death as he ducked around the mess hall and headed for the steel building where he kept his ultimate weapon.

—∾—

Morgan struggled to assess the situation. The gunfire must be from Jack and his friends. And the militia returning fire. But what exactly was happening out there?

Trainer had left the door open, which gave Morgan the opportunity to step through without worrying about any explosives on the door.

She found herself in an anteroom that led to another door. It was also open, and she could see morning light pouring through.

Cautiously she stepped forward, and saw Jack running across an open area. His two friends were right behind him.

"Jack!"

He stopped in his tracks, a wealth of emotions crossing his face as he took in her appearance.

"Are you all right?" he shouted.

"Yes."

"Thank God, but I've got to get Trainer," he answered. "Before he kills us all."

From the side of the building, someone started shooting. Morgan ducked down as the Rockfort men returned fire. After a moment, there were no answering shots.

Shane ran up to her. "It's not safe for you out here. Get back inside."

Her throat clenched as she watched Jack heading for a steel structure with a barrel roof.

"He's in danger," she whispered as he disappeared from sight.

"He'll be okay."

She gave Shane a fierce look. "You don't *know* that. Give me a gun, and let me go with him."

"Not a chance." Shane's expression was just as fierce as hers. "If something happens to you, Jack…" He stopped and started again, a pleading look in his eyes. "He risked everything to come back here for you. Don't let it be for nothing."

She swallowed hard because it was true. And not just for Jack. His two friends were risking just as much.

When Shane put a firm hand on her arm, she knew he was only trying to keep her safe. "Come back inside."

She did as he asked, her ears tuned for the sound of gunfire, and her skin crawling as she stepped back into the torture chamber where Trainer had held her.

Shane followed her and stopped short as he took in the room. She watched his eyes go from the metal bed to the rack of implements and back again.

"Christ. This is where he had you?"

She nodded. "And it's probably where they were holding Jack."

Shane looked back at her. "You need to get some clothes on."

He unbuttoned his own shirt, shrugged out of it, and handed it to her. "Put this on."

She did, grateful that she was no longer standing around in her underwear.

Shane turned and pointed his rifle toward the door. "We'll stay here until we hear from Jack."

She nodded, praying that he would be okay.

"What happened? I mean, how did you get here?" she asked.

"We came in on glider planes and mostly used tranquilizer guns to put the militiamen out of commission. We'll be out of here before they wake up."

"Trainer and I were fighting when we both heard gunfire."

"You were fighting him? How did you get loose?"

"I used a screw head on the bed to saw through one of the ropes holding my arms."

"Good girl!"

"Where did Jack go?"

"Trainer's got some kind of Doomsday device. Jack and Max have got to stop him from setting it off."

She winced. "A bomb? He told me the door to this room was booby-trapped with a bomb."

"Oh yeah? Let me just take a look at that," Shane answered, stepping quickly out of the room again.

—∾∾—

"He knows he's defeated, and he's planning to take us with him," Jack said as he and Max arrived at the door to the steel building. It was locked.

"Shit. We've got to get inside."

Both he and Max raised the weapons they had liberated from the militiamen and started firing at the lock, losing precious seconds before they were able to turn the mechanism to shreds.

Jack slammed the door open, and they both rushed into a room whose walls were filled with racks of armament. Parked around the floor were various vehicles including a steamroller, a troop carrier, a backhoe, and a front-end loader.

"I don't see him," Max said, starting to search behind the vehicles. "You're sure he came in here?"

"I didn't see him go in, but he was heading this way." He dragged in a breath and let it out. "From the way he acted, I know there's something important about this place. It's not just for equipment storage." In the dim light, he pointed to a smaller flat-roofed building at the end of the long room. "In there."

They both ran to the small structure. Again, the door was locked. When Max raised his weapon, Jack shook his head. "No. We could set something off in there."

Jack looked wildly around for something he could use to break through the walls. There were grenade and missile launchers, but again he hesitated to use firepower.

As he searched for another alternative, Jack zeroed in on the front-end loader. The keys were in the ignition, and he climbed into the cab, glad that Trainer had made all the troops work at moving earth around as part of their training.

"You might want to get out of the building. There's something deadly in there," he called to Max as he worked the gears, lurching forward.

"I'm staying."

Jack nodded and jerked the big machine forward, then moved more smoothly as he picked up the rhythm of working with the construction equipment. Lowering the scoop at the front, he rumbled forward and caught the bottom edge of the metal building, rocking it back and forth before slamming it back down.

He was gratified to hear a curse from inside. Trainer was in there all right. He'd thought he was safe from interference. Now he was finding out he wasn't quite so secure.

Jack manipulated the controls, shoving the scoop farther under the little building. Then he raised the mechanism, tipping the cube-shaped structure onto its side, exposing the bottom surface, which looked to be of thinner material than the top portion—probably because Trainer had never considered that the floor would be vulnerable.

As Jack backed up and moved forward again, he prayed that Trainer hadn't already unleashed something deadly. And if he had, would it be better to leave him in there with it?

Maybe, but there was no guarantee that it wouldn't get out.

Making a decision to keep going, he bashed at the exposed bottom of the building with the scoop, opening a wedge in the material, then maneuvered the teeth under the flooring and peeled back the skin.

When he'd made a two-foot opening, he jumped down from the machine, and he and Max moved cautiously forward, rifles at the ready.

"We've got you covered. Surrender," Jack called out.

For answer, gunfire erupted from inside, and they both backed away.

Jack scrambled up on the construction equipment again and hooked the teeth of the scoop under the portion of the floor that he'd peeled back.

Lifting the cube, he slammed it into the concrete pad of the vaulted building. Then lifted it and did it again, hoping he was turning Trainer to jelly in there. As he kept up the assault, he heard some kind of noise from inside.

Once again he slammed the cube on the concrete, then climbed down. Still cautious, he and Max approached the cube, and Jack stuck the muzzle of his rifle inside. When Trainer didn't fire, Jack took a quick look into the cube.

Trainer was lying beside a long metal table that had tipped on its side. Small drawers from a large cabinet were scattered around the little room.

Trainer was clasping a metal box, his fingers frantically working at the catch. Jack leaped inside and yanked at the box. Trainer tried to hold on, but his grip finally gave way, and Jack fell backward with the box clutched to his chest.

Trainer scrambled for the gun that had been lying beside him. Raising the weapon, he took aim at the box. Before he could fire, Max put a bullet in the middle of his forehead, and he went still.

Jack looked over his shoulder. "Thanks, buddy."

"What the hell is in there?"

Jack gingerly lifted the box and hefted it in his hand.

"It's not heavy." He looked at the cover. "It's got a stamp from Fort Detrick on the top. You know— the place where they make and test the biological weapons."

"Anthrax?"

"My guess is it's something worse."

"What do we do with it?"

"Unfortunately, I think we need to take it with us. We don't want anyone opening this damn thing by mistake."

Max handed over his knapsack, and Jack made sure the box was securely latched before shoving it into the bag. He also reached into Trainer's pocket and found his cell phone, which he put into his own pocket.

They were just heading for the door of the storage building when they were greeted by the sound of automatic weapons fire.

The man who called himself Arthur Cunningham lived on a very nice estate outside Frederick, Maryland. Close enough to D.C. to be near the action and far enough away to be out of the danger zone when Trainer pulled off his attack on the Capitol.

He was sitting in his comfortable family room, waiting

by the phone, expecting to hear that the Rockfort Security problem was taken care of. He'd told them he wanted to stop Trainer. It was just the opposite, of course. He'd be prepared to rat out Jack Brandt at the crucial moment to keep him from stopping the D.C. attack.

Impatient for news, he slapped his right fist against his left palm. Maybe he never should have hired Rockfort. But he hadn't been able to stand the idea that he'd have no sure source of information on Trainer. Even though the man was the best there was at what he did, you could never entirely trust anyone.

He'd learned that the hard way.

He turned back to his computer and brought up one of his favorite Web sites. He monitored a number of bulletin boards and sites frequented by guys who were dedicated to overthrowing the government of the United States. He'd known most of them didn't have a chance in hell of carrying out their grand plans. But he'd seen something in Wade Trainer that he hadn't seen in the others.

The man had a divine sense of purpose, determination, and the ability to follow through. And he had guts. Don't forget about guts.

Arthur had met him at a convention, where they'd started talking. He'd become more and more excited, the more he'd learned about the man. But he took a couple of months before deciding that Trainer was the guy who could put a large infusion of cash to good use.

And Arthur was willing to use the money he'd inherited to avenge the death of his son. Well, a lot of it. He had to keep enough to live on in the style to which he'd always been accustomed.

Once he'd been a patriotic American, so proud of his son graduating from West Point. An officer and a gentleman. That was Pete through and through.

They'd talked about the wars. Both of them had supported the invasion of Iraq. Both of them had been shocked that no weapons of mass destruction had been found.

In retrospect, it was too bad that Iraq had taken the U.S. focus off of Afghanistan. If the government had done what we should have there, the conflict might have been over before Pete had to go over there.

When his son got through one tour okay, Arthur had breathed a sigh of relief.

That second tour had started to change his mind about America's foreign policy. Pete had only had a couple of weeks to go when his Humvee was hit by an IUD. If the Congress had authorized the proper armor, his son would still be alive. But they'd scrimped on this damn endless war. Because it wasn't *their* sons being sent to a godforsaken foreign country to die.

Nor had they considered how many other people they were hurting. His sweet, loving wife, Louise, hadn't survived more than a few months after Pete's death. She'd suffered a massive stroke and mercifully died a few hours later.

That was on their heads too.

And very soon they were going to pay the price for the way they played with other people's lives.

He'd given Trainer a lot of money. And found a biologist at Fort Detrick who'd been willing to unleash hell on the U.S. Capitol because his own son had suffered the same fate as Arthur's. Of course, the man was now dead, so he could never reveal what he'd done with that batch of ZR 427 that was never supposed to leave the level four containment lab. Nobody even knew it was missing, because almost nobody had access to the stuff. It was like ricin, only better. A whiff could kill in a matter of minutes.

Jack and Max both leaped to the door of the storage building and looked out. The two medics and Duffy were circling the building attached to the infirmary, the building where he'd left Morgan and Shane.

Christ! He'd thought he'd left them in a safe place. As he saw the militiamen closing in on them, his heart leaped into his throat.

The troops fired toward the structure, and someone inside returned fire. Probably Shane. Or if Shane was down, was Morgan shooting? Oh Lord, no! But the three men were spread out, coming in slowly, making it difficult to go after all of them at once.

"Over here," Jack shouted.

With most of their comrades down, the three men had lost any semblance of military discipline. And now they were caught between Jack and their original target.

They scattered, but Jack took down Duffy. Max got one of the medics, and the other got off a burst of fire.

Shane blasted him in the chest, and he went still.

"We got them," Jack shouted. "For Christ's sake, tell me you're all right in there."

"Ready to party. Is that the last of them?"

"Yeah. Including Trainer."

A moment later, a bare-chested Shane Gallagher came out. He was followed by Morgan, who was wearing Shane's shirt.

"Thank God," Jack breathed.

Before he could caution her, Morgan dashed from behind Shane and crossed the open space between the buildings, landing in Jack's arms. He caught her and held tight. "Are you all right?" they both said at the same time.

"Yes," they both answered.

He held her for a moment longer, wanting to say so much to her, but he couldn't do it now.

"We're getting the hell out of here," he said. "But I've got a couple more things to do." Jack turned to Max. "You get one of Trainer's Land Rovers." To Shane, he said, "Take Morgan into Trainer's office, and see if you can find anything useful. You know which building?"

"Yes," Shane answered.

"I'll clear away the mess at the gate and meet you in the office. If you touch anything, wear gloves."

He headed back to the main gate, finding the defenders where he'd left them. He dragged the unconscious men to the side of the road and pulled the dead ones into the bushes where maybe Morgan wouldn't see them.

His mind was still processing what had happened. They'd made it out of Trainer's death trap, but he wasn't quite ready to leave the compound.

When he returned, the Land Rover he'd requested was parked outside the office.

"Find anything?" he asked Max as he joined the others inside.

"Lots of nut job books on political theory and rebellion. The records must all be in the computer."

Jack sat down at the computer. When he touched the keyboard, the desktop lit up. It was a picture of the Murrah Federal Building in Oklahoma City—after McVeigh had destroyed it.

After typing in the password, Jack took a thumb drive from his pack and downloaded the contents of Trainer's hard drive. Then he found several bulletin boards that the militia leader subscribed to as well as email addresses of the White House and some prominent Congressmen. To each of them he sent a message that said,

"This is a final message from the leader of the Real Americans Militia, Wade Trainer. I am preparing to carry out my main mission. By the time you read this, I will have launched a deadly attack on the U.S. Capitol."

When he was finished, he wiped off the keyboard.

"We'd better split," he said as he turned away from the computer.

"Why did you send that message?" Morgan asked as she followed him outside.

"Because it will look like he was getting ready to deploy—and someone prevented it."

He gave Morgan and Shane a serious look. "I think we'd better stop at one of the barracks so you can both get dressed."

They ducked into a cabin that had been used for sleeping quarters, and Jack found her some pants.

They were a reasonable fit, although she had to roll up the legs. And the only shoes she could find that came close to working were a pair of rubber flip flops.

Shane quickly found a shirt.

Outside again, they all climbed into the Land Rover, and Max pulled away.

As they sped through the front gate, Jack was thinking that they still had a couple of jobs to do.

They had to turn the deadly box over to someone who would know what to do with it. Probably that would be the Department of Homeland Security. In exchange Jack was going to get them all immunity for what had gone down at the militia camp.

Chapter 31

NOW THAT JACK HAD DONE EVERYTHING HE COULD, he flopped into the backseat of the Land Rover beside Morgan. She reached for his hand, and he wove his fingers with hers.

"Thank God you're all right," he whispered as Max drove out of the militia compound. There was a lot he wanted to say to her, but he couldn't do it yet. And certainly not in front of his friends in the front seat.

"And you," she answered.

He leaned his head back and closed his eyes. He needed to rest, but he had another motivation as well—avoiding conversation. When the car came to a stop, he looked up. They were at the airfield where they'd been towed up in the glider.

Shane went to do a preflight check on the helicopter. When Jack had confirmation that they were ready to take off, he pulled out Trainer's cell phone and dialed 911.

"What is the nature of your emergency?"

He lowered his voice to a gravelly whisper. "This is Wade Trainer. I want to report an incident at my militia compound." He gave the address.

"Can you be more specific, Mr. Trainer?"

"Just get over here," he said and clicked off.

Morgan looked at him. "When the troops who are tranquilized wake up, won't they tell the authorities what happened?"

"Maybe. But I'm betting Trainer didn't tell them my real name—or Shane and Max's either. They won't be able to identify us. And even if they come up with information, the local authorities have that fake message I sent where he's declaring his intentions to attack."

She breathed out a sigh. "Yes.

"And I've got something to give Homeland Security that will get us immunity."

"What?"

"Some kind of deadly biological weapon from Fort Detrick. My guess is that Cunningham got it for Trainer."

"How?"

"I guess they'll find out."

They climbed into the helicopter, and Max took them up. As they headed for the safe house, Jack could see police cars on the road speeding to the militia compound. He didn't know if it was in response to the 911 message or the Web message. Or maybe both.

While Max piloted the helicopter, Shane used the communications equipment to check on some of their unfinished business.

When they disembarked at the safe house, Shane was grinning broadly.

"What?" Jack said as they climbed the steps to the porch.

"I have an ID on Arthur Cunningham."

"How?"

"Before we left, I took a few extra minutes to send

his fingerprints to a friend in the FBI. His real name is Arthur Crispin. He's a lawyer, and he was a five-term Congressman from Maryland. He also inherited a boatload of money from his parents. They made millions from cold remedies and liniments."

Jack gave him a long look. "You know I would have told you not to take the time."

"Yeah."

"I'm glad you did. Good work."

"We know where he lives," Shane said.

"And I have an idea about what to do to him," Morgan said.

They all turned to her. "You do?"

"You know he's the one who brought me to the militia compound?"

"Yes."

Her face contorted. "I knew something was wrong, but I couldn't get away from him."

"Not your fault," Jack answered.

She gave him a little nod, and he could see tears in her eyes.

"I said it's okay."

"I caused you all a lot of trouble. You could all have gotten killed because of me."

"No. Not you." Jack pulled her close and held her for a moment before easing away. "Never think that. It was them—Trainer and Crispin."

He knew she was struggling to get control of her emotions.

When she finally spoke, her voice was stronger. "When you told me about the biological agent, that gave me an idea."

As she began to outline her plan, the men grinned.

"Can we pull it off?" she asked.

"Yeah," Jack answered, thinking how much courage this woman had. She'd just been through an ordeal that would have left most women an emotional basket case. But she was thinking about how to turn the tables on the bastard who had captured her.

Arthur Crispin blinked when he saw the lines of type come across the bulletin board.

"This is a final message from the leader of the Real Americans Militia, Wade Trainer. I am preparing to carry out my main mission. By the time you read this, I will have launched a deadly attack on the U.S. Capitol."

He jumped up and whooped. He'd been worried, but that son of a bitch Trainer had done it! He'd taken care of Rockfort, and now he was on his way to the U.S. Capitol.

He'd known the man was good. Apparently he'd decided to go right from cutting down the Rockfort men to the endgame.

He called Trainer's cell phone on his speed dial and punched the button. There was only a recorded message, but the guy was busy and probably on radio silence.

He waited for the beep and left a message. "Big congratulations."

Next he snatched up the TV remote and turned on CNN. They were deep in the middle of a stupid debate about tax increases with the usual guys giving their usual opinions.

Where was the news of the attack? Maybe it hadn't

happened yet. He started scanning the online news services, thinking that maybe they'd get it first. Or maybe all the reporters down there were dead. That thought had his heart beating faster.

How many thousands would die? He hadn't thought about that, just those legislators taking other peoples' lives in their hands.

They were done for now. And that deserved a celebration. He brought out a bottle of Krug Clos d'Amonnay, 1995, opened it with a flourish, and took down a Waterford flute from the set Louise had brought home from Ireland on their last trip together.

On second thought, he got down two. One for her. He had no doubt that she was in heaven with their son and no doubt that they were both looking down on what he'd done with approval.

He had pulled off a master coup. All it had taken was a great deal of money and the right man. And if they caught Trainer, so what? He could never tell anyone who had financed his chicken-shit militia because he didn't know Arthur's real name. And he was sure that none of those Rockfort guys were still alive to finger him, either.

He had just taken a sip of the champagne when he heard a knock at the kitchen door. He wasn't expecting anyone. Maybe it was something he'd ordered from one of the online stores where he liked to shop for coffee and cheese.

As he started to call out, "Who is it?" the kitchen door blew off its hinges, and four white-clad figures stepped in.

His mouth gaped open as he stared at them. It took

a moment to realize they were even human—men wearing white hazmat suits that looked something like space suits, enclosing them from their large yellow boots to their insect-like helmets.

Each of them wore an air tank on his back, attached by wide black straps. He could hear them breathing through the respirators, but he couldn't even see their features because of the thick faceplates on the helmets.

Why were they here? And why now?

A sudden thought struck him. The attack had begun. And since he was a former Congressman, they were going to whisk him to a secure underground location until the government knew the area was safe again.

He tried to grasp at that explanation, but it swam out of his mind as they surrounded him, closing in, making him feel like he couldn't breathe.

"What… what are you doing?"

None of them answered as they formed a circle around him. He'd thought they had come to help him. Now he trembled as he tried to figure out their purpose.

His eyes danced from one of the frightening figures to the other, looking for a way out. Seeing an opening, he tried to dart through, hoping he could make it to his den and lock the door. From there, he could get out a window.

His plans went up in smoke when one of them grabbed him and spun him around, and he realized he'd never really had a chance to escape.

"Don't," he choked out.

"Where were you going?" a hard voice boomed.

"You're frightening me."

"Oh, sorry."

He still couldn't identify any of them. But there was something familiar about one of the voices. And one of them was smaller than the others. Maybe it was woman.

"Arthur Crispin?" a grating voice asked.

"Yes."

The figure turned to the champagne bottle on the counter. "I guess you were celebrating the attack on the U.S. Capitol. But there's been a change of plans. The fun will be here."

He tried to make sense of that.

"What? What attack?"

"You know damn well," a hard voice said.

"No," he protested again, looking from one to the other, searching for some signs of human compassion.

The small person stepped forward. He tried to figure out who it was, but he stopped focusing on the figure's distorted features when he caught sight of a metal box, about the size of a toolbox, with the words "Fort Detrick Labs" and "Extreme Biohazard" printed across the top.

Arthur gasped, and his heart started to thump inside his chest when he saw it. "What... what's that?" he quavered.

"It's that nasty biological agent you arranged to steal from Fort Detrick."

"No. Trainer took it to the Capitol. He said so."

"Actually, no," the figure holding the box corrected him. "Wade Trainer didn't really send that message. It was Jack Brandt who did it—after he finished off Trainer."

Arthur's mouth had turned so dry he could no longer swallow. Through his terror, he looked at the figure more closely—and recognized the pretty nose. The bow of a mouth. Her blue eyes were fierce. It was the woman he'd kidnapped and taken to Trainer's compound.

"How…" He couldn't finish the sentence. It had become impossible to speak as she sprung the latch on the box. Inside was another container, this one with a skull and crossbones on the top. There was an elaborate mechanism to hold it closed.

When her gloved hand began working at the latch, he felt his whole body go cold.

"We're protected, and you're not," she said as she opened the box. Inside was a white powder. She gave it a shake, waving her gloved hand over the contents. The powder flew up in a little cloud that drifted toward Arthur.

He began to cough and choke, his eyes watering as he tried to protect his face. But there was nothing he could do. The stuff clung to him, and he felt warmth spreading in his pants. Looking down, he saw that he had wet himself.

"Why did you want to attack the Capitol?"

"They killed my son."

"And you didn't mind killing thousands of innocent people to get them," the woman said, her voice a buzzing in his ears.

"The Congress…" The words ended in a fit of choking.

Two of the others in the white suits grasped Arthur's arms, holding him upright so that he couldn't collapse. The door opened again, and four more men stepped into the room.

Arthur's eyes bugged out as he stared at them. They weren't wearing any kind of protection. They were dressed in ordinary dark business suits.

One spun him around and cuffed his hands behind his back.

"Department of Homeland Security. Arthur Crispin, you are being held under indefinite suspension on suspicion of treason."

He realized he had been deceived, that the men and woman in the white suits had wanted him to think he was being exposed to a deadly biological agent.

"That wasn't ZR 427?" he choked out.

"No. It was an irritant. How did you like getting tricked?" Jack Brandt took off the helmet of his hazmat suit and gave Arthur a satisfied smile.

His terror was replaced by anger. "You son of a bitch."

"It was just a joke, Arthur. Not like what you did to us. You really thought you were going to get us all killed, didn't you?"

The others took off their helmets, and he saw Shane Gallagher along with Max Lyon and Morgan Rains.

He focused on the injustice of what they'd done to him, not the way he'd used the Rockfort Security men and Rains. They'd been a means to an end. That was all.

"I want a lawyer."

One of the Homeland Security men spoke. "Maybe later. Under the Patriot Act, we can hold you without legal counsel."

"But—"

They marched him outside to a waiting vehicle, a van with no windows, and he was thinking that perhaps he would never see the outside world again.

—〰—

Jack watched Crispin go. He should hate the man, but he thought he understood him. Grief had driven him to extreme acts. Jack knew how that could happen.

But if you recognized what was happening, maybe you could stop it. Especially if you had some help.

Chapter 32

MORGAN STRIPPED OFF HER BIOHAZARD SUIT AS SHE watched the van with Crispin drive away.

"What happens now?" she asked.

"Crispin's caught in a system he isn't going to like—where his money isn't going to do him a damn bit of good."

"He put himself there."

"Or we did," Shane said.

The three men had also taken off the special suits.

They'd come from an old Navy SEAL friend who now worked for Homeland Security. Bud Lewis. After Jack had explained what had happened, Lewis had gone along with Morgan's plan to turn the tables on Crispin. He'd taken charge of the deadly compound from Fort Detrick, provided the gear, and also arranged for Crispin's arrest.

Morgan was still looking at Jack. And she realized that the other two Rockfort men had left the room. When she heard an engine start, she looked outside. The other car drove away, leaving her and Jack alone.

"Where are they going?"

"Back to the office to deal with the authorities. There's a lot of mopping up to do."

She moistened her dry lips. "What about us?"

The question could have meant a lot of things. He chose to say, "We're going somewhere else."

She climbed into the other vehicle, and Jack slid behind the wheel. When she saw the rigid set of his jaw, she clasped her hands in her lap. This could be good-bye, for all she knew. And if that's what Jack had in mind, she was going to fight every way she knew to change his mind.

To her surprise, they drove back to the property where she'd been in hiding, but they bypassed the main building.

"We're not going there?" she asked as they passed the Victorian farmhouse.

"Not after Cunningham—I mean Crispin—broke in."

She appreciated that he didn't go into details. He continued up the road. When he rounded the helicopter hangar, she saw a small building nestled in the woods that might have been a farmworker's cottage.

Jack pulled up in front, cut the engine, and got out. She joined him outside, steadying herself against the car door as he came around to her side of the vehicle.

"What are we doing?" she asked in a voice she couldn't quite hold steady.

"We have to talk."

"Are you getting ready to leave me because you think it's the right thing to do?"

"I should."

The words made her throat go tight.

"But I don't think I can."

"Thank God."

She reached for him, pulling him into her arms.

"Oh Lord, Morgan," he whispered as she held him to her. "What are we going to do?"

"Love each other."

"I finally admitted to myself that I loved you when I knew Crispin had taken you."

"I knew it before that. I knew that I'd only been half-alive for the past year and a half, and then I met you and everything changed. I wanted to live. I wanted a life with you. Starting right now."

He looked dazed, as though he'd thought she was going to object.

"I assume there's a bed in this house," she said, reaching for his hand and leading him toward the front door.

The door wasn't locked, and they stepped inside. She got only a quick impression of a comfortable living room as they hurried through to the next room which was furnished with a wide bed. She took him down to the horizontal surface with her, where they clung together, rocking in each other's arms.

She'd held back her emotions the whole time they were planning the scam on Crispin. Then she'd been afraid of what Jack was going to say.

Not now.

She clasped his shoulders, pulling him close, her body pressed to his, sending her blood pounding hotly through her veins.

"I never did thank you for saving my life," she whispered.

"Leaving you there would have been like my own death," he answered in a rough voice.

He brought his mouth to hers for a kiss that said everything he hadn't yet put into words.

When they came up for air, she said, "I think we need to get rid of these clothes."

They discarded jeans, T-shirts, and underwear quickly, then rolled toward each other again.

She made a small sobbing sound as he clasped her to him, overwhelmed by the feel of his naked body against hers.

He held her for long moments, then reached between them, shaping her breasts in his hands, then playing his fingers over her nipples, bringing them to throbbing points of sensation.

When he took one hard peak into his mouth, drawing on her as he used his thumb and finger on the other side, she cried out with the pleasure of it. And when he stroked his free hand down her body and dipped into the hot, slick folds of her most intimate flesh, she came to a jolting climax.

As she caught her breath, she looked into his grinning face. "That took me by surprise."

"Me too," he agreed. "But it was kind of fun."

He began to kiss and caress her again, and this time she was better able to focus on each thing he did as he aroused her to fever pitch once more.

He dragged in a ragged breath, raising his head so that his eyes could meet hers. "Are you ready for me?"

"More than ready."

He covered her body with his, and as he sank into her, emotions flooded through her.

He began to move inside her, and she matched his rhythm, her breath coming hard and fast.

Again, climax grabbed her, and she heard him gasp, "I love you" as he joined her.

"I love you so much," she answered, as she came

down from the heights, stroking her hands over his sweat-slick back.

He shifted off of her, and they lay together on the bed, both breathing hard.

"You are so good at that," she murmured.

"I could say the same thing."

They lay together for long moments, until he said, "Something I should tell you."

"Good or bad?"

"Crispin gave Rockfort a down payment on the job of finding out what Trainer was up to. But he obviously had no intention of paying the rest—since he was going to eliminate me and the rest of the Rockfort men."

She nodded against his shoulder. "That's behind you now."

"Yeah, well, I got Trainer's bank account number from his computer. I transferred the money in it to Rockfort."

"How much?"

"A million dollars."

She gasped.

"I think we deserve it, considering what he put us through. The guys and I decided that half of it's mine."

She found his hand. "Yes, I think you do."

He swallowed. "Enough for a down payment on a nice house, with cash to spare, if we can figure out where we're going to live."

"Is that a proposal?"

"You don't want to just live with me?"

"No. I want commitment."

When he licked his lips, she felt herself tense.

"Is that going too far for you?"

"I thought I could ease into this."

"Not a chance. I know you're the man I want."

"You move fast."

"When I have to. And I've been thinking about where we should live."

"Oh yeah?"

"At the end of the semester, I'm going to resign from George Mason and go into clinical practice. In Rockville, so we'll both be close to work."

"Clinical practice? Even after what you told me about that guy who hanged himself? And—uh—the way our hypnosis session ended?"

"Oh Lord, thank you for reminding me about that. Trainer told me why it happened. Well, he didn't know the importance of what he was saying."

"What do you mean?"

"When he had me spread-eagled on that bed, he bragged that you weren't breathing after the guy hit you on the head in his office. His medic had to revive you."

He swore under his breath. "Lucky for me he wanted information."

She moved closer and hugged him tightly. "Lucky for me, too."

For long moments, neither of them spoke, and then she inclined her head so that she could look at him.

"I've changed from the woman who found you outside in the woods. You've changed me. I'm a lot more confident of what I can do. And I hope you are too. You got us out of a lot of scrapes, and then you came up with a rescue operation nobody else could have pulled off."

He nodded tightly, yet there was still a look of doubt on his face.

"What?"

"I'm in a dangerous profession. Your husband was shot and died. What if…"

She pressed her fingers to his lips. "There are no guarantees. I understand that better than most people. What I want with you is to live every day to the fullest."

"Maybe you can teach me."

"Glad to."

And glad that this extraordinary man had stumbled into the woods near her family's old cottage. He'd had a hard life, but it was going to be a lot better from now on. And so was hers.

About the Author

New York Times and *USA Today* bestselling author Rebecca York's writing has been compared to Dick Francis, Sherrilyn Kenyon, and Maggie Shayne. Her award-winning books have been translated into twenty-two languages and optioned for film. A recipient of the RWA Centennial Award, she lives in Maryland, near Washington, D.C., which is often the setting of her romantic suspense novels.

Betrayed

Rockfort operative and former Army M. P. investigator Shane
Gallagher is working security at S & D Systems, trying to
learn who's stealing vital secrets. Systems analyst Elena
Reyes is the one with access to the most sensitive files and
Shane is ready to close in—until he begins to understand
Elena's terrible dilemma.

Coming July 2014
from Sourcebooks Casablanca

Rev It Up

Black Knights Inc.

by Julie Ann Walker

He's the heartbreaker she left behind…

Jake "the Snake" Sommers earned his SEAL codename by striking quickly and quietly—and with lethal force. That's also how he broke Michelle Carter's heart. It was the only way to keep her safe—from himself. Four long years later, Jake is determined to get a second chance. But to steal back into Michelle's loving arms, Jake is going to have to prove he can take things slow. Real slow…

Michelle Carter has never forgiven Jake for being so cliché as to "love her and leave her." But when her brother, head of the Black Knights elite ops agency, pisses off the wrong mobster, she must do the unimaginable: place her life in Jake's hands. No matter what they call him, this man is far from cold-blooded. And once he's wrapped around her heart, he'll never let her go…

Praise for Hell on Wheels:

"Edgy, alpha, and downright HOT, the Black Knights Inc. will steal your breath…and your heart!"
—*Catherine Mann*, USA Today *bestselling author*

For more Black Knights Inc., visit:

www.sourcebooks.com

In Rides Trouble

Black Knights Inc.

by Julie Ann Walker

—◦◦◦—

Trouble never looked so good...

Rebel with a cause

Becky "Rebel" Reichert never actually goes looking for trouble. It just has a tendency to find her. Like the day Frank Knight showed up her door, wanting to use her motorcycle shop as a cover for his elite special ops team. But Becky prides herself on being able to hang with the big boys—she can weld, drive, and shoot just as well as any of them.

Man with a mission

Munitions, missiles, and mayhem are Frank's way of life. The last thing the ex-SEAL wants is for one brash blonde to come within fifty feet of anything that goes boom. Yet it's just his rotten luck when she ends up in a hostage situation at sea. Come hell or high water, he will get her back—whether she says she needs him or not.

—◦◦◦—

Praise for Hell on Wheels:

"Edgy, alpha, and downright HOT, the Black Knights Inc. will steal your breath...and your heart!"
—*Catherine Mann*, USA Today *bestselling author*

For more Black Knights Inc., visit:

www.sourcebooks.com

Thrill Ride

by Julie Ann Walker

~~~

He's gone rogue

Ex-Navy SEAL Rock Babineaux's job is to get information, and he's one of the best in the business. Until something goes horribly wrong and he's being hunted by his own government. Even his best friends at the covert special-ops organization Black Knights Inc. aren't sure they can trust him. He thinks he can outrun them all, but his former partner—a curvy bombshell who knows just how to drive him wild—refuses to cut him loose.

She won't back down

Vanessa Cordera hasn't been the team's communication specialist very long, but she knows how to read people—no way is Rock guilty of murder. And she'll go to hell and back to help him prove it. Sure, the sexy Cajun has his secrets, but there's no one in the world she'd rather have by her side in a tight spot. Which is good, because they're about to get very tight…

~~~

Praise for the Black Knights Inc. series:

"Walker is ready to join the ranks of great romantic suspense writers."—*RT Book Reviews*

For more Black Knights Inc., visit:

www.sourcebooks.com

Cover Me

by Catherine Mann

It should have been a simple mission…

Pararescueman Wade Rocha fast ropes from the back of a helicopter into a blizzard to save a climber stranded on an Aleutian Island, but Sunny Foster insists she can take care of herself just fine…

But when it comes to passion, nothing is ever simple…

With the snowstorm kicking into overdrive, Sunny and Wade hunker down in a cave and barely resist the urge to keep each other warm…until they discover the frozen remains of a horrific crime…

Unable to trust the local police force, Sunny and Wade investigate, while their irresistible passion for each other gets them more and more dangerously entangled…

Praise for Catherine Mann:

"Catherine Mann weaves deep emotion with intense suspense for an all-night read." —*#1* New York Times *bestseller Sherrilyn Kenyon*

For more Catherine Mann, visit:

www.sourcebooks.com

Hot Zone

by Catherine Mann

He'll take any mission, the riskier the better...

The haunted eyes of pararescueman Hugh Franco should have been her first clue that deep pain roiled beneath the surface. But if Amelia couldn't see the damage, how could she be expected to know he'd break her heart?

She'll prove to be his biggest risk yet...

Amelia Bailey's not the kind of girl who usually needs rescuing...but these are anything but usual circumstances.

Praise for Catherine Mann:

"Nobody writes military romance like Catherine Mann!"
—*Suzanne Brockmann*, New York Times
bestselling author of Tall, Dark and Deadly

"A powerful, passionate read not to be missed!"
—*Lori Foster*, New York Times *bestselling
author of* When You Dare

For more Catherine Mann, visit:

www.sourcebooks.com

Under Fire

by Catherine Mann

—⁓—

No holds barred, in love or war…

A decorated hero, pararescueman Liam McCabe lives to serve. Six months ago, he and Rachel Flores met in the horrific aftermath of an earthquake in the Bahamas. They were tempted by an explosive attraction, but then they parted ways. Still, Liam has thought about Rachel every day—and night—since.

Now, after ignoring all his phone calls for six months, Rachel has turned up on base with a wild story about a high-ranking military traitor. She claims no one but Liam can help her—and she won't trust anyone else.

With nothing but her word and the testimony of a discharged military cop to go on, Liam would be insane to risk his career—even his life—to help this woman who left him in the dust.

—⁓—

"Absolutely wonderful, a thrilling ride of ups and downs that will have readers hanging onto the edge of their seats."
—*RT Book Reviews* Top Pick of the Month, 4 1/2 stars

"Wild rides, pulse-pounding danger, gripping suspense, and simmering, sizzling, spiraling passion." —*Long and Short Reviews*

For more Catherine Mann, visit:

www.sourcebooks.com

The Night Is Mine

by M.L. Buchman

—◦—

NAME: Emily Beale

RANK: Captain

MISSION: Fly undercover to prevent the assassination of the First Lady, posing as her executive pilot

NAME: Mark Henderson, code name Viper

RANK: Major

MISSION: Undercover role of wealthy, ex-mercenary boyfriend to Emily

Their jobs are high risk, high reward:

Protect the lives of the powerful and the elite at all cost. Neither expected that one kiss could distract them from their mission. But as the passion mounts between them, their lives and their hearts will both be risked… and the reward this time may well be worth it.

—◦—

"An action-packed adventure. With a super-stud hero, a strong heroine, and a backdrop of 1600 Pennsylvania Avenue and the world of the Washington elite, it will grab readers from the first page." —*RT Book Reviews*

For more in The Night Stalkers series, visit:

www.sourcebooks.com

Wait Until Dark

by M.L. Buchman

NAME: Big John Wallace

RANK: Staff Sergeant, chief mechanic and gunner

MISSION: To serve and protect his crew and country

NAME: Connie Davis

RANK: Sergeant, flight engineer, mechanical wizard

MISSION: To be the best… and survive

Two crack mechanics, one impossible mission

Being in the Night Stalkers is Connie Davis's way of facing her demons head-on, but mountain-strong Big John Wallace is a threat on all fronts. Their passion is explosive but their conflicts are insurmountable. When duty calls them to a mission no one else could survive, they'll fly into the night together—ready or not.

Praise for M.L. Buchman:

"Filled with action, adventure, and danger… Buchman's novels will appeal to readers who like romances as well as fans of military fiction."
—*Booklist* Starred Review of *I Own the Dawn*

For more M.L. Buchman, visit: